WE'LL SLEEP WHEN WE'RE OLD

WE'LL SLEEP WHEN WE'RE OLD

A Novel

Pino Corrias

Translated by Antony Shugaar

ATRIA BOOKS

New York London Toronto Sydney New Delhi

ATRIA
BOOKS

An Imprint of Simon & Schuster, Inc.
1230 Avenue of the Americas
New York, NY 10020

First Atria Books hardcover edition December 2017

ATRIA BOOKS and colophon are trademarks of Simon & Schuster, Inc.

For information about special discounts for bulk purchases, please contact Simon & Schuster Special Sales at 1-866-506-1949 or business@simonand schuster.com.

The Simon & Schuster Speakers Bureau can bring authors to your live event. For more information, or to book an event, contact the Simon & Schuster Speakers Bureau at 1-866-248-3049 or visit our website at www .simonspeakers.com.

Interior design by Dana Sloan

Manufactured in the United States of America

10 9 8 7 6 5 4 3 2 1

Library of Congress Cataloging-in-Publication Data
Names: Corrias, Pino, 1955– author. | Shugaar, Antony, translator.
Title: We'll sleep when we're old / Pino Corrias ; translated by Antony Shugaar.
Other titles: Dormiremo da vecchi. English
Description: First Atria Books hardcover edition. | New York : Atria Books, 2017.
Identifiers: LCCN 2017017448| ISBN 9781501144950 (hardback) | ISBN 9781501144981 (ebook)
Subjects: LCSH: Motion picture producers and directors—Italy—Rome—Fiction.
 | Performing arts—Italy—Rome—Fiction. | Missing people—Italy—Rome—Fiction. | Psychological fiction. | BISAC: FICTION / Literary. | FICTION / Psychological. | FICTION / Thrillers. | GSAFD: Suspense fiction.
Classification: LCC PQ4903.O74 D613 2017 | DDC 853/.914—dc23 LC record available at https://lccn.loc.gov/2017017448

ISBN 978-1-5011-4495-0
ISBN 978-1-5011-4498-1 (ebook)

To Gi Bi, who's gone now.

If you need a friend, get a dog.

—GORDON GEKKO IN *WALL STREET* (1987)

There was nothing sweet about the dolce vita,

it was horrendous.

—DINO RISI

Contents

Part One

LA DOLCE
ROMA

Ashes

Before the ashes, before the flames, it was a pleasant warm Roman evening like so many others that blossom in June, from the villa overlooking the windows of the homes around the beautiful Orange Garden, amid the flowering magnolias and the metallic Bentleys of the Aventine Hill. And this story contained an infinity of colors. As many as could be found in the Persian carpets laid out the length of the mansion's front hall—the last villa as you climbed the steep street, with architectural spaces and arches in a florid art nouveau style—carpets woven with Sufi techniques in Kāshān and Tabrīz. All of it gone up in smoke now, along with the Flemish tapestries hanging at the foot of the spiral staircases, and the Shirvan hall runners in the corridors, and the contemporary art decorating every single room, bathrooms included. Everything, devoured by flames and reduced to ashes—so long. All of it crumbled to cinders, cold now and smeared together with the flame-retardant foams unleashed by the firefighters, transformed now into a monochromatic expanse of gray verging on white, not unlike

3

the most famous painting of the collection so recently destroyed, a Piero Manzoni Achrome, renowned for three surprising reasons. First: for being appraised at close to €2 million. Second: for representing the indecipherable epitome of its owner. Third: for stirring in all those who beheld it, along with admiration for the artwork and its owner, the unsettling possibility that at least one of the two, artwork or owner, might be sumptuously fake.

❧

Everything that comes before the fire belongs to Oscar Martello, a millionaire producer of high-impact cinema and lowest-common-denominator television series—God-fearing out of vested interest—and the owner of Anvil Film Studios by personal vocation. Who, as he saunters onstage with his hands in his pockets, produces much the same effect as the Manzoni painting: an impression of solid wealth and a highly valued solitude. The kind of things that at first glance shoot out beams of hope to starving directors, screenwriters without ideas, unstable actors and actresses; and at second glance seduce into a hypnotic state; and with each successive glance annex and incorporate. But as they annex, they reduce the functions of the annexee to one and one alone: obedience. As well as a hairy gratitude that serves only to facilitate the digestion of the great Oscar Martello, digestion that is never devoid of a hint of disgust, a disgust that comes over him with every episode of gastric reflux, when for psychosomatic reasons his digestive juices, rather than remaining where they belong to grind up oysters and champagne, choose to come and pay a visit to his throat. Forcing him, reflexively, to emit a tiny, saliva-less spit. The mimesis of a spit, if Oscar only knew what "mimesis" meant.

The sequence of absorptions and expulsions has been speeding

WE'LL SLEEP WHEN WE'RE OLD

up since Oscar Martello, climbing from success to success, from benediction to benediction, took ownership of a nice fat slice of the assets of La Dolce Roma, over which he skates, encountering no emotional interference save for the black surge of resentment for the family he was born into, so poverty-stricken that he still feels shame, rage, and the surge of intolerance that so many years ago drove him from Serravalle Scrivia out toward the world he yearned to sink his teeth into. The world of money, the world of the movies. The world of Helga and the cougar women on their expense accounts. The world of stories, where the soul of the narrative is never to be found in the plot twist, only in the characters. Where, by manipulating them, you can manipulate the audience that sits gazing up at them openmouthed—physicians, lady doctors, police detectives, homely but good-hearted schoolteachers, street thugs on the road to perdition, brave mothers, priests, fraudulent saints, bloodthirsty saints, and even popes, all of them deployed for the common good of the viewing audience, which turns out to match the private—and privately invoiced—interests of none other than Oscar Martello.

Oscar Martello is the first character of this story. He's forty-six years old, married to a wife who's as cutting as a shard of broken glass, but stunningly beautiful, Helga, a Buenos Aires–born Argentine, and he has two young daughters, Cleo and Zoe, one aged three, the other aged five, for whom he feels an automatic tenderness every time he lays eyes on them, and a yearning to take them in his arms and protect them from the jutting nails of this world. But then he promptly forgets about them, because he lacks the time, he lacks the patience, and he entrusts them to safely sterilized nannies and expensive toys because he always has something else usually super urgent to do: drive nails into the world.

Oscar has the face of a bandit, a face worn haggard by sleeplessness. He lives on the run, he thinks on the run. Like all the filthy rich, he's unhappy, especially at night, when the shadows come flying through the dark. And again at dawn, when he finds himself awake and alone.

By day, he's a guy who travels in a straight line, even when there are curves in the road. He's never read a book from cover to cover, but he knows men, he knows women, and he pays them both, though for different reasons. When he closes his eyes, he makes up stories. When he opens them again, he has them written down. With those stories, he makes money. With the money, he leads a sumptuous life, he buys houses and apartments in Rome and around the world, the latest a palazzo on the Grand Canal in Venice. ("But don't you think there's a curse on the place? Get me a priest and have the fucking place blessed.") He has a broker who buys him stocks ("I want ten thousand shares of Pfizer by end of business today, get busy!") and he purchases canvases by contemporary artists, provided they're very expensive and all the latest rage. He has three Jaguars parked in his basement garages, three Filipino houseboys, all of whom he calls "You there" ("I'm no racist, it's just that I can't tell them apart"), and nine carbon steel Masamoto knives for cutting fish. He considers himself the lord of seafood and stories. He has an endless sequence of private sins that he conceals behind a luxuriant public devotion, and which he offsets with lavish donations to the pagan coffers of the Vatican. Somewhere, beneath some mental false bottom in the suitcase of his brain, he truly believes that heaven exists. Some time ago he reserved himself a chunk of it with a panoramic view, as if it were something to which his native aggressiveness entitled him, but in the meantime he haggles with the Lord Almighty over the price per square foot and skims every penny he can on the expenses.

He steals for himself and his dream on earth: to become the number one Italian movie producer and moreover—hear ye! hear ye!—to buy for himself the most spectacular and pretentious dream factory of them all, the hundred-acre production lot of Cinecittà, the facilities where Maciste, Totò, and Federico Fellini invented the world and where at least two dozen divas—from Isa Miranda to Sophia Loren—made it fall in love. Cinecittà, the factory of all stories, the twenty-two soundstages crumbling into decay little by little, including the broad boulevards that with their maritime pines once smacked of salt air, distance, and adventure, whereas now they smell of nothing but exhaust fumes and the traffic that clogs the vast commuter quarter of Tuscolano. Oscar Martello yearns to awaken Cinecittà, like Sleeping Beauty in the fairy tale, using millions of euros instead of a kiss, and then screw it royally, from above and from behind, fertilize it with great movies, great box office takes, make it throb once again with its own light, provided it reflect on his own.

Oscar Martello is an extrovert. And extroverts generally kick up tremendous clouds of dust so they can then hide in them.

⁂

Andrea Serrano is the second character of this story. He's thirty-nine years old, he lives and walks by himself, except for brief and fleeting love affairs. His physique is still lithe and fit, his eyes are still quick. And yet he gives the impression of someone who thinks slowly, whose thoughts chase slowly after comets, especially when he sits there, with his elbow braced on the armrest and his

face propped between thumb and forefinger, his forefinger resting across his lips. He makes his living by writing screenplays of
average intensity, meant for an average audience that he imagines
along with the screenplays, as he sits there that way. Occasionally
he is distracted by the sudden, painful revelation of how time is
passing without ever leaving behind anything that resembles an
explanation. Usually, this revelation makes him don the special
Neutral Working Expression that keeps him at a safe distance
from the battles of life, all of them too concrete or too risky. He
calls that elegance, but deep down he has a vague suspicion that
it's really nothing but run-of-the-mill cowardice. He's a shy man.
And shy men, when they have their backs against the wall, can
become dangerous.

✌︎

Jacaranda Rizzi, the actress, is the point of departure. And actually, also, the point of arrival. She's thirty-two years old, but you
might guess she's twenty-two because of the whiff of peach or a
freshly plucked flower. She descends from a cloud, she lives on a
cloud: her cloud contains hundreds of photographs, plus several
memorable scenes from the movies she's acted in. For instance,
one in which she dives off a boat on the high seas, saying, "It's time
I go now." Another one in which she sobs with her arms around
a sick little boy. And one in which she undresses—though not entirely—and then lets herself fall back on the sofa, spreading her
legs in front of the man who's staring at her, and then says to him
in a whisper, "Is this the way you want me?"

Because of her sweet little bipolar heart and the sheer quantity
of pills she ingests, and her beauty, made up of honey-colored eyes,
blond hair, and pink freckles, she contains a shadow of darkness

that she once tried to slice with razor blades. But that shadow still hovers beside her.

This time, Jacaranda is laying the groundwork for vengeance, certain that she will emerge victorious or at least unharmed, finally free from the evil ghosts that visit her in her sleep and from the sense of vertigo that attends her morning awakenings. But the ghosts and the senses of vertigo come from far away, they're stubborn enemies, they're hunters who run and never grow tired. She is the prey. And Oscar Martello is her escape route.

The how and the when are in the first scene.

La Dolce Roma Was Turning Slowly Beneath the Stars

The first scene takes place at night, five weeks before the fire. It's April thirtieth, but it's already as hot as if it were summer, the moon is almost full, and it's so bright in the dark-blue sky that it looks like someone has just polished it. A light breeze tosses the leaves.

Andrea Serrano and Oscar Martello are sitting across from each other, inside the movie screen of Andrea's plate glass picture window overlooking the Tiber. They're on the top floor of the corner building across from the Ara Pacis and the church of San Carlo al Corso. All around them, Rome projects its sequence of shooting stars and lives in transit.

Fernanda Liberati, also known as Ninni, costume designer and would-be playwright, black hair and black nails, red lips, skin freshly scrubbed by a shower spray, has just been filed away with a kiss into the elevator. Immediately after she rode down, Oscar Martello rode up.

He's made himself comfortable in an armchair and he's talking nonstop. It's nine days to catastrophe and that makes him furious and at the same time terribly calm. He twists his neck, he smokes Cohibas, he coughs, and he spits a couple of times, though rather politely.

"In nine days, the movie's going to open in four hundred theaters. It'll hold out for a day, maybe two. Then word of mouth will set in. They'll rip that asshole director to shreds. They'll destroy the cast, starting with Jacaranda Rizzi. The film critics will start dumping their shit on it. And then on me, the finest producer of them all. They'll stab me in the back. And it's going to be that miserable, microscopic Lea Lori who'll turn up her nose and lead the charge for that pack of frustrated dry asses. The critics! Just think what a thrill it will be for them to rip me to shreds. It's going to rain blood and I'll have lost six million euros, a dozen lines of credit, and all self-respect. They'll sink their fangs into me, they'll gnaw at my liver. They can't wait."

"Threaten to fire her daughter."

"What?"

"The 'miserable, microscopic' Lea Lori's daughter. Didn't you give her a job at Anvil to cover your ass?"

"My ass I ever hired her. I slip her a thousand euros a month under the table. I keep her warm and comfortable and in the meanwhile I grab her diminutive mother by the ovaries." Oscar sucks on his Cohiba and puffs out smoke. "You know how I do it?"

"How you do what?"

"How I pay her under the table." Bragging excites him and relaxes him. "I send her to London every two or three months on one of those twenty-euro easyJet flights. She goes, she picks up the cash in an envelope from one of my rent-an-accountants, she goes shopping at Harrods, buys a shit ton of crap, and comes home. She's happy. Her mother covers it. I cover it. We're both in cahoots and no one gets hurt."

"One of these days, you'll wind up in the news."

"Now don't you start jinxing things."

Andrea has been listening to Oscar's unbroken stream of words for a quarter of an hour. He senses the electricity that Oscar's been emanating, he has to take care to stay out of his trajectory. But Oscar can go on for hours, overboosting the voltage relentlessly. So Andrea decides he's had enough. "I didn't write that pile of bullshit that your director shot."

The movie they're talking about is called *No, I Won't Surrender!* In the poster, Jacaranda's angelic face is at the center of a crosshair, and in the background is Palermo, imprisoned beneath the black sky of the Mafia, with the remarkable innovation of the silhouette of a Kalashnikov instead of the more traditional sawed-off shotgun. "I know. Your script was long, slow, and romantic, but at least it was decent, and the best things in it I'd dictated to you verbatim."

"Oh, really? Then why did you reject it?"

Oscar ignores him. "I just happened to miss the fact that Fabris, asshole that he is, completely lost it on the set, all charged up on testosterone and cocaine: every day he was shifting the scenes around, stretching them out or slowing them down. He thought he'd become Andrei Tarkovsky, the fool. And by the time I saw what he'd shot, it was too late. I should have beat him black and blue and then fired him."

"Which is what you actually did do, though."

The scene, a week ago, had been unforgettable, with the whole postproduction studio savoring it, motionless.

"I should have done it sooner! It's all my fault." From the strain of his confession, Oscar snaps the Cohiba in two, gets to his feet, drops it in the trash, and rubs his head as he thinks back to the pointy, blood-engorged face of Attilio Fabris whining like a child, *waaah, waaah*, as he crawls across the floor, leaving a trail of tears and saliva. "Get me something to drink."

"You still haven't answered my question."

Answering him costs Oscar Martello a vast sigh. "I never rejected it, I just trimmed it down, I snipped off the curls, the intellectual dogshit, the boredom. And I was planning to pay you. After all, it belonged to me. It needed to be rewritten by a new pair of hands and you weren't on the right wavelength."

"Says you."

"Of course, says me, I'm the producer and I know what I'm doing."

"So we've seen."

Oscar is skinny, tense. In comparison, Andrea is a long, lazily lingering wave. Oscar is a well-dressed clotheshorse, impeccably groomed. Andrea, on the other hand, is wearing a pair of technical trekking shorts and a cotton T-shirt with a slogan emblazoned on it, LE ROI DE RIEN ("The King of Nothing"), which is a small auto-biographical touch. He's barefoot, as if he were at the beach. "I've got some grass that comes from Salento. Maybe that will calm you down."

Oscar sighs, sits down, loosens his tie. "Then get me something to drink, give me something to smoke, and make me something to eat."

"Will that be all?"

"Don't you get started. I already have a goddamned ulcer that's scorching my soul."

"You're just somatizing."

"Fucking right I am, I'm somatizing my life."

"That's a good one, we can use it for the scene with the lesbian girl who outs her mother."

"Asshole," he says, then he stops and looks at him. "But you know, you might be right . . ."

"About what?"

"Lea's daughter! Maybe she really is a lesbian. She always acts so weird, so standoffish, a girl who doesn't like cock."

"I wasn't talking about Lea's daughter."

"I know you weren't. But you have involuntary intuitions that open my eyes. You focus down. That's what I like about you. You wouldn't happen to have a bowl of hot chicken noodle soup for your old friend, would you?"

"But I thought you'd already eaten."

◦※◦

Oscar Martello, hero of the Superworld that pumps out cash, projects, and vendettas, shows up uninvited in Andrea's apartment at midnight, hastening the eviction of Fernanda, a.k.a. Ninni. He's coming from one of those benefit banquets thrown by Donna Angelina Casagrande, known as the "Queen of Flowers" not only because she loves the San Remo Casino (the suit of clubs in English cards is the suit of flowers in Italian, you see), but also because as a girl she was a flower vendor, with a kiosk on the street, or at least so the legend has it. Since then, millions of euros have flowed through her legs. A high-profit pair of legs: "When I was young, every time you stuck your dick in her, out came the receipt," says Oscar. Over time, she became an aristocrat, like certain other former penniless waifs, sucking down the earthly possession of three husbands, a meat wholesaler from the Marche region who went hurtling at top speed into Lake Maggiore at the wheel of his stupid Ferrari; then the nephew of a sheik from Dubai who vanished into the flames of some holy war, bound and determined to win himself his seventy virgins; and finally a false French baron who stuffed himself silly with pâté and Château Lafite and had finally even come down with a terminal case of diabetes, but who ultimately died in his bed, choking on a supine nocturnal reflux. And now Donna Angelina, a happily spruced-up widow, freely sprinkles a few crumbs of the fortune she's piled up, tax free, in Monte Carlo and Luxembourg, giving back with sumptuous dinners prepared by Michelin-starred chefs, at which all the laymen and high prelates gulp down such molecular delicacies as suckling pig, duck in vermouth, citrus shrimp, raw scampi in jars of ice and lime, and thousand-euro bottles of Dom Pérignon, just so they can ship a little millet flour, powdered milk, and aspirin past its sell-by date to some village in the Sahel, destined to be wiped off the maps by the next sandstorm. For three hours, Oscar dutifully ate what was put before him ("Surrounded by those old hags loaded down with gold and those nimble-fingered bankers who make money out of the sandstorms in question, I don't know if you take my point") pretending all the while that he too was good-hearted enough to deserve a benediction, along with a lobster and mayonnaise and a dozen smiling photographs to celebrate the world hunger that had made them all filthy rich. Camouflaged in those surroundings, Oscar was scheming some plausible alternative to murdering the director who, that very afternoon—before fleeing in tears, protected by the shrieks of his miserable Milanese agent—had shown him for the hundredth time rushes of the film, fresh from the Moviola, once again shattering his metabolism, mood, and vocal cords.

Where are you now, Attilio Fabris? Where are you now, Attilio the Phenomenon? As Oscar walked into Donna Angelina Casagrande's home, he'd looked for him everywhere, sniffing out his scent from room to room, among dozens of guests, until he reached the Tiepolo room, walking at Helga's side; to bolster her demeanor she strode through the guests erect like a flag at the Olympics, with the grace of a pink flamingo. Oscar dreamed of finding him, dragging him soundlessly into one of those aristocratic drawing rooms lined with volumes of the Treccani encyclopedia, a crackling fireplace, and at least one Morandi on the wall, jamming a fat wooden pencil into his ear and applying pressure on it until it pierced his eardrum, and then finally pissing into that ear.

When he discovered that no one had so much as dreamed of inviting that asshole of a director, much less his odious agent, he went on drinking. And just before getting into a fight with Helga in public because she was telling him to calm down ("I'll calm down when and if I feel like it, you bitch. And get that stick out of your ass. Relax. They're every bit the criminals that we are, no less and no more.") he started off down the enfilade of baroque drawing rooms toward the exit. At the last door in the sequence, the queen of the poor black orphans Donna Angelina Casagrande tried to plant a kiss on his lips. He pushed her behind a brocade curtain, realizing in that brief instant of exaggerated proximity that the little old grandmother—some indeterminate age between fifty-one and sixty-nine years old—had once again had her tits redone and she was just looking to give them an inaugural run. So he slipped his hand down the front of her dress, gave her nipples a squeeze, and told her, "I'm hard as a rock, sweetheart, but if I let you kiss me, I'd probably catch your case of the wrinkles."

She burst out laughing right in his face and he caught a whiff of her bad breath. "I only have two wrinkles, asshole. And I'm usually sitting on them. Care to check me out?"

"Some other time, sweetheart. But only if first you'll suck my cock with both hands tied behind your back."

She laughed again and he took advantage of the opportunity to make his getaway down the pink marble staircase, leaving the chauffeured Jaguar coupe to Helga and setting off on foot down Via Condotti and Via della Fontanella di Borghese, then taking Via Tomacelli until he reached the bridge, ignoring along the way, in order of appearance, a little Indian girl begging for spare change and offering incense, a Romanian playing the accordion and singing "Roma capoccia" before the half-empty tables of a trattoria, a Chinese man selling phosphorescent necklaces, and a couple of homeless men wrapped up in their filthy cardboard boxes, whereupon he finally took a breath of Roman night air. Time to recharge his batteries. Time to perfect his plan.

Now he's heading for Andrea's kitchen. "Don't think for a second I didn't see her."

"Who?"

"The superbabe who rode downstairs in the elevator."

"Her name is Fernanda. Ninni to her friends."

"Spectacular: great tits, great ass, fiery eyes. Where did you find her, on Amazon?"

"She's a costumer."

"Of course she is. She knows how to put them on or take them off—ha ha ha!"

"Both, actually, it depends."

"Hmmm. Anyway, I need you unattached."

"What?"

Oscar is wearing a pin-striped charcoal gray suit, an off-white dress shirt, a gray tie with tiny red polka dots, and a pair of black Allen Edmonds wingtip oxfords. On his wrist is a brand-new €170,000 extra-flat white gold Patek Philippe watch, and on his pinky finger is an old ring with a skull etched into iron that can't have cost anything more than 20,000 lire. The watch represents his point of arrival. The ring represents his point of departure. He stops, turns to look at Andrea with gunfighter eyes, and repeats, "Unattached. Don't you even think of starting up a relationship right now."

"Why not?"

"Because I suddenly just connected the wires."

"Which means what?"

"Which means I may have figured out a solution."

Andrea has rolled a joint. Oscar lights up and takes two drags, luxuriantly. He's enveloped in a cloud of white smoke, dense with aroma, that crackles as it makes him squint. "Now let's get comfortable and I'll tell you all about it, then you'll see whether I'm not the lord of stories."

"Sure, just don't say it every five minutes."

They've decided to make a giant pitcher of ginger margarita. They start messing around with bottles of tequila, salt, lemon, ginger, and crushed ice.

"Do you have crackers and olives?"

"But weren't you just out for dinner with the good white matrons who are going to save the world?"

"Very funny. When I'm surrounded by those old whores, my stomach always ties itself up in knots." He gulps down more flaming smoke, puffs some out, spits, passes the joint, and says, "And now it's unknotted again."

"I have some goat cheese, salted anchovies, and butter, and if you like I can heat up some bread."

"I adore you."

"Why do you go?"

"What?"

"Why do you go to those dinners."

"Because if I don't, Helga sulks for a week. She's convinced that if she socializes with the better nature of those burnt-out society dames, they'll make her a princess one day."

"Or else they'll make you a prince."

"I couldn't care less. I'm an ex-proletarian, but I'm not an ex-anarchist yet."

They both know there's not a speck of truth to it, but it's all part of the masquerade that Oscar loves to hide behind. Just as he likes to pretend he's not climbing the social ladder that keeps him up nights chasing after Helga's ambitions; Helga, to whom he's been married for the last seven years, Helga who has already scrambled up to the sky and above in her stiletto heels, a long way from the mud-floor hovel in the favelas of Buenos Aires, and who made it out alive from a first marriage to the bodyguard of an admiral who used to whip her with a leather belt, and now they say that she's resting up for her spectacular last act: waiting for the heart attack that will carry off the great Oscar Martello, so she can stage a princely funeral, then dump his corpse in a potter's field and inherit the whole tamale.

"Where's Helga? Did she go on home?"

"I left her on a slow simmer at the party. I need to be able to think without having her talk to me about producers that need killing, priests that need feeding, apartments that need to be bought, daughters that need to be sent to the French day school, and charcoal tablets to be taken to stop aerophagia."

There was a time—he told Andrea in detail, greedy eyed, unaware of the recklessness of what he was doing—when Helga gave him blow jobs to die for. And she'd slide all her fingers between her legs while she was going down on him and moan while he came in her face. That was love. Then they got married. "And now the bitch always has a migraine."

Oscar has taken off his jacket and tie, rolled up his shirtsleeves, and now he's starting to prepare their beverage, squeezing lemons, filling the pitcher with crushed ice, adding just a couple of drops of raspberry juice, the ginger, six healthy shots of tequila *reposado*, and a pinch of crumbled chili pepper, his own personal invention to add a smidgen of character to the dancing Mexican soul of the cocktail.

Andrea pulls everything else out of the fridge and turns on the toaster.

Oscar says, "I adore your apartment, everything's within reach. At my place, I just get lost."

※

Oscar lives on the Aventine Hill, in that rose-colored art nouveau mansion, with green shutters set in cornices and columns and cream-colored flowers. The front door, surrounded by Virginia creeper, is made of heavy crystal, brass, and hardwood; the main staircase rises in a spiral; the floors are hardwood, mosaic, and marble. The ceilings—frescoed with branches of grapevines, pink ribbons, ochre scrollwork, and blue flowers—are high and arched. The house is four stories tall, each floor set back, with a large terrace between the third and the fourth floors. Aside from the reigning family, it contains the three Filipino factotums, Helga's personal maid, Miriam, a nameless Siamese cat that's been getting fatter for years and won't let anyone touch it, and a tiny, hysterical bulldog named Napoleon that, when it's not sleeping, chews up everything within reach. Oscar hates both cat and dog and whenever he can, if no one's looking, secretly kicks them. Then there are two immense living rooms that open out onto the main terrace, an array of sitting rooms, the dining room, the rec room, half a dozen bedrooms, each with its own bathroom, two kitchens, a gym with sauna and Jacuzzi, a sunroom, a greenhouse full of flowers, and a sixty-foot swimming pool with two lanes.

All told, sixteen thousand square feet of floor space—plus his own personal turret, known as the Castle, where he has his study, furnished in sage green, and with windows on four sides overlooking the terrace below, the cupolas of Rome, and his two and a half acres of gardens. A house that Oscar is rapidly transforming into a museum, since his latest obsession—after money, cocaine, women, movies, TV, real estate, and *naturally* Cinecittà—is buying art. This is his way of feeling like a college graduate without having to go to the trouble of studying. He started a few years ago, purchasing the banal beauty of the figurative painters of the dreary novecento, such as the various painters of the Roman school, Scipione and Mafai among them, plus a couple of De Chiricos, five sketches by Boccioni, and even a few horrid Guttusos. Then he figured out that conceptual art offers identity only at stratospheric prices, multiplied by the sheer incomprehensibility of the work. He had to have them as pure exhibitions of wealth, which was exactly what he was looking for. The most famous piece in his collection, aside from the shark in formaldehyde by Damien Hirst, the heaps of rocks by Richard Long, the colorful puppets by Jeff Koons, and a couple of installations by that genius of cheerful bullshitting Maurizio Cattelan, is Piero Manzoni's Achrome, for the three celebrated reasons that all La Dolce Rome talks and gossips about incessantly.

It was Massimiliano Urso, the contemporary art critic, as he walked arm in arm with Oscar, sipping champagne, who explained to him with a certain perfidious enjoyment that the young Manzoni, who died of alcoholism and heart disease at the tender age of just twenty-nine, had done more or less 300 artworks. Whereas nowadays the catalog of his work magically numbers 1,229. "Which doesn't include the fact that, in public auctions and private galleries, at least twice as many are in circulation."

"So what you're telling me is . . . ?"

"That it's probably a fake."

The revelation left Oscar speechless. When he regained his ability to speak, the words that came out were the wrong ones. "Then what should I do?" he asked in alarm, staring with a new understanding at his stupid Manzoni.

"Keep it. And when you find another fool, sell it to him."

Oscar wasn't fast enough to respond with a head-butt, a face-slap, or at least a "How fucking dare you, you miserable hobo," before Urso wandered off nonchalantly, leaving him standing there in surprise and frustration. The humiliation still smarts, all these years later, whenever he thinks back on it. Not that it did a lot of good to strike Urso from the list of his future invitees. Nor did threatening to sue him if he so much as ventured to say a bad word about his Manzoni. That time, too, the damned critic simply shrugged and wrong-footed him. "Go ahead, and we'll have some fun."

❧

"Have I ever told you how much I hate critics?"

"A hundred times or so."

"They're parasites. They're frustrated. They sit there in the dark spitting out decrees about those who have the courage to venture out into the glare of daylight. They have to demolish others in order to exist."

"So who do you have it in for now?"

"Everyone. At Angelina's party there must have been at least a dozen, all of them gathering crumbs from under the table."

In the hierarchy of living things, according to Oscar Martello, critics are below dogs, even when the dogs in question are canine nonentities, such as the farting dachshunds that contessas tend to keep, or his own blasted bulldog, Napoleon. He has personally threatened many of the working television and movie critics, while he has put others on his expense reports, which he usually doles out in the form of plates full of Spanish *pata negra* ham and tiny lines of coke to make them feel like they're part of the in-crowd. The idea that a critic might do his job for the pure intellectual pleasure of the thing has never even crossed his mind, no more than his imagining that a politician is there for some reason other than the take.

"Did I ever tell you the story of Angelina Casagrande?"

"No, that's one I haven't heard."

"Well, when she was a girl she was beautiful, sexy as hell, and, who knows why, between one marriage and the next she fell in love with a literary critic, I can't remember his name, just that he wore these dreary boiled wool jackets and traveling salesman ties. He made a living by gnawing at novels and selling reviews. He said he wanted to save the world with beauty, but actually all he felt toward the world was hatred. After a couple of years of German poetry and canned tuna from the supermarket, she dumped him and hooked up with one of these bandits from the Roman political world. The great Achille Marchesi, do you remember him?"

"I didn't know that she'd been his lover, too."

"No one knew it, he was the vice president of the Senate, he had seven children, a great defender of family values, on close personal terms with the Vatican cardinal secretary of state. An unrepentant cocksman, and a great friend of mine."

"And then what happened?"

"Then what happened is that Angelina told me that she'd never laughed so hard in her life as when she ate, drank, fucked, and thieved with Marchesi. And to entertain her he would have his bagman summon a handful of these piece-of-shit critics, her ex-boyfriend among them, these highfalutin' art professors, these archaeology sniffers, and he'd keep them waiting for hours, promising them the chairmanship of some foundation or academy or public toilet. But he'd promise all of them—one by one—the same chairmanship, if you get the point. Telling them it was a secret. Then he'd leave them on a slow boil for the months that followed and watch them struggle to slit each others' throats."

Andrea considers the viciousness of the prank, then an old story comes to mind. "I knew three girls in high school, friends of mine, who'd do more or less the same thing, on a smaller scale. They'd get comfortable in a café, and they'd call in succession all the biggest losers in their class, the fat boy, the pimply boy, the skinny pigeon-chested boy, promising each of them they could cop a smell. And then they'd make bets on which of them would be the first to get there."

"Then what would happen?"

"The boys really would show up. But the appointment had been made for the bar on the opposite side of the street and they would enjoy the scene from their café."

Oscar thinks it over. "I hope they all wound up old maids, your three young sluts."

"No, even worse, all three of them are married."

"Ha ha! That's a good one."

"What about your friend Marchesi—he came to a bad end, I'm guessing. Cancer, leukemia, something like that?"

"Ulcerative colitis. Practically speaking, he died in a pool of shit."

"Oh, fuck. Would you pass me the ice?"

℈

They're hanging out in the kitchen as if it were nine at night, but it's actually two in the morning. They've each put together a plate for themselves. Then they head out into the living room to drink and eat, in the pink armchairs by the plate glass window.

For a couple of years now, Andrea has been living in that 750-square-foot penthouse apartment, plus 200 square feet of terrace, within which he has limited himself to scattering his emptiness on the hardwood floor, a parquet the color of Virginia-blend tobacco, mild and sweet. The bed, the built-in armoire, and the bathroom are all on the interior side, which overlooks the roofs. The kitchen is just a corner of the living room, which then opens out toward the expansive picture window that looks down over the Tiber. The living room is empty, except for a black carpet, a glowing sand-colored glass cactus, a large canvas by Mario Schifano—two couples drawn in white against a black background—

titled *Assenza di gravità*, dated 1990, a screen on the wall, twelve tiny speakers bluetoothed to an iPad that's filled with a hundred hours or so of jazz. The walls are white except for the far wall, which is orange and gold with luminous yellow threads, like the Dan Flavin neons that run along the four sides of the perimeter. Aside from the two armchairs, there's a dark hardwood table, unadorned, without drawers, and without chairs except for the padded office chair. Then there's the computer, the printer, three red oversize cushions on the floor, a dozen shelves full of books and CDs, all of them survivors of the death of paper publishing, the disappearance of records, and twenty or so years of moving.

At night, the lights on the orange wall give the impression that the apartment is the interior of a magic box where the air floats in a warm iridescence, while the speakers put out the crystalline music of the Esbjörn Svensson Trio—piano, string bass, and drums—filled with that northern European sweetness capable of chilling even the baroque amplitude of the Roman night. Taken as a whole, the apartment communicates comfort and a solitude that is, all things considered, self-aware. An entirely untrammeled solitude.

⌘

"Tell me about the wires that you've connected."

"You should have seen the spark, when your name came up," Oscar tells him seriously.

Every alarm bell starts ringing in Andrea's head. "What does it have to do with me?"

Oscar talks as he chews his food. "Your name and Jacaranda's are made to be together. I don't know why it never occurred to me before this."

"What the fuck are you talking about?"

"I'm talking about the idea that hit me, a way to save the movie and save all our asses."

"Leave me out of this story."

"It's not a story, it's a plan."

"Leave me out of your plan."

"Like fuck I will. You're in it, up to your neck: If I go under, how are you going to pay for this lovely apartment that comes complete with sunsets? Or have you forgotten that I plucked you out of a manhole in the Milan sewers?"

Andrea bursts out laughing right in his face. "You never plucked anyone out of anywhere; I came to Rome under my own steam, leaving behind me the nice bright sunshine of spring."

"Ooooh! Ooooh! You were down a manhole, and a nice deep one, too, under siege by three or four hysterical Milanese women. I tossed you a rope and hauled you all the way up here, to the most beautiful city on earth, a place that has existed for two thousand years without honor, or law." Oscar is emptying one glass of margarita after another and the tequila is just winding him up. "And now, instead of living in the midst of Milan's miserable poplar trees, you live in the heart of the world. You write for the big circus. You fill your tank with pussy on a regular basis. You eat late at night with the producer. And last, but not least"—he points his fork in all directions—"you look down on the Tiber that flows over the miseries of mankind. And you know what?"

Andrea sighs. "What?"

"The idea has never occurred to you that you might wind up down there, in that water, has it?"

"Oh, fuck."

"I wouldn't want you to start thinking about it tonight."

"Why on earth should I?"

"Because if the movie's a flop and I'm out six million euros, holy Christ, I swear I'll ruin all your lives, one by one, and throwing yourselves into the Tiber might not be the worst solution you can find."

"Don't come complaining to me: what with pay TV and broadcast networks, home video, and all the other bullshit that's out there, in the end you won't lose a penny even if it flops in its theatrical release."

"Fuck that! It can't flop anywhere. I'm asking you to do one thing for me, after I've done hundreds for you, is that clear?"

This time, the shameless smile that he normally wears when he improvises something to amaze or defraud vanishes. That threat comes not from the tequila, but from his plan: *He has thought about it*. And deep in his dark eyes, a light full of heavy metals and viciousness has just condensed. Andrea notices the change. But instead of memorizing it—because this is the moment when this story begins—he shakes his head, takes another gulp of margarita, and forgets, instead. Allowing Oscar to unfurl the smile that turns him into a fucking wooer with a snarl, always ready for a threat followed by a caress: "Did you get scared, you little bobbing dickhead?"

The Film to Be Saved

The movie is called *No, I Won't Surrender!*, with an exclamation mark that in the trailers is pierced by a bullet as the foreground is filled with the pouting face of Jacaranda Rizzi, staring the audience right in the eyes in an extreme close-up.

It doesn't take a film critic to see that the movie lurches along, fails to engage, makes promises, and then disappoints. It takes just Oscar Martello, the lord of the box office.

It's the story of a young woman in Palermo who goes to war against the Mafia clan that killed her beloved husband by mistake. Technically, a random killing on the sidelines of a shoot-out, a case of collateral damage.

Once she's dried her tears, instead of bowing her head to destiny, the star of the movie sets about planning her vendetta. She reassures her son. She takes him to safety, to stay with a sister of hers who lives in Urbino. Then she goes back to Palermo to face off, one by one, with the Mafiosi who have robbed her of her life. She gets a gun, she learns to shoot, she learns to use her head, her

29

vicious impulses, gasoline and arson. She adopts their methods. She harasses them with phone calls in the middle of the night. She threatens them. She shoots bullets into their front doors. She destroys a speedboat that belongs to one of them. She finds out where another one parks his cars and sets them on fire. She burns down the mob boss's villa, then she destroys his reputation and his family with photos of his secret trysts with his lover.

Her plan is to fill their lives with terror and anguish for as long as possible and then kill them, one after the other, when she decides it's time to take back her own life. Unfortunately, fate is not entirely in her hands. Even though those hands are very beautiful, and any sensible fate would be happy to let itself by fondled by her.

Jacaranda Rizzi has the face of a Sicilian woman of Norman descent, a peaches-and-cream complexion, that blond hair, those honeyed eyes, those sparse freckles scattered like stars, a body that would enchant any male, the kind of body that promises fire and nectar, perdition and paradise.

But even the people in the movie struggle to fit together. They're all too beautiful, too well dressed, their hair too perfectly groomed, all that blood, all that viciousness. Or maybe it's the director's fault, maybe he just couldn't figure out how to knead all the ingredients together properly. Jacaranda's too luminous to go unnoticed, to live in hiding the way she plans to, and the bad guys are too naive to be truly dangerous. Palermo is icy instead of steamy, and the vendetta is too hot, when it really ought to be ice cold. What the audience wants is suspense, surprise plot twists, and instead there's too much comedy for there to be cruelty and vice versa. In the end, what reigns supreme is confusion. And then there's the finale, which just leaves you baffled. The star, after killing the last Mafioso soldier and finally facing off with the mob boss, who's helpless, back to the wall, simply stops, lowers her gun, and decides not to kill him, satisfied with the terror that she's glimpsed in his eyes, a terror that will torment him forever. She vanishes into thin air, just as the cops from the mobile squad come along to sweep up the aftermath, because she's left enough evidence to convict them all. What's become of her? Has she managed to save herself, or has good luck abandoned her? Does she now lie buried in some reinforced concrete highway pier?

Only after a solid fifteen minutes—by which time you're ready to ask yourself why the fuck you ever paid to see a story you can't make head or tails of, full of shoot-outs, chase scenes, helicopters, speedboats, etc.—does the main character reappear in a small German town with neatly tended flower beds. She goes to pick up her son at school, and when she says to him, "From now on, we'll live one day at a time," half the theater laughs and the other half cries. Half the audience complains and half is stirred emotionally.

If it had a theatrical release without any fanfare, it would surely be a flop. But fanfare is Oscar Martello's specialty.

The Plan

"Tell me about the plan."

"It came to me after watching the movie ten times in a row, emerging first depressed and then furious."

"Can't you recut it? Usually you can find a way out." Andrea and Oscar both know that the history of cinema is full of mediocre films that, once they're recut, become smash hits. The great Franco Cristaldi locked himself in the Moviola room with *Cinema Paradiso*—which was long, slow, and dull—and by cutting fifty minutes, transformed it into a film that won everything, even too many awards.

"That's the point: we can't, there's no way out. The asshole shot an endless quantity of tracking shots. If you move a single thing, you're moving too much. And if you cut, you're cutting everything."

"Didn't you notice it when you watched the dailies?"

"No, that's my fault."

"So what are you going to do?"

"Instead of doctoring the movie, we need to doctor the premiere."

"Interesting. How are you going to do that?"

Oscar smiles. He leads into it without any haste; he likes to drag out the anticipation. He says, "I hired two freelance muckrakers."

Oh, this is starting out well, thinks Andrea. Instead he says, "Well good for you."

"They're Totò Guerra and Mirko Pace."

"I know them. Guerra and Pace. They have the nerve to desecrate all that is sacred by doing business as War & Peace."

"They're the best in the business."

"They're garbage."

"Nice work, genius. Their job is to fabricate garbage."

"They destroy people."

"Not always. Sometimes, instead of sending them to hell, they launch people into the firmament."

"Is that the case here?"

"You can bet your life on it."

⁓

Totò Guerra and Mirko Pace, the muckrakers, are each about forty years of age. They're exactly the way you'd imagine them: skinny, angular faces, necks and arms swathed in tattoos. They come from the outskirts of Milan. They go everywhere with mini-cameras, mini–tape recorders, and family-pack portions of sheer ruthlessness. They wear skintight black suits, white shirts, narrow black ties. A couple of morgue assistants, here for the news. To hobble their victims they use hidden video cameras and escorts in plain view. They invent scandals on commission for all the celebrity magazines, as well as for a couple of websites specializing in gossip. And, likewise on commission, they make those same scandals disappear.

In the early days, in search of easy money, they'd focused on the good-for-nothing scions of the jet set: two days of stakeouts and they were sure to have handfuls of photographs with young girls, hot to trot, cocaine, Thai masseuses, transsexuals with bulging biceps, swinger clubs, the whole nine yards. At the time, the point of the work the duo did was almost never to publish the photographs, but to ensure they weren't published. Their fees spiked heavenward, the agency was riding high. But since it was like shooting fish in a barrel—and with all the shooting that was going on, a platoon of investigating magistrates had developed the habit of summoning them for questioning as "individuals with information about what had happened"—after a dozen or so exploits they started to get scared about all those investigations that were threatening to dry up their sources, and leave them with third-degree burns on their buttocks. They were starting to get sick and tired of those muscle-bound, overtattooed assholes who always wound up begging for mercy through their tears, and especially of the unscrupulous lawyers who first represented them and bought back all the compromising photos under the table, only to turn around and hit them with bills that were more expensive than the blackmail they'd just paid.

So War & Peace began to be curious about the lawyers themselves, about their fingertips so well trained at ferreting out cash, delving deep into the deposits of showbiz, under the monuments of the eternal city, down the infernal circles of muck and gold that made up La Dolce Roma: a landscape of interchangeable living rooms, telephone conversations destined to be tapped, movies, television, soccer, music, jet set, politics, worlds on a continuum so intimate that they overlapped and become one single universe, inhabited by men and women willing to sell their souls and their sleep at night for a well-placed photograph or an appearance on television, a love affair or a betrayal in the gossip papers, a contract, an election, a gram of cocaine and a gram of power.

Thousands of transactions from which War & Peace try to skim their attendance fee and drop it into the slot of the wheel of fortune, which inevitably, after turning and turning, lines up the three fatal red cherries, followed by the corresponding shower of tax-exempt coins. A rain that now irrigates the entire crop of privates and corporals that work under them, the scoundrels paid by the day to spread contrived news, the platoon of unfaithful cops who arrange to identify license plates and tap phones illegally, sub-blackmailers and women willing to train rent girls. All of them people with their heads back and mouths open, waiting for a drop of grease to spill from the perennial feast of the Superworld.

"How can you trust a couple of attack dogs like those two?"

"I pay them and they bite whoever I tell them to."

"I don't want anything to do with this."

"Why, are you afraid of getting your hands dirty?"

"You said it."

"Oh, fuck! We have a virgin trying not to wallow in the mud."

"I've always tried to write things I don't need to be ashamed of."

"Are you sure?"

"I've never written about gossip or other bullshit from some keyhole."

"Sure, but now you write TV drama. And I assure you that even War & Peace are ashamed of the things you write." And he bursts into loud, unaccompanied laughter ("Ha ha!") as he gulps down his margarita. Then he calms down and says, "You'll never even see them. And anyway, *they'll* be taking care of *you*."

"So you're determined not to understand."

"No, I understand, and I understand everything. If you'll just be quiet, I'll explain." Oscar Martello gets up, walks over to the parapet of the terrace, looming up in shirtsleeves against the blackness surrounding the embroidery of the cupolas and the shooting stars of the automobiles traveling along the opposite bank of the Tiber, the Lungotevere embarcadero. Then he comes back indoors to the center of the room. He's creating, now: "Thursday night you and I are going to a party in Sabaudia at Milly's place, the fat woman who hates me. There are going to be lots of people, and Jacaranda will be there, too."

Milly Gallo Bautista, the fat woman who hates Oscar and adores Andrea, grew up in an orphanage like in all the worst fairy tales. And on the strength of her guts, muscles, and resentment, she became one of the most powerful agents in Roman show biz. She gives a living to a hundred or so actors, directors, and screenwriters. In exchange, she sucks between ten and fifteen percent of their blood. She endows them with life, feeds off of them, and in the meantime, she gradually kills them.

"Okay, we meet Jacaranda. Then what?"

Oscar spreads his arms wide, imagining how to frame the unexpected turn of events: "Then you'll disappear together."

Andrea evaluates the information.

Oscar smiles.

Oscar relishes the silence.

The revelation hovers in the night air and then slowly glides down to the point where Oscar's gaze and Andrea's gaze meet, while a seagull passes by outside the glass doors, just skimming the roofs, screeching like the wails of a newborn child.

"What do you mean we'll disappear?"

"To Paris, a romantic getaway. The actress and the writer. Beauty and the Beast, tell the story however you like. But they won't know that right away. First the suspense. First the mystery. Think about it. The mystery of the disappearance of Jacaranda Rizzi, the star of *No, I Won't Surrender! Pam-pa-pa-pam!* A great, courageous actress takes a stand against the Mafia and now she may have been *kidnapped* by the Mafia. It'll froth up like whipped cream on all the front pages. I can already see the banner headlines."

"And you think that's going to be enough to launch the movie?"

"Don't you worry about that. The two of you will just stay holed up in Paris, no phones, no communication with the outside world, while back here War & Peace kick up a storm. And all this on the eve of the premiere! It's bound to work."

"It's a crime."

"What? Which crime?"

"It's called raising a false alarm."

"And who gives a damn?"

"I do. We'd run the risk of looking like fools and we'd run the risk of being put on trial. First we'd be seen as fakers and then we'd be seen as criminals. I'm not joking around: it's a crime."

"No, my friend, it's the movies." Oscar Martello's face emanates flashes of pure happiness when he utters the words "the movies."

"Of course: it's the movies. This way we can all wind up writing soaps for the Albanian national television network."

"No one puts anyone on trial and no one goes to jail in this country, unless you're some fucking gypsy. Crimes just help to bulk up your résumé. And after all, we're the ones who decide what the truth is; we can act as well *outside* of the movies as we do *in* them."

Oscar's idea has started to open a breach through Andrea's

mental pulsations, which are dripping tequila as they illuminate a close-up of Jacaranda sitting next to him at a table in La Coupole, in Paris, while the continental evening descends. The image isn't all that bad, after all. "Go on."

"Once the mystery has built up, we'll blow it wide open. And while people are rushing to their movie theaters, that's when Jacaranda will leap out of the woodwork and be back, good as new. She was never kidnapped by the Mafia. Jacaranda is simply, wonderfully, romantically head over heels. And in love with whom? With the writer! The Mafia doesn't have a fucking blessed thing to do with it; she was just on the run with her beloved. Happy ending for her, double the publicity for us. Do I make my point?"

"That way, everyone will assume I wrote that tremendous piece of shit."

"Look at the positive side and stop getting lost in the details, for Christ's sake. I'll put your name on the screenwriting contract, and you'll even get a share of the royalties."

Suddenly he doesn't mind the idea quite as much. "You will?"

"I will. A nice chunk of cash for your trouble, no?"

"And then what will happen?"

"What will happen is that unfortunately you'll have to pay taxes on it. Ha ha!"

"No, I'm asking a serious question."

"You and Jacaranda are going to play boyfriend and girlfriend for a couple of weeks, War & Peace will tell your fantastic Paris story, and then we're all friends like before."

"What about the director?"

Oscar makes a face as if he's just bitten into half a lemon. "To hell with the director! He doesn't know a thing and it has to stay that way. I never want that asshole underfoot again."

"But he's also her boyfriend."

"Whose boyfriend? Get caught up with events. Jacaranda gets a new boyfriend every time she needs one, especially when she has a movie coming out. And that asshole Fabris does the same thing."

"Let true love triumph."

"Fuck, but do you write films or just read about them in the gossip mags? No one loves anyone. Get that into your head."

Meanwhile, Jacaranda

So events grind into motion that night. And as they grind into motion they determine their first consequence, which ricochets not all that far from that conversation on the terrace—at least, not too far as the crow flies—landing in Monte Mario over near the Hilton. The reverberation has reached the fourth floor of the small white villa that stands midway between the grand villa that once belonged to the valorous Cecchi Gori clan and the four hundred rooms of the hotel Hilton, where at that hour Jacaranda is asleep, with no company other than the little lamp on the night table that designs an infinity of stars on the ceiling and, at their center, the sweep of the Milky Way, which has the same color of sand and silk as her nightie.

She sleeps clutching tightly the secret that for all these years has been tormenting her, like a bad memory that won't let itself be forgotten. The secret that even presses on her dreams, sometimes turning them so sour that it awakens her.

Jacaranda opens her eyes, looks at the time, sees that it's three in the morning. Someone is thinking about her. But whether lovingly or malevolently she cannot say.

And already in the dimension between wakefulness and sleep, there's that sensation of not being in her own home but in some provisional place, which is something that's happened to her ever since she was a tiny girl, when she first moved with her mother. And as a teenage girl, when she went to live in at least three different apartments with her aunt. And after her adolescence, with her girlfriends, living in cramped rooms and filthy kitchens and bathrooms packed with lipsticks, panties, and bras: those were the years she attended the Academy of Dramatic Arts, a time of short-order hamburgers, when she played Blanche DuBois in *A Streetcar Named Desire*, the role created by Vivien Leigh in Elia Kazan's film version of the play, the one who is raped by Marlon Brando at the end. A role that cut into her like a knife wound, as she learned the part, so that she burst into tears at the end of the final audition, right in the middle of the round of applause, because she felt suffocated by it, that time and forever after.

Then there were the apartments of her boyfriends, even the short-order boyfriends, whose names she doesn't even remember anymore, but the furnishings, yes, she remembers them, especially the sofas and the beds she had sex on, pretending to have orgasms that never came through, and the milky light that filtered in through the windows at dawn while they snored and she lay awake, watchfully eyeing her beauty as it dripped away, nourishing nothing.

All of those places were homes that she put on like someone else's overcoat, to feel a little warmth against the cold, and sometimes, like the scripts that offered her the haven of a well-written character, a destiny, a meaning. Always sensing that that home, that boyfriend, that script, would have a provisional duration, a limited time outside which, she knew full well, what awaited her was the void that wasn't a blank space, but rather a black, cold one, where it sometimes poured down rain.

That void frightened her and, at the same time, attracted her—just as she was attracted by the idea of bestowing herself freely on men who were useless for anything other than to bring a little light into that blackness, whether in real or cinematic life, each of those lives paying a bit of oxygen to the other. Letting her public—but also her directors like Attilio Fabris and producers like Oscar Martello—go on believing that her suspension bridges over life remained standing, still capable of taking her somewhere. And that (instead) they hadn't long ago begun crumbling, and were by now being held together by nothing but benzodiazepine—or alcohol when she was younger, or cocaine when there was someone to buy it for her—to support the weight of her magnificent body, but only one step at a time, one reawakening at a time. Which was, after all, the quantity of suffering that she could tolerate, or at least so she believed.

With her eyes wide open, she thinks back to the movie, and the tragic dimension that it contains, at least for her, since it is the story of a woman who won't surrender, played by a woman who has done nothing but surrender in real life.

She still hasn't seen the whole movie. The producer and the director had a fight. Punches were thrown. That's not usually a good sign. But how would she know?

Attilio, the director, is worthless. He's one of those guys who live in their mirror and already by the third night they're snoring.

But not Oscar. Oscar never sleeps. Oscar, bandit that he is, says that now he's found the solution. He has an idea up his sleeve to launch the movie the way it deserves. With the spotlights trained full on it and a skyful of fireworks. He told her, "Get ready for a full-frontal assault of television cameras, film festivals, and awards seasons."

So now she knows that this will finally be the right time. The moment she's been awaiting for years, the time to empty her gut and, finally, also her head. To utter that story in public and to cry enough to rid herself of all the salt that's burned her inside. To set down the brick that for too many years she's been carrying, the brick that every now and again she's tried to forget, to conceal in her secretmost hiding place, and that then suddenly reappeared in the center of her chest, choking off her breath, like what happens to Nicole Kidman, the mother of a little boy killed by a hit-and-run driver, in a movie that always brings tears to her eyes, *Rabbit Hole*; a hard, flat, sharp-edged grief that, however, she can no longer do without because *it keeps her company*.

By now, she's sick and tired of that company. She has to do it. She can do it. And at last she'll stop letting herself be overwhelmed by things, even when she is the protagonist of those things. To be done, once and for all, with this sensation that has been devouring her little by little, with the feeling that she's being lived much more than she's actually living. And finally free herself, vindicate herself. Fill the void, be able to breathe once again. Or at least that's what Jacaranda believes she's revealing to herself in the confusion of her half-waking state, in that hundredth night she's lived through alone, when even the most senseless thoughts seem like so many arrows bringing luminous revelations.

Oscar Martello, the Story

Oscar Martello has a handsome face, like some fifth ace tucked up a sleeve, short hair, dark eyes, and a smile that calls for a straight-armed slap. He usually wears dark silk-and-cotton sweaters without a shirt, custom-tailored jackets and trousers, handmade leather ankle boots. In the course of his lifetime, he's taken plenty of punches. He's returned them. He's learned to feint from them. Aside from movies, he also produces detective shows for TV. And then there's the long-running series, more spectacularly unbelievable than fiction, of his own real life. He got his start in raggedy patched pants and now he goes everywhere with fat wads of bills wrapped in a rubber band, and when he pays stratospheric hotel bills or restaurant checks, it seems like cinema. He's becoming a bandit, and perhaps it was fated so, because he came up from the street. As Helga likes to say—and she knew knife dancers from the toughest outlying areas of the cities of Argentina—"Those who come up from the street have no limits."

As a boy, Oscar wanted to be an actor. He studied mime in

44

Milan. He dreamed of working for Julian Beck's Living Theatre. And perhaps he could have achieved that dream. But at the end of his first apprenticeship, on the stage of the Palazzina Liberty in Milan, Julian Beck started kicking him during an improvisational performance. The kicks were part of the show, but after the second one Oscar spun around, dodged the third one, and started slapping Julian Beck's face, to a loud burst of applause from the other students. Before stepping down off the stage, he said to him, "I am a free man and you're a dickhead." The next day he left for Rome.

In Rome he got a job driving cars for weddings, during which he'd proposition the girlfriends of the bride, cadge meals, fill his pockets with the traditional Jordan almond confetti and with phone numbers. One day he bought himself a camera. He discovered that he had a talent for framing a picture. He had a good eye. In those days, he lived in a studio apartment in the San Lorenzo quarter, he dreamed of getting work in the movie industry.

Instead of the movie industry he found a hack producer, a movie industry wannabe, Eusebio Reverberi, a "Roman from Frosinone," a producer possessed of a certain sly genius for big box office, lusting for money and work, who happened to need a driver, a personal assistant, and a sidekick for his routines as he foisted off lies on his potential investors. Reverberi had gotten his start with light, low-budget comedies, a bit of soft porn disguised as light entertainment, an unremarkable side business in girls to fill the beds of Roman politicians in the interests of pillow talk. In his way, he loved the movies, he believed in the magic of a darkened theater. But he was one of those fragile men who are sure to lose everything sooner or later.

Oscar watched, drove, and learned.

He learned that in the movies, everyone claims they're penniless, but money circulates constantly because there are always
installments to be paid, ex-wives who demand alimony, beautiful
Cuban girls who ask for diamonds, and sons and daughters who
need rehab clinics where they can dry out. At first, Oscar skimmed
a little off the top on the fuel, the restaurants, and the girls, cadg-
ing blow jobs in the car, high atop the Aventine Hill, with a view
of the sunset. But even though the Aventine was one of the seven
hills, it was still just a way of looking at life from the lowest point,
a bequest of his father the doorman, his mother the housewife.
Both of them tenants of the world of before, the world of losers,
the world with the scent of the bouillon cube in the front hall, the
swayback sofa in the cramped little living room, the lightless life
of Serravalle Scrivia, an Apennine town on the age-old highway,
in the province of Alessandria, which is to say, nowhere. The horrendous colorless North, frigid girls who kiss with icy tongues, the
priest from the parish youth club with a raging hard-on, the flaking
plaster walls of the vo-tech school, the movie theater in the town
piazza that showed two movies every Sunday, an old-fashioned
Western and Cecil B. DeMille's *The Ten Commandments*. Until the
night that Oscar went to a movie theater in Novi Ligure and saw
the Californian epic of *The Strawberry Statement*, the universities
of Berkeley and Columbia, occupied in the sixties, building up to
1968, police, kisses, fists and nightclubs, grass, liberation of Viet-
nam, with a West Coast soundtrack, and "The Circle Game" as
sung by Buffy Sainte-Marie, a movie that had opened his eyes, his
heart, and his imagination, and had convinced him to leave that
filthy pit of fog and gravel behind him and go out and capture the
world. And, sooner or later, buy that world for himself.

Within six months he learned to think bigger and bigger all the

time. Not only to use the custom-tailored shirts of his boss, Eusebio Reverberi, but also to order them for himself from the tailor
Piero Albertelli with the exact same air of nonchalance. And also
to use his visual talent, his facility for memorizing names, places,
circumstances, and films. To imitate the way that those born to
money act. To transform his lack of manners into sheer arrogance
in order to compete with them. To despise them and, at the same
time, to admire them. He used to say, "I'm an anarchist, I disman-
tle power and I pocket it."

He also learned—protected by his brash ignorance—to pocket
the workings of the film industry. To express his opinions about
scripts, discovering that he also had a talent for good stories. To
track down affordable locations and services. To offer pesky actors
small parts, saying to them, "Now you owe me a favor." And as he
built up a backlog of favors, he learned how to redeem them.

Open Up, It's the Police!

The opportunity of his lifetime came the day a platoon of policemen from the First District burst into Eusebio Reverberi's penthouse apartment in Vicolo del Divino Amore. It was six thirty in the morning: "Open up, it's the police!"

They said they were searching for documents concerning a suspicious corporate bankruptcy. They didn't find them. To make up for that, they did find a half-naked underage female fast asleep, twenty grams of cocaine, a slab of hashish, five Rohypnol pills, amphetamine tablets, counterfeit prescriptions for codeine, and an unregistered Colt Python .38 Special, a six-shot, short-barrel revolver.

Reverberi started whining, he said that someone, who knows who, must just have left the coke and the amphetamines there to set him up; the naked minor was a girlfriend's daughter, he'd had no idea she was a minor and anyway he'd never touched her, he was just giving her a place to stay because the poor thing had been locked out of her home; the prescriptions for codeine and the Ro-

48

hypnol were all just to help him get to sleep; and the handgun was to protect himself from certain Sinti gypsy loan sharks who had been threatening him. He called his lawyer. He called a cabinet minister he'd been supplying with girlfriends. He called Oscar to hold off the journalists, the lawyers, the busybodies, and the cats. He wound up spending nineteen days in Regina Coeli prison, where a huge gorilla of a convict tried to shove him up against the wall in the showers and rape him, and he wept and shouted so loud that the guards came running to rescue his virgin ass cheeks. When he was released, he told the press that he'd been framed, he was innocent, he had complete respect for the entire Italian magistracy with the exception of those two judges who had put him behind bars just to drum up some favorable publicity for themselves, and he swore he would make a social protest film about his odyssey through the criminal justice system. Then he went home, threw himself a party with three Brazilian girls who took turns sucking his dick while the other two stuck balls of cocaine up his ass to send him cartwheeling through space as far as possible from the stench of prison that had imprisoned his nostrils. On the third night of carousing, as he was sitting in the bathroom and counting the passing angels, Eusebio Reverberi felt a surging wave of pure heat descend over him from the ceiling or perhaps direct from heaven, said, "Oh, fuck!" and died on the spot of a fulminant myocardial infarction.

Oscar, in the days following Reverberi's arrest, had set up housekeeping at his apartment. While waiting for him, he'd organized dinners, cocktail parties, and future films. When Reverberi got out of prison, he'd found his apartment reduced to a pigsty. The two of them had fought, and Oscar had been fired summarily on the landing. But as he left, he'd realized he still had the key. The key of fate, considering that when Reverberi kicked the bucket, falling face-first onto the marble bathroom floor, the three Brazilian girls decided to call Oscar's cell phone and then take to their heels, without even stopping to brush their hair. He went over, opened up, saw, thought, and decided. He cleaned up the scene of the death. He threw open the windows. He dressed the corpse in a pair of pajamas and a dressing gown that was worthy of an English gentleman. Then he called the doctor and the lawyers to arrange the scene: the great producer had died while he was already hard at work on the screenplay inspired by his legal ordeal. The death of an innocent man. His heart hadn't withstood the many humiliations piled on him by the judges, the press, and the world at large.

At dawn, Oscar Martello left behind him that old life and set out on a new life with his nice fat severance pay: five and half ounces of cocaine that Reverberi, God rest his soul, had purchased with his assistance on the day of his release from prison, plus his address book with all the phone numbers, plus a Vacheron Constantin pink gold wristwatch that he was just crazy about, a few cashmere jackets, a small stack of cash, and the keys to the Jaguar Executive XJ6 that he'd been driving for a year and which he'd grown quite fond of. And it was only to be the first in a long series of such cars.

With that treasury of phone numbers and cocaine—cut with cornstarch and shameless confidence—Oscar dug the foundations of his fortune, making home deliveries in the movie industry, for private parties and dinners. He became everyone's best friend. He sold. He bought. He doubled his prices and then offered insane discounts. He was likable, he was munificent, he offered advice. He listened to secrets. He dispensed opinions.

And in the meantime he absorbed ideas. He learned how to observe the backstage workings of the movies, which are invisible to the naked eye, but much more instructive than what you see in the movie theater. And, even more useful than that, he learned to navigate the backdrops of the Roman night, with its crowd of narcissistic actors, irritable actresses, scoundrels and thieves, politicians with way too much testosterone, genuine artists, fake artists, homosexuals both cheerful and on the brink of despair, depressed daughters, good-for-nothing sons devoted to bodybuilding, sharks with the teeth of CPAs, money launderers, young heiresses with bad breath, lawyers from the Locri area of Calabria, dripping dandruff and cash, widows covered with wrinkles, rubies, and hysterical Jack Russell terriers that pee on the couches, barricaded in their pink and yellow mansions in the Parioli district or in their funereal villas on the Appian Way. Everyone needed the bit of help he could give them, Oscar Martello's little helping hand, Martello the consoler of solitary nostrils, propman with a face you want to slap and a heart of gold for all the poor drug fiends out there in circulation. His cell phone rang constantly at all hours. And he always answered, and he listened and listened and listened. They'd open his heart, and he'd open their billfolds.

From Coke to Cinema

I n those days, peddling between ten and twenty grams of coke a day in exchange for cash, free sex, the occasional extortion, invitations out on yachts and speedboats, all-expenses-paid vacations at the Hotel Cristallo in Cortina, Oscar had produced his first movie. A cyberpunk reenvisioning of the story of Saint Francis in which the saint cut his oppressive father's throat, screwed Saint Clare, talked to the birds of the forest only to lure them in so he could catch them and roast them over an open fire, and recommended sex as the viaticum toward the ineffable, along with sexual charity, as a critique of the vested powers. A tremendous piece of trash that aroused the indignation of the press, arguments among theologians, and the eager excitement of the moviegoing public on account of Saint Clare who, thanks to Oscar's ever vigilant and innovative mind, appeared fully nude, and completely shaved, in the throes of an ecstasy that her faith perfected into a pair of resounding orgasms every bit up to the standards of the Living Theatre.

His debut in the world of filmmaking was greeted by his customers with the occasional sarcastic comment, a certain amount of admiration, and a great deal of envy. From that moment on, Oscar, as he steadily dusted the cocaine off his heels, increasingly wallowed in cinema. He learned to perform the part of the producer: he'd earn ten and boast a hundred. He envisioned international blockbusters and put together passable TV series featuring good-hearted doctors, lawyers hunting for justice, priests hunting for sinners. All of it canned cat food for unhappy families.

But the whole time, he was making money. He was milking cash out of the Ministry of Performing Arts. He pocketed political recommendations from the notary Alfonso Davanzati, the head of the Freemasons, and from that aging queen Amedeo Castelli, who was building the new outskirts of the city, and a functionary of the Vatican's Opus Dei. From them he had learned that politicians are like certain smartphone apps: they cost you a few euros every month but they come in handy, providing you with what you need, a workaround or a recommendation, at any hour of the day or night. And when they've served their purpose, you leave them in background mode, ready for their next use.

He learned from his mistakes. His TV series got better and his doctors got meaner. He perfected his aptitude for sensing the things that were in the air. He'd picked up a fragment of Dan Brown, the heretic. He'd toss in a dash of Padre Pio, the saint, and a pinch of Paulo Coelho to tamp down the blood from the stigmata with a little New Age talc. He'd add the chill of a murder victim. Or else the flames of a cheating wife. And even the mystery of an alien asleep in the catacombs of Rome.

He took a couple of trips to Los Angeles, but instead of coming home a reconverted *ammerikano* like all provincial producers, he came back filled with simple, national-popular ideas. Like:

Husband and wife, leading a standard life. In the fourth scene, roundhouse punch: the adolescent son dies of leukemia. Boom! The couple slips into a dark crisis. Grief, reexamination: Who are we, where are we going, why are we alive? "The kind of bullshit everyone wonders about at times like that, right?" Tears. Pitiless analysis, husband and wife go at it brutally. It gets so bad that maybe the two parents orphaned of their son are on the verge of a breakup.

But that's not how it goes; instead, there's a turning point: it is revealed that their late son had a first sweetheart, and they never knew it. The parents want to get to know her. They invite her over. She has freckles and a button nose. Her name is *Luciiia*. "Just listen to how musical it is!" And the young thing tells them about the time they skipped school together and had their first kiss: pure love bubbles from her naive lips. The parents listen: it's a surge of fresh water churning the pond of their opaque, adult love. They feel envy, they feel nostalgia: How long has it been since *their* first kisses? And what have they turned into now?

That nostalgia stirs their emotions back up again.

The father and the mother look at each other with new eyes.

They touch each other with new hands.

They speak to each other with new words.

So it's possible to start living again after all. "Music! Long shot, zoom in on their faces as their cheeks brush. Close-up: a kiss. Tears: tremendous, spectacular sex!"

The Narrative Foundations

One thing that Oscar inherited from that blessed, deeply rotten man, Eusebio Reverberi, was open access to the drawing room of Donna Angelina Casagrande, which meant a direct
line to the Vatican, which in turn brought him his first half-price
penthouse on Piazza Mignanelli, discounted mortgages, foreign
exchange to foreign exchange, inside tracks with God-fearing
politicians—men in the finest political alignments of the former
Christian Democrats, the former Socialists, the former Fascists,
all of them now tributaries to Berlusconi's New Right and the
old lunatic-asylum Roman Left without so much as a change of
wardrobe, bank accounts, or lovers—and good news concerning
the permeability of Catholic morality, making it possible to rob
whatever's not screwed down, and only afterward to cultivate in
blessed peace one's own sacrosanct sense of guilt.

He reduced his use of cocaine virtually to zero. The "virtually" went up his nostrils on weekends, when he'd roam the city in
search of good reasons not to go back home at night, home where,

nowadays, Helga had taken up residence. Helga, his sweet dam-
nation, who had in the meantime popped out two baby girls so
fragile that they brought tears to his eyes every time he looked at
them—though, truth be told, he usually didn't look at them at all.
He started smoking the contraband Cohibas that he had smuggled in from Cuba, and providing hot meals free of charge to the
hordes of starving screenwriters—screenwriters more accustomed
to eating hamburgers and contracts for pitifully small multiples
of euros, journalists who couldn't wait to abandon the depressing
open-plan cubicles of their ink-on-newsprint papers, and who believed, as they swallowed a dozen oysters, on a terrace with Filipino houseboys and candles glowing in the night, that they were
finally tasting Hollywood.

He liked to call money "large," but that term applied strictly
to payments in the thousands of euros and above, the next level
up being "rocks," which stood for millions. Anything beneath
the thousand euros were "yards," or spare change, or even better,
"nothing." Four yards for a dinner with a babe at Dal Bolognese,
in the Piazza del Popolo, five yards for raw fish at San Lorenzo.
Ten large for a long weekend at the Quisisana on Capri—the
Italian name, which meant "Here you heal," changed jocularly to
Quisiscopa, or "Here you fuck"—with a couple of whores, ideally
a mother-and-daughter set. Fifty large for a fucking vacation that
can hold its head up, with sailboat, a crew, and champagne, for
instance, a week with Helga in that volcanic psychiatric institution
for the wealthy known as Pantelleria.

Then one day he saw the ocean liner *Rex* set sail across the black
sea of *Amarcord*, an unforgettable scene shot entirely on Sound
Stage 5 at Cinecittà, and it had the effect of a dazzling revelation:
all he needed if he wanted to buy the world was to purchase the

world-in-a-box represented by the movies. And then expand it, using the infinite spaces of the imagination and stories, which are the only sea capable of keeping us afloat. And allowing us to tolerate the death that every goddamned day sends our lives straight to the bottom.

This was his dream. It became his secret project. He needed to make his money grow exponentially, and fast, too. And so he grabbed every production he could lay his hands on, taking work from the state television networks and the private networks. He siphoned money out of the ministry. He multiplied the teams of screenwriters. He learned to play fast and loose with the advances on signature, which he knew were the first spark of any movie, the seed that instilled it with life and triggered the creative churn. He promised more than other producers and beat them to the punch. He actually laid out advances on signature of five large to screenwriters, and ten large as a second installment. As a result, everyone hurried home to rack their brains and draft the treatment of this imminent masterpiece and then rushed back to Oscar to deliver, hoping that the promise of a second installment wouldn't crumble to dust in their hands. They had no idea that watching second installments crumble to dust in their hands only stimulated Oscar Martello's creativity, reawakened his old love of theatrical improvisation, drove him to all his finest performances, the ones where he played the furious producer, a role that usually started with this line: "You've written a giant steaming piece of shit, every last one of you is fired," he'd say, freezing his audience to the spot. Then he'd indulge in a full minute of silence as he paced back and forth, while the screenwriters gasped like beached whales, inventing excuses or absurd questions, such as, "Why are you being so negative?" or even, "I don't know if you read all the way through to the end, because the last scene has a wonderful plot twist and we were thinking that—"

At that point, Oscar Martello would let his eyes bug out, suck in all the oxygen in the room, emit a series of sounds, emit an array of vibrations, and then shout, "I wipe my ass with wonderful plot twists in the last scene!" He'd stop, and then slowly and clearly enunciate, "Wonderful plot twists belong at the beginning, in the middle, and at the end of any good story: chapter one in the handbook of a professional screenwriter."

Then he'd take a wide stance to get a solid balance as he felt the gales of inspiration begin to gust inside him. "Open your ears wide: stories are like buildings. If I'm going to construct a building, where do I start, from the roof, from the foundations, or from the plot twists?" He never expected a reply, he just relished the absurdity of the question in silence, savoring the looks on their faces and the air hissing out of the air conditioner.

"That's right! Good boys, just keep your traps shut, that way you won't piss me off even worse. And do you know why you've all so royally screwed the pooch? Because instead of starting from the foundations or even from the roof, you went straight ahead and started with the flowers on the windowsills. You decided to dabble in a form of fucking literature that nobody at all gives a damn about, much less the TV industry. You've produced a piece of Mannerism, which as far as I'm concerned, amounts to so much mental masturbation. *Man-ner-ism*," he would say, acting it out. "Got it?"

He'd take pleasure in the overall effect. Then he'd go and sit down, pick up a Cohiba; he'd bite off the end, spit it out, light it up, suck down the smoke, and cough. By taking away his oxygen, the smoke would soothe his nerves. From there, slumped in his armchair, he'd say, "I don't give a damn about the flowers on the windowsill. I want nice, spacious foundations, nice, solid foundations, I want *nar-ra-tive foundations*," enunciating as he held his arms out horizontally to indicate the vastness of the concept and the depth of the challenge. "Do you all know what the fuck I'm talking about?"

As he looked around the room he'd lock eyes with the screenwriters' darting, evasive gazes, he'd imagine their cute little hearts in frantic palpitation. In fact, no one in the room knew what the hell he was talking about, and for that matter, neither did he. All the same, he looked out at them from the center of these entirely fictional narrative foundations, shrouded in clouds of smoke, in the throes of a full-blown brainstorm—which absolutely ruled out any trivial sidetracking toward such thorny issues as advances deliverable in either "large," "yards," or "nothing," much less the purely fictional second installments. There was just no time for it. The new plot was growing and speaking through him. Through the great Oscar Martello, the oracle.

"Imagine . . ." he said amid the silence.

And he'd tell stories, or really he'd create them, getting to his feet, pacing in circles, miming, working himself up, smoking and spitting. And he'd shout, and shout, and shout until the screenwriters, overwhelmed by their sense of guilt for their own miserable narrative ineptitude, finally convinced themselves that what they'd turned in was a fish skeleton without flesh, a lifeless story, an inert mass of words with a sprinkling of literary cream.

"What the fuck good to me is cream, when I'm starving for meat, when I'm starving for big emotions?" Oscar would shout, staring at them one by one. "What am I supposed to sink my teeth into if I don't have a story?" he'd yell, the veins bulging in his neck, as they all looked at the floor.

They'd promise rewrites, retouches, inventions. And the minute the meeting was over, thanking the good lord above that they
hadn't heard those terrible words "You're fired!" again, they'd
hastily gather up their notes. They'd leave without so much as
mentioning the long-forgotten promise of more large, just thanking their lucky stars that they'd ever received the old money.
They'd hurry home to get back to work, pleased that they'd managed to get a second chance.

But by that point they were in the trap. He would call them
the next day and continue their indoctrination, "I want it to ooze
sentiment, you understand?" he'd tell each of them. And the next
morning he'd call them again, "Did you write? Summarize."

But working with so many different teams on so many different projects at the same time, surrounded by the confusion of
Helga, the whims and complaints of his young daughters, and the
inefficiency of the household domestic staff, every so often even
the great Oscar Martello, king of the catch-a-sucker-every-minute
narrative approach, would hit a logic fail and get his teams and
his sentimental clichés mixed. At seven in the morning he'd yank
one of his screenwriters out of bed with a call: "Listen up and listen good. The scene is that she hears footsteps and runs. Outside
it's snowing, this is the night of the living dead, do I make myself
clear?"

"Certainly," says the guy, who's still struggling through the fog
of sleep.

Oscar would work himself up, "She runs toward the car.
There's snow everywhere. She gets in. The car won't start. The
shadow's getting closer. She tries again, it won't start! The shadow
gets even closer. She screams, the side window shatters into bits,
the engine finally turns over, the tires screech, a hand is about to

grab her, she screams with all the breath in her lungs, the tires finally grab the asphalt, and the car rockets forward. She survives by the skin of her teeth. Fuck, Rodolfo, you understand how?"

A long pause, as if it were snowing in the telephone, too. "But I'm not Rodolfo," the screenwriter says, finally wide awake.

"Huh? What? Then who the fuck are you?"

"Roberto. I'm writing *Orphans of Love*, not *Werewolves of Milan*."

"Ah, Roberto! One of my eighteen fucking Filipino houseboys thinks it's funny to hide my fucking eyeglasses. I can't see, I can't write. And this desk diary is written with a fucking microscope. But what are you doing, Roberto, resting on your laurels? Are you making progress? Did you write the big sex scene yet?"

Oscar was a vicious beast who loved to sink his fangs into his screenwriters' asses. He'd summon them for a meeting, sit them all down, and say, "Open your eyes and ears." Their gazes of admiration were the power driving his stories, feeding him images and words. They would pump his imagination. And then and there, live, in front of them, the great Oscar Martello would chew up plot twists, grind out stories, digest cliff-hangers and, to general applause, shit out scripts.

Andrea, Last of the Serranos

Andrea is the last of the Serranos. His father was called Giaime, and he died of a heart attack when Andrea was just eleven. He remembers him as a great tree casting a long shadow. Like a big fish and a broad wake of bubbles. Never and never again would he ever have imagined the frailty of his solid heart. They lived in Milan, and they were so happy that they had no idea of it. That day, twenty-eight years earlier, the sky fell on the shoulders of his mother, who had blue eyes and was named Eleonora, affectionately called Nora, or by her loved ones Neretta, and because of that burden she began to shrink, shedding the pounds of all the smiles that had nourished her. She became a wandering soul, then a glass always full of cognac with sugar cubes, and finally an empty hug goodbye, leaving him and his older sister, sweet Alice, all alone.

His mother died, overwhelmed by a sorrow that she could no longer combat, or that she had gotten tired of fighting, but giving them in those eight years of daily survival the certainty that they were loved—which is, after all, the only map needed to find the treasure of life.

Alice set sail in pursuit of a marine equipment designer who lived in Australia. She vanished, leaving behind her a cheerful shower of picture postcards every time she moved to a new Australian city or state, until the day that she announced she was getting married in Queensland, in a Baptist church made of light blue sheet steel. From that day forward, he'd hear from her only every time she popped out another baby.

Andrea chose cities on terra firma—Milan, London, Buenos Aires, Rome—even though his blood came from a big island, Sardinia, the place that had generated his family's history, only eventually to wipe out all traces of it. He discovered that fact the day his cousin Marco took him to an out-of-the-way piazza in the city of Cagliari and pointed to a flower bed in the middle of it, and told him, "There, that's where your house was, the home of the Serranos."

"There, where?"

Ignoring the question, Marco continued to tell him about things that couldn't be seen. "Your family bought and sold horses. You had land and stables. When the war broke out, the men left for the front, the women for the countryside. The horses were all requisitioned and butchered. Then came the bombing raids and all the rest vanished too."

From that day on, the house of his past and the blood of his roots had become the air above a flower bed. And what little Andrea knew about his father vanished into that air. Including the way he swam, pushing aside masses of water. As if in that revelation of vanished places, he and his sister and his mother had also been liquefied, lost forever in a time that was no longer even nostalgia, but just a piazza full of traffic.

From that day forth, Andrea always lived alone. He learned to cook the bare necessities. He knows how to wait for sleep or a friend who's gotten lost. He's learned to travel to find his way home. He spent three years of his first life reading one detective novel a day. And three more years watching television until dawn, including the on-air auctions, the cooks, the quarreling couples, the drooling bodybuilders. As a young man, and later as an adult, he's never feared death. After the deaths of his father and mother, however, he's always feared memories. That's why he's never even thought of getting married, much less putting a child on this earth. He read Leskov's *The Enchanted Wanderer*. He was stirred to emotion by Goya's white clouds and the rain in *Blade Runner*. He learned to travel without money and to get drunk without a reason. He's thrown punches in self-defense, to hurt others, to defeat fear, and for sheer pleasure. And he's fallen in love for more or less the same set of reasons.

He's built his lean physique by walking and swimming. And then he's broken it back down by overdrinking. He's studied life, judging it to be a largely messy affair, but one that needs to be worn with a certain elegant nonchalance. And as he's studied it, he's started to rewrite it. And as he's rewritten it, he's made it his work, one episode at a time, according to the grid of the handbooks: the hero's challenge of life, the descent to the underworld, the return to the surface. Knowing that the three acts are almost never as important as the liberation of intermission in the theater, when the lights come back up, and you can see the faces of all the other audience members, including *her* face, and the ice cream vendors come through. To live in that moment of intermission is his dream.

Andrea Serrano is five foot eleven inches tall. He has black hair, combed back. His eyes are almond shaped, his face is hollow cheeked, his nose is narrow. He has fleshy lips, the dark skin of the sea-dwelling Sardinians, prominent veins and muscles on his neck. And a body that makes way for itself, when he walks for hours through the city in search of ideas for his neoromantic adventures.

In his free time, he's always worked. He's filled the rest of his time with love affairs that were more than just love affairs and girlfriends who were never just girlfriends, but also friends, confederates, and deep down, mirrors, in which they'd make themselves up, and the makeup was him. Until a certain evening five years ago, when the mirror broke once and for all.

⌘

It happens in Milan and it starts with the first ring of the telephone. It's Luisa, a divorced blond biologist, who suffers from minor stress-generated headaches, but is proud of her large breasts and her body—a body that knows how to devour a man—until she eventually loses him. She doesn't even say hello, she just asks him, "Do you mind telling me why you never call me?"

As Andrea is trying to come up with an adequate answer, he hears the beep of call waiting. His phone might lie there in silent slumber for hours at a time, but once the first phone call wakes it up, the others waste no time piling on. The second call is from the delectable Tereska, who comes from Prague, plays the cello, weeps every time she hears Mahler's Symphony no. 4 in G major, has smooth skin, and expresses her love the way children and puppies do, eyes wide open: "My looove, are you there?" And at that exact same moment the downstairs intercom buzzes: it's Francesca, who's shouting through her tears, "I'm pregnant, asshole, will you buzz me up?"

He just can't go on like that. He should have thought of it before, but that night, unequivocally, he realized that being loved without loving in return is a miserable condition. And so he consoled Luisa, said farewell to Tereska, waited with Francesca for the negative results of the pregnancy test, but didn't stick around to hear her justifications for having made the whole thing up. The decision to leave that life behind him must also have influenced, through some mysterious channels, the real estate management company that sent him a registered letter informing him that the apartment building would be undergoing a renovation, the condominium fees were going to double, and if he couldn't pay he'd be evicted. Just one week later it was his agent's turn: the man was named Massimiliano Testa, and he usually wore life like an ascot, but instead he showed up with a face that looked like a floor rag, his hands in his pockets, and his eyes downcast, to tell him that Giorgio, his boyfriend, had gone back home to his wife, the literary agency was teetering with debt, and he was thinking about leaving for San Francisco, where he planned to become a piano player in a bordello.

Saturation had triggered a wide-scale, generalized weariness. The weariness had stimulated loneliness. The loneliness, thoughts.

⁂

For many years, Andrea navigated his way across the surface of life that way, and was perfectly satisfied. He'd constructed that existence during the tough years of his adolescence, while fate was chewing up his family. Then came his time at the university, studying literature, only to quit in utter contempt, followed by months

of insomnia, and grueling trips through Greece, Morocco, and the
Balearic Islands. After all that cutting, wounding sunlight, he finally allowed himself to be won over by the gray hues of London,
a city he explored for a solid year, living for the first six months
in a thoroughly beatnik hovel in Camden Town, a bartender by
night and a poet by day, full of beer and dreams, with only Dylan
Thomas's starry skies to comfort him. But then he climbed straight
up to the dizzying heights of a luxurious penthouse in Chelsea—
the guest of a young woman, Jane Allison, who had been using a
camcorder to film faces on the Underground in order to devise
an encyclopedia of the world, and had extracted him from that
world. At the time he had been twenty-one, with a clean-shaven
head and a powerful physique, and would take hour-and-a-half
runs along the Regent's Canal, past the zoo, do fifty pull-ups, jump
rope, work the heavy bag, and occasionally get into brawls in pubs
with the troublemakers of Tottenham.

Jane Allison was beautiful, elegant, and gleaming like a young
doe. She was a banker's daughter. But she was shooting up heroin
twice a day, and it inundated her eyes with light and her heart
with an irreparable emptiness.

Andrea hadn't gone to London to save her, he'd gone to save
himself. He dumped her, along with her two-bit artistic videos,
and her Chelsea penthouse. He took a job that he'd found in the
Guardian's classified ads selling prosthetic limbs and medical de-
vices. He saw other bits of real life. Among them the sweet, sweet
eyes of Susan, who was forty years old and had been living for
the previous five in a wheelchair in one of those little one-story
red brick houses that fill the suburbs of Chiswick, where he had
gone to deliver replacement parts for certain defective wheelchair
gearings.

Susan had been a high school chemistry teacher until the day that the father of one of her Arab students had thrown her down the stairs. The man had told her he was in love with her, but she'd turned him down, and with just one punch he'd knocked her into a whole different life.

Andrea was enchanted by her eyes, by her face, which bore none of the marks of rancor. Susan lived alone, read Emily Dickinson, rooted for Arsenal. She offered him a cup of tea. Then some marijuana, which she'd gotten from the Jamaicans in Brixton and which made your head spin like an amusement park ride. When the evening lights turned on, she asked him if she could undo his trousers, look at him naked, caress his body and the youth that had abandoned her once and for all. And she did it with a maddening slowness, sticking her head between his legs, sniffing at him, kissing him. And then explaining to him how to take her in his arms, lay her out on the bed, slip into her, but gently, a little at a time, seizing her lips in his.

Their relationship lasted for three months. Andrea took half an hour on the Underground or two hours by car to go and see her. But every time he got there, the sorrow stored up in that house seemed insurmountable. She realized it and, to bid him farewell, she let him come in and find her naked on the bed, with a tie around her neck, a dinner of sugary fritters, and a gift of a T-shirt that said ITALIANS DO IT BETTER. And when it came time to say goodbye, she didn't shed a tear.

Leaving London behind him, Andrea returned to Italy for a year. He tried teaching, selling insurance, writing entries for the *Encyclopedia of Art*. He'd seen Bob Rafelson's *Five Easy Pieces* and he'd learned from Jack Nicholson to wear black turtlenecks, light-colored corduroy jackets, pipestem trousers. And he'd also learned to think that by moving constantly from place to place he too would be able to escape whatever it was that was going wrong.

He left for Buenos Aires, where one of his best friends, Paul Carezza, had opened a restaurant facing the Plaza República de Paraguay, in the Recoleta neighborhood. But the tango and the tragic love affairs that inhabit the hearts of Argentine women wound up consuming all his good will in less than four months. Transforming it into nostalgia, yearning for home.

The Police Blotter at Night

Milan gave him a way out. At the last afternoon daily still eking out an existence, they were looking for a beat reporter to cover the police blotter at night. The managing editor was a guy he'd met in Camden Town one evening when the young Anglo Pakistanis, in the aftermath of a brutal murder of one of their compatriots, were roaming the streets with cricket bats, on the hunt for white prey. Andrea had run into him and rescued him as he wandered the neighborhood like a terrified target. He had said to him, "Are you Italian? Stay close to me." He'd led him down secondary streets, while cars were being set afire on the main thoroughfares. He'd kept him from running, he'd calmed him down. The guy was called Daniele Barbieri, and that night he reeked of sweat, adrenaline, and fear. And the next day, he'd handed him his business card as a managing editor, wrapping his arms around him and telling him that he owed him his life.

In exchange for that life, a year later Andrea walked through the front door of the newsroom to offer him his own. Daniele welcomed him as a fellow veteran of a war they'd fought together. He became a beat reporter on probation. He started with a dog show, the inauguration of a neighborhood hospice, the story of an aging comedian who had attempted suicide but had failed even at that. But when it came time to cover his first murder, Andrea Serrano discovered his true calling. It was a story of Calabrian gang wars, a father and a son playing cards in a bar in Cesano Boscone, when two guys pull up on a motorcycle wearing full face helmets and lay them out with fifteen shots, and then tell everyone else, frozen to their chairs, "You talk, you die."

The story got him six installments about the 'Ndrangheta in Milan, a few threatening phone calls, and a full-time contract. From that moment, he started spending time under the fluorescent lights of police headquarters. He learned to recognize the cop's slow footsteps, the lies of suspects, the smells of apartments that had been visited by the flaming tail of crime reporters. And he learned that there's nothing better at keeping readers' lives alive than someone else's death.

At last, he found he liked that black and white. It was a good way to simplify the world: good and evil, the innocent and the guilty. He worked at night. He didn't sleep much. He earned good money. He fell in love with newly graduated lawyers, policewomen, emergency room doctors, and fellow broadcast journalists from local television stations. It was one of them—the pretty Ginevra Oliva who wore Prada and came with her own mirror—who taught him that navigating the surface certainly didn't mean you were superficial, but rather "deep in a different way." It was possible to tell the tale of an entire life in just eighteen lines, and the reasons for a murder in a forty-second news broadcast. It was possible to spend time with other people's bad blood without ever turning bad oneself. It was possible to stitch up other people's wounds without carrying the scars. All one had to do was make one's way through the operating rooms of life along the right trajectory, the trajectory of the surgeon or the anesthesiologist. And when the day was over, say goodnight to everyone. Get out of there. Carry your private life out of the newsroom. And if possible, lie down to sleep next to a person who cares for you but asks nothing much more. And then go away in time.

He decided he liked that strategy. He perfected it—after Ginevra—with Carla Risi, the anatomical pathologist; Sabrina Sideri, the lawyer; Marina Zani, his colleague at the Ministry of Foreign Affairs. It entailed detachment. It entailed silent overall views.

And he wound up perfecting it during his only journey into a genuine war zone, a month that he spent in the black-and-white slaughterhouse of Grozny, Chechnya, where the Russian militia castrated separatists and watched them bleed to death, as they smoked Sobranie cigarettes and drank vodka. It was all so cruel, so violent, so intolerable, that his everyday life filled him with an unexpected tranquility and, for the very first time, as he looked at himself in the mirror in a dreary hotel room at the foot of the mountains of Dagestan, it suggested to him the full awareness of that detached gaze—which he redubbed the Neutral Working Expression, borrowing it from the members of the French Foreign Legion, veterans of the massacres in Indochina—that he would don from now on to watch the operetta of his own first world.

❧

His newspaper job lasted eight years and brought him a regular series of raises, some savings, a book of noirish short stories titled *When Blood Becomes Printer's Ink*, the purchase of a romantic garret apartment on Via Scarlatti, near the central train station, an immense archive of armed robberies, murders, and deliriums, which he tended the way you do in coal mines and sentimental quarries, excavating more and more new tunnels, shoring up the old ones, but always keeping an eye on the light of the exit to make sure you're never trapped by the overwhelming darkness.

When the newspaper folded due to a lack of readers, Andrea turned down a new position. He'd had enough of fluorescent lights, bitter coffee, policemen who show you their Beretta 7.65 and a photograph of their girlfriend. That's to say nothing of the grim atmosphere that you could already sense in all the news-rooms, the first signs of decline, the restructuring plans, the new editors in chief chosen because they knew which knives and forks to use at dinner, the publishers with their crushing debt loads and the favors they needed to repay.

He had met Massimiliano Testa, the literary agent, and a couple of producers who were decently impassioned aficionados of the movies and bank accounts. Everyone was looking for television treatments; they paid well and they paid promptly. They too wanted their surfaces in black and white with a dusting of basic emotions—hatred and love, friendship and vendetta—to keep the gears turning. He said okay and his story started all over again from scratch, this time as a writer of multiple lives destined for millions of eyes.

In that new Milanese life punctuated by a regular order that re-assured him—writing from the early morning until five in the af-ternoon, walking, reading, doing a hundred abdominal crunches a day, turning in at the end of every month, picking up a paycheck at the end of every month—the usual emotional chaos began to build up again, aggravated, this time, by his condition of solitude, which is the fate of all professional screenwriters. Sailing into that chaos came Luisa, Tereska, and Francesca. Each of them along a trajectory that wound up derailing into the two others due to lack of space, due to lack of time, due to lack of care. The epilogue hit him first as a revelation of the state of his emotions, and then suggested to him the possibility of considering those three final relationships as simply the beginning of a new series.

Once again, it was time to leave.

Falling in Love with Rome

Five years ago Rome spread out before him on his arrival. The city had introduced him to the rest of the world that manufactures stories in series. Many writers, with considerable talent and surprising imaginations, many directors enamored of the gaze. Actors with soul, actresses with the fire of their calling. But together with them, also the clamoring crowd that Oscar Martello calls the "Superworld of La Dolce Roma," its inhabitants armed with tooth and claw and secrets to be used as so much ammunition. Sometimes dangerous, sometimes amusing.

All of them on the march—politicians in gray tweed, writers with performance anxiety, television functionaries with headaches, directors with penthouses, producers with lovers on the side, lovers with developer husbands building subdivisions, builders and developers with loan sharks, loan sharks with politicians in gray tweed—to conquer something, anything to keep them far away from all that outlying sprawl that they still can't help seeing as they drive past it. Sprawl punctuated with vast barracks-like apartment houses and acres of garbage, long lines at bus stops, hardworking immigrants, panhandling immigrants, broken sidewalks, old men who walk along hugging the walls, children, mothers, and fathers all wearing the same synthetic tracksuits, the same rubber track shoes, fat bodied and skinny gazed, marching down the elegant Via del Corso on Sunday afternoons.

All of them in search—so distant from those quarters of the real world—of a little light, a little money, a little good fortune to stave off at all costs the current of the drowned, to remain in the dry, warm world of the saved. But all of them also eagerly awaiting the enchanting instant (that Rome reserves in certain postcard sunsets and at dawn in the empty streets of the center and in certain piazzas of the early twentieth century and among the gardens of the residential buildings and on the terraces from which it is possible to glimpse the outlying areas of heaven) when for once they'll no longer feel all alone.

"We are," Oscar recited for him one evening, inspired by alcohol, looking him in the eyes, "the ones who prepare the show, who never travel incognito, and are always zipping by in the passing lane. We are the privileged few. The ones who'll always be shown in through the private side door. The ones who get the 'complimentary' seats. And even when we're behind the scenes, we always control the center of the stage. Because we are the current that powers the spotlights. And when we leave the theater, we are the ones who leave the darkness behind us."

And then, "We are the ones people talk about because they have nothing else to talk about. The ones that people dream about because they have nothing the fuck else to dream about. And then, of course, we are the idiots. We are the actors that strut and fret their hour upon the stage. We are the ones destined never to sleep, because there's no time, my friend. There's no time." The great Oscar would quote Shakespeare, but in practically the same breath, he'd also quote that great prince of the street Franco Califano, God rest his soul, when he'd say, "I hope I get old five minutes before dying."

❧

Andrea fell helplessly, head over heels, with Rome. After two short-term apartments, one in Prati without light, the other in Trastevere without peace, he found his top-floor apartment overlooking the Tiber. And an adorable next-door neighbor, on the same landing, Margherita, eighty-two years old, blue hair, the youngest daughter of the engineer who had designed and built the palazzo in the 1920s. She had inherited it a half century later and sold off one apartment after the other, one floor at a time, withdrawing into the top floor, where she now lives without ever sleeping, with the sole consolations of Mozart, the flowers on the terrace, and a whisky and water after dinner.

For him too, Rome unscrolled its sky full of blue light that rendered more nuanced the shadows of men, put women's hearts on alert, mixed up lives, nourished passions, illuminating them with a Renaissance light just as it has always done with the facades of the palazzi. It then transforms them into pixels, providing theme songs and casts, arranging the debuts and entrances, seating the orchestra. And as if it were the most natural thing in the world, behold as the music descends on the city, even though almost no one hears it on account of the traffic that saturates the space, the buses full of tourists, police escorts with sirens wailing, motor scooters, wailing newborns, the Senegalese street vendors running away from Ponte Sisto. Still, that music's there. And that music makes the air dance all the way up to the pompous tops of the maritime pines that climb the Janiculum Hill, where young couples go to kiss and feast their eyes on domes so perfect that they strip everyday life of its drama, reassuring us that it's just a passing thing, with all its damage and its remedies, in the face of such utter eternity. They don't know that that, too, is an illusion. "And if they do know," says Oscar Martello when he's had enough to drink to find wisdom, "they pretend not to. Otherwise they'd have to kill themselves."

Fast Friends

Andrea and Oscar became fast friends one Saturday morning in that first year. It was late September, the sun was shining brightly, casting shadows. A group of Nazis had a stall in the market bedecked with fluttering Italian tricolors and crosses, on the right-hand side of Campo dei Fiori. Oscar and Andrea were cutting diagonally across the piazza, talking about murders to recalibrate and incidentally about leaving for Sperlonga, to Oscar's villa, which had been thrice enlarged, thrice placed under judicial seal, and thrice issued a zoning amnesty.

The guy walks toward them; Andrea sees him only at the end: twenty years old, black leather jacket, black denim jeans, black combat boots, blue Celtic tattoos, fucked-up pimply face, skinny nervous chicken neck, and bobbing Adam's apple.

He asks him, "Do you want to sign, sir?" He places himself square across their path.

Oscar grunts. The guy steps aside, but without taking his eyes off him.

79

Andrea feels the blood circulating a little faster through his veins. He stops. He asks him, "Sign what?"

"Against drugs," says the Nazi, proud of his mission, with his chin jutting into the air, emitting a stinging vibration.

"No, I'm not signing," Andrea calmly replies.

The Nazi's eyes spin with a hint of confusion. He balances his weight and asks, "And why would that be?"

"Because I'm in favor of drugs, all drugs," he says to him, even though he doesn't even really believe it. He just says it to piss him off.

It's one of those mornings that make Rome glow as if its millennia were solid gold: Campo dei Fiori rocked gently by the west wind still has the smell of summer, a whiff of apricots and basil. A light, light breeze that tousles the flowering terraces, spreading the aroma of coffee among the round outdoor bar tables, the market stands, and the conversation of the tourists.

The guy looks at Andrea and doesn't stand aside. Another, bigger guy comes over, with a round face, the same gravedigger's uniform, a scar with stitches on his forehead, watery eyes, arms teeming with tattoos. He and Oscar lean in, shoulder to shoulder. The big guy has a disgusted look on his face: "What the fuck did you say?"

Oscar, who is the more extroverted of the two, tells him point-blank, "Here, do this: take what the fuck he said and just fuck yourself with it, and also wash your mouth out before you speak."

The smaller one takes a step back, as if baffled by the reaction. "Fucking drug addicts."

Stepping back, the little guy makes way for the bigger one, who has targeted Oscar's face and is winding up for a right hook. But he commits the unforgivable error of opening his mouth. In these situations, whoever talks loses, that's the rule. And so as the big guy's muttering "You filthy fucking drug addict," Andrea aims his knuckles straight at the soft saddle between the big guy's Adam's apple and the jugular, also known in Italian as the *acquasantiera*, or "holy water fount," hoping to knock him flat immediately, so that he'll be able to turn and anticipate the reaction of the little guy, who has the appearance of a nasty weasel. He pulls back and lets fly. The big guy, who isn't expecting the punch, dodges it at the last second, but in the wrong direction. Andrea lands all four knuckles smack against the guy's ear, and can feel in his own shoulder the reverberation of the burst of energy that is unleashed into that big broad face, shattering cartilage and sharply dislocating the jaw, which emits a loud crack and shoves inward. The big guy screams in pain and collapses. The little guy lets loose with a kick meant to strike Andrea in the balls, but Oscar is quick enough to shove him off balance with a quick blow of the knee to his other leg and then a hard backhanded smack that smashes his nose in. The big guy is struggling to his feet. Andrea hauls off and kicks him, aiming at his still-unhurt cheek and his nose. Andrea's shoe transmits the second crack of another breaking bone.

The scene is spraying blood in all directions. Passersby on all sides reel in horror. There are screams. The stand covered with Italian tricolors is knocked over. A young woman, heavily tattooed and bulked up from weightlifting, the third member of the group, screams even though no one's touched her. The big guy and the little guy are both on their knees, both of them clutching at their faces, which are swelling up visibly. An entire platoon of Chinese tourists explodes around them. Andrea and Oscar allow themselves to be swept along by the flow of the crowd, which opens up and closes back around them, absorbing them like a breaking wave and carrying them off, to safety.

Oscar leaps and prances euphorically, rubbing the hand that hurts him like a bitch. "I can't stand Nazis." Andrea is spraying adrenaline in all directions, huffing, doing his best to regulate his respiration and slow his galloping heart. "What do you say, did they notice?" They exchange a glance. They burst out laughing, overloaded with tension. The tension holds them together like an embrace.

~

That night Oscar took him to his favorite place on earth, number 1055 on the Via Tuscolana, outside the gates of Cinecittà, which Fellini called the Threshold. And he told him—as the Jaguar purred in the darkness and kept them warm—that in those days the gates were watched by a certain Pappalardo, the security guard, who wore a long loose coat and visored cap, and above the visor was written CINECITTÀ in letters that looked like solid gold.

There was darkness and silence. They split two lines of coke. They smoked some grass. They got out of the car.

"One day, I'll turn all the lights back on in this fucking place. I'll roll in here in my white convertible. There will be a couple of secretaries waiting for me. And two dozen screenwriters, notebooks in hand." Oscar looked at Andrea with an intensity heightened by grass and coke, but perhaps also by the sheer emotion of the moment. He leveled his forefinger at him. "You'll write the first movie of the new era. One of these days, I'll tell you the title."

Andrea started laughing.

They jabbed fists like soldiers in a gang.

He asked him, "Why me of all people?"

Oscar answered, as if it were the most obvious thing imaginable, "Because starting today you and I are fast friends, do I make myself clear?" And for once, he wasn't entirely lying to him.

On the Run toward Sabaudia

Since then, they've ground through three movies, six TV series, two international coproductions, a dozen or so writing projects, and five winters.

Now it's seven o'clock on a warm May evening. They're riding along in the very latest Jaguar that Oscar has managed to purchase under the counter and below market price, directly from the importer, a Jaguar C-X17 Crossover, a concept car that is going to be presented in four months at the Frankfurt car show, the color is Liquid Gold, interiors in cream leather, central dashboard console with touch screens, 4.2-liter, 6-cylinder gas engine, 460 HP.

The sirocco wind continues to blow in this early sample of Roman summer that runs from one curve to the next along the coastline to heat up like a steam iron the traffic jams that inch forward at walking speed, every weekend between Ostia and the Via Pontina.

The radio stations broadcast news reports about record temperatures, the first fires of the season in Sardinia, the stock market collapse, a former member of parliament fleeing the country, the opening of auditions for *X Factor*, plus the notable fact that over the past twenty years, twenty-four thousand rivers have vanished in China, all of them sucked dry to produce dams and hydroelectric power. "Fuck," says Oscar, puffing out smoke now that Helga isn't there to forbid it, "one of these days the Chinese will cut off their dicks to make Vienna sausages and sell them for half a buck each. And they'll be happy for the profit."

It's only a week until the movie's catastrophic premiere, even though if you look around there's nothing to suggest the imminence of the general state of mourning that so obsesses Oscar—aside from the little shrines that pop up here and there along the sides of the Via Pontina, where young men swerved and crashed on their motorcycles, leaving behind, nailed to the trees, bouquets of flowers, smiling photographs, and the inconsolable farewells of mothers and girlfriends. But these relics can be glimpsed only out of the corner of the eye, memorized and immediately deleted by the living who continue to race past in cars that reek of overheated families and synthetic deodorants.

Oscar and Andrea get on the road after sunset, heading for Sabaudia, and those indicators of death, to their eyes, glitter along the curves like some easy-to-overlook interference of the real world with the one they're busy inventing.

They've decided to eat dinner by themselves before going to Milly's party; "there they'd probably poison us and shatter our eardrums." They stopped at Saporetti, where they've just put the tables out, overlooking the last beach along the littoral that bows in adoration before the looming rocks of Torre Paola: spaghetti with clam sauce, fried crayfish and squid, espressos, two chilled bottles of Sanct Valentin, whisky to finish off the dinner and start up the evening.

The evening's topic is the Plan. Which is getting fine-tuned now. Oscar's opening gambit, at the start of the evening, was one of his usual gasconades: "I'll give you the essential outlines, then you can color in all the empty spaces. Ha ha!"

And so. Andrea and Jacaranda will go to Paris, where Oscar has just purchased a very chic apartment in the Denfert-Rochereau area, fourteenth arrondissement. "The deed still hasn't been approved and registered, but the apartment is perfectly inhabitable. Milly Gallo can't know a thing about the plan, much less about the trip."

"You already told me that."

"I don't trust that woman."

"Okay, go on."

"You'll make the drive tonight. Once you've crossed the Italian border, you can slow down and take it easy. The important thing is to avoid using your cell phones. You're going to have to forget about them entirely."

The idea is that his disappearance and, most important, that of Jacaranda, should appear to be so mysterious, so sudden, that it will trigger a surge of alarm among family members and the press. "Not that we give a damn about the family members; I think she might have a female cousin somewhere up around Trieste. Instead it's the press that War & Peace will be working methodically, with a steady drip of toxic news reports, such as the notion that Jacaranda had been receiving anonymous threatening phone calls. And that maybe over the past few days she'd had the distinct sensation that she was being followed." He fills the glasses with ice and pours a generous slug of whisky for them both. "Nothing too precise, just clues, that way if we need to, we deny it all, and we're done, am I making myself clear?" The police will do their best to ignore the whole case, but after the first few articles, they'll "kick up a nice big cloud of dust."

"And you'll be ready with a fan to kick up more."

"Exactly." At that point, Oscar the oracle predicts, there's bound to be one of those overzealous judges who'll start an investigation so he can get his own name in the press as soon as possible. He grimaces in disgust. "I detest judges."

"More or less than you detest critics?"

"Only a little lower down the scale. And I especially detest the fucked-up procedurals those judges write on the side. Because in the end, they never hold together, their plots are riddled with holes, just like their real investigations, when they throw some poor sucker in jail and then oil off to take a long vacation."

Andrea bursts out laughing. "When did you start reading the right-wing press?"

"I don't read a fucking thing about anything. And the things I think, I think on my own."

"Are you sure?"

Oscar sighs in exasperation, ponders, and takes a drink. "Don't play the philosopher with me. And don't go off on tangents."

The investigations, the idle chatter, the hypotheses, and the talk shows will all ensue: "What on earth has become of that tremendous hottie Jacaranda Rizzi?"

The social networks will make their usual noise, confusing all the issues.

A couple of girlfriends will be hired to go on TV and cry convincingly.

Another couple of days and the muckrakers will come out into the open to say that maybe it's not the Mafia at all, but a romantic getaway. "Remember that when you want to kick up a cloud of dust and elude all pursuit, you always need to have two solutions to the mystery. When people aren't sure, they argue about which one is right. And the more they argue, the more confused they become. And the more confused they are, the more passionately they care."

The executives of Anvil Film will play dumb, saying, "Jacaranda may be in danger. But we have implicit faith in the magistracy." And in the meantime they'll bring up the imminent release of the movie every chance they get.

No visits to Parisian friends. No letters, no postcards, no texts. "Get Jacaranda a hat, get her a pair of sunglasses." Absolute radio silence for at least three days. No, make that four, or even five days. "You can just say that you lost track of the time." That'll give them the time they need to whip the general state of paranoia up into a froth. "When your name emerges as our little kitty cat's new boyfriend, you can always just say you didn't want anyone to come around bothering you, not even during your brief intermissions to go and scrub your cock and enjoy a half-dozen oysters in blessed peace, am I making myself clear? Ha ha!"

The whisky melts the ice and strengthens their union. The story expands. And so does the plan.

As the wave of fear of a Mafia kidnapping begins to decline, the general jubilation will swell over the new love story starring Jacaranda Rizzi, the diva. She will reappear in the same couple of days that the film premieres, at a sumptuous press conference held in her honor. "Someone will get hold of a couple of pictures of the two of you in Paris along with a few salty details, like how you liked doing it in the elevator."

"Why in the elevator?"

"I don't know. But it's one of those things straight out of the gossip mags that make boys and housewives dream."

Instead of some grim Mafia plot, what will pop out is a story of radiant passion. The movie will go great guns. And nobody'll get hurt.

"Does Jacaranda already know all about it?"

"I talked to her."

"And?"

"She played a little hard to get, but just because she enjoys busting my balls, making me yearn for her, and then upping the price. No two ways about it, she's an actress. You know her, don't you?"

"No."

"Really?"

"I've talked to her once or twice by mistake. I doubt she remembers me."

"Oh, yes, she does. She remembers you *perfectly*." Oscar always knows how to apply tiny areas of pressure to the imaginations of his audience. "You're not going to tell me you don't like her?"

"She's pretty and off the balcony." Oscar smiles, drinks, and takes tremendous pleasure in laying out the net.

Andrea is walking into it with both feet: "She's what?"

"Off the balcony, a little bit nuts."

"Those are the ones we usually like, aren't they?"

In fact. The idea of running away with Jacaranda Rizzi, acting out a love story with her, spending time with her, completely free of any of the anxieties attendant on performance or courtship, at this point piques his curiosity more than it worries him. He'll see what it's like to live in someone else's shoes. And maybe even in his own shoes, and in the shoes of the divine diva—you never know.

Oscar keeps pouring. He asks the waiter for more ice, then he slips his hand into his inside jacket pocket and pulls out a roll of bills, held tight with a rubber band. "Let me advance you a roll of large for your pocket expenses; that way nobody will use credit cards or fuck things up some other way. Count it."

Andrea looks at the stack of cash, hefts it, and whistles.

Oscar specifies, "That's five thousand."

"Fuck. Why are you so generous all of a sudden?"

"I feel like it. But you have to promise me you'll take her out at least once to Le Boeuf sur le Toit, just a couple of blocks from the Champs-Élysées, the food is fantastic and one night Helga and I even had sex there, slipping into the women's bathroom and fucking. That was our first trip to Paris."

"While you're at it, why don't you tell me what to order."

"Asshole. Do what you like, but if you made an effort to fuck her in that restaurant, you'd make me happy. A memory that blooms once again. You know what a romantic guy I am."

They laugh, they drink a toast with the last of the whisky. And they even hug before paying the check. They're so in tune, so on the same wavelength, that Andrea doesn't even begin to suspect that anything could possibly go wrong. The movies are so much more innocuous than real life. Even when real life seems like an innocuous dinner among friends.

The Big Villa, the Party

Milly Gallo Bautista's oversize villa is on the beach of Sabaudia.

Sabaudia is the consolation of all of La Dolce Roma. It speaks of adventures from years gone by. It has white villas designed by Michele Busiri Vici, set since the long-ago thirties between the green of the maquis and the sand dunes, locations that make one imagine before-dinner aperitifs at sunset among the columns of Villa Volpi, matrons with broad hats and Dalmatian dogs. Here there has been real estate speculation, illegal construction, and general slovenliness, and yet the aesthetic harmony has never been lost. There has been the messy disorder of certain movie sets built out on the dunes, not only the sentimental shadows of Germi's *Divorce Italian Style*, but also the cheerful bright light of Salce's *Crazy Desire,* with an unsettling Catherine Spaak, the queen of the cinema of those years. And then the technicolor assault of mass holiday-going, the famous swims of Alberto Moravia, king of horny writers ("A guy with his dick always slung over his shoulder," says

Oscar, the oracle), the hastily organized soccer games of Pasolini, before his atrocious murder, the new millionaire monsters, the soccer players, the fashion models, the producers, the paparazzi, and the latest generation of beachside houses, just a shade less ugly than those of the seventies, like Milly Gallo Bautista's huge imperial villa, entirely disproportionate in every detail, to give you some idea of the sheer wealth of majestic ignorance.

The low green sea is perfectly suited to the place. Certain days it's transparent to the point of perfection, buffed to a gloss by the north wind, and certain others it transforms into a green the color of the bottom of a bottle, deaf to light like the seacoast in August, crushed by the heat, by the automobiles caught on land in traffic jams, and by the swimmers who fill the water. Or else it's perfectly immobile under the May moon, as it is now.

☙

Oscar and Andrea come screeching up to the front gate, which opens automatically, revealing the trees of the grounds beyond, the terraces descending, and behind them, the sea. A bodyguard in black gestures for them to park farther on, toward a cluster of other automobiles with aggressive bodywork clogging up an oblique clearing. They wedge the golden Jaguar between a metallic convertible and a camo-patterned Jeep. Once they get out, a breeze charged with salt air and music caresses their faces.

Before locking the car, they put on their jackets. Oscar's wearing a navy blue Tasmanian wool suit with a dove-gray shirt buttoned to the collar. Andrea is wearing a black Paul Smith suit in light corduroy with a steel-gray crew neck T-shirt.

Oscar looks him right in the eyes. "All right then, are you ready?"

"I'm ready."

"We're about to go onstage."

"Okay."

"To the bitter end, don't forget."

"To the bitter end."

He hands him the silver-and-leather keychain with the Jaguar tattoo. "Treat my baby right," he says, pointing to the hood of the car, which is emitting a glowing warmth.

"What time is the driver coming to get you?"

"I told him to be here at sunrise, when you and Jacaranda will already be at the Swiss border."

"Is there anything I should know about the car?"

"Yes: that a beauty like this one is well beyond your reach. So if you wreck it, you're in trouble."

"Nice, what else?"

"It has a turbocharged gasoline engine. It'll do two hundred miles per hour. If you try it and they catch you, they'll tear your license up in front of your eyes and then handcuff you. So do as you think best."

"I know how to take care of myself. Relax."

"I'm already relaxed, what about you?" And as he says it, he clicks open the trunk, sticks in his head, and snarls, "Fuck, I should have guessed!"

"What?"

"That bitch Helga never even took the luggage out of the trunk from her trip to the mountains."

In the dim luminescence of the luggage compartment there are three bags in rigid blue plastic, covered by canvas, and tucked so far back you can't even see them.

"Well, what's it matter to us? We'll just leave them there. Let's go see what that cokehead Milly has cooked up for us."

Even while they're still under the portico they greet faces that emerge from the darkness. A couple of babes call out loudly and cheerfully, "Oscar, my love!" A guy in a white jacket with a face to match gets up from his table: "May I introduce you to my new girl-friend?" he asks, pointing to a big-eyed blond with crossed legs. Oscar says, "I just got here, give me a chance to catch my breath." And the other guy, "Of course, sorry, it's just that I never see you. I have a new story I'd love to have you read." Oscar, without even slowing down, pats his cheek and flashes a broad, cardsharp smile. "In that case, I'd rather have you introduce me to your girlfriend," he says, still walk-ing. "What's the story?" The guy tags after him. "Actually, it's two stories, a psychological intrigue between a man and a woman that eventually turns sexual. It's set in the world of stocks and bonds."

Oscar slows down. The blond has stood up, after the guy in the white jacket did. The blond is a bombshell and well deserving of a halt. Oscar stops entirely. The blond smiles at him without break-ing eye contact. Oscar drinks her in; the blond laughs instantly, and the connection is established. As Oscar heads off, he says to her, "Don't wander away."

Andrea grabs a vodka from a passing waiter, says hi to Antonia Morganti, the screenwriter of the multiple-prizewinning movie *Love and Sand*, and she gives him a hug. "You and your Oscar go every-where together, you wouldn't be a little gay for each other, would you?" He kisses his friend Fernanda, a.k.a. Ninni, who says to him, "I just signed up for the new movie. I'm moving to London for two months. All right with you if I pop you into my suitcase?" Andrea smiles at her, and as he gives her another kiss, he remembers her per-fume. "I'll think it over. I might have to leave for a while myself. But trust me, I adore you." Continuing toward the front door he ignores a fat man who offers him a sparking, sizzling joint, a guy reading the tarot cards of a dazzlingly beautiful young black woman, and a bunch of people farther on, sitting in white armchairs, surrounded by candle flames, gusting whiffs of hashish, hands brushing, all of them apparently reliving a long-ago time of their lives.

When they walk in through the villa's two sets of front doors, first the outer doors, then the inner ones, Andrea and Oscar find themselves plunged into a weltering bedlam that reeks of an array of different deodorants, nicotine, and fried foods. The music tumbles down from on high like a thunderstorm. The herd of human beings mills around beneath. Getting drenched.

$\approx$

"Jacaranda must be down there." Oscar and Andrea walk into the semidarkness of the party, heading for the maximum density of bodies and furnishings that, at the end of the second hallway, lay siege to the big living room. Among the moving bodies they recognize the producers of the two series *Wait for Me* and *The Crocodile's Heart*, both recipients last year of awards at Capri, Siracusa, and Capalbio; the two leads in *Indecent Love*, who've just finished writing a book about their favorite vegan recipes; the star of *Robbery Squad*, Vittorio Migliore, muscle bound from bodybuilding, with his third wife, Anouk, ex-model and ex-junkie; the French financiers behind the series *Isn't Life Grand?* as they drink toasts with the two lead actresses, Sissi and Margot, still a longtime couple ever since the days when they were picking up gigs in the network of apartments used for couple swapping.

For everyone Oscar had a hug, a smile, as if they really were friends. *How are you? How long has it been? Do you have good shit?* The usual things, then the wave of bodies slackens, the music in the new living room towers over them.

"If we run into Milly, don't tell her anything about the plan."

"Ah, good to know. You hadn't mentioned that."

They shout at each other.

"What?"

"About the plan!"

"There are only three of us who know: you, me, and Jacaranda. And that's already too many."

"What about the two muckrakers?"

"Who?"

There are people dancing. Percussions, synthesizers, and lights make the air vibrate.

"The muckrakers!"

"All they know is what I told them and they don't ask questions. They obey and nothing more."

There's more human flesh sprawled all over the sofas, young women zapped by alcohol, barefoot men and men wearing ties, a couple of girls touching each other, a zoned-out DJ with a headful of dreadlocks, surrounded by spinning colored lights, transforming the walls into a multitude of shadows that loom and depart in surging waves. And even a little beagle, in the throes of a canine trance induced by excessive noise, spinning on his tail. The percussions bombard the walls. The walls tilt and sway.

Out of a reef of shoulders with clouds of smoke pops a fat woman dressed up in strawberry-colored latex and blue enamel. She points both her forefingers straight at Oscar, opens her mouth wide, and shouts, "You filthy goddamn son of a bitch!" Then she bursts into a loud laugh when she sees Andrea. "You're here, at last!" This is the mistress of the house. This is, in fact, Milly Gallo Bautista.

Milly and Her Two Hundred and Forty Pounds

Milly has an inner world that you can't see, covered up by her two hundred and forty pounds of white fat. Not satisfied with the outer shell, she adds into the bargain the laughter, the embraces, the slaps on the back. All methods for steering attention away from her black heart, which beats in silence from down there, pumping aggressivity, resentment, thirst for revenge, and a sugar-sweet rage that she savors in solitude.

To look at her now, you'd never imagine how slender and sweet she was in her youth, as melancholy as a frightened pit bull puppy, clear confirmation of the rule that the dogs that are most timid as puppies will become the most aggressive adults, if only to even up the score.

From age zero to age eighteen, Milly was just another out-of-sorts inmate at the orphanage of Our Lady of Sorrows, in the hills around Narni, in Umbria. In those grim days, she possessed a rag doll named Ophelia, a bed, a little woolen overcoat, and no memories that made her particularly unhappy. All of her torments belonged to the present: she loved music, but she was forbidden to dance. She loved life, but she was forbidden to live. Released from the orphanage with a teaching certificate, she took off. In Rome, after a year of substitute teaching, she finally found a job that allowed her to breathe. She was working as a cashier in a pastry shop in the Trieste neighborhood, and she loved it. She adored chatting with the customers. She adored the smell of the custard, the little brightly colored pastries lined up in the display cases, the fragrance of the chocolate, the sweet blizzards of confectioners' sugar dusting the *maritozzo* currant buns: all of these were things she'd only drawn pictures of as a girl. She was lovely as only freshly blooming wildflowers can be. She was just waiting for the sunlight that would let her stretch her body in sensual elasticity, filling her fleshy lips with passion and her eyes with emotional flame. A young theater director fell in love with her and became that light. His name was Filippo Parodi, Genoa born, a little nutty and kindhearted, with the soul and the literary gifts of a poet, and he'd bring her camellias and tremble as he took her clothes off. She even became an actress for him. She put on a beauty mark and a blond wig to play a Marilyn from the Ligurian provinces in a play that was as half baked as it was romantic, and in the course of that experience, as she learned to perform someone else's life, she understood things that had never even occurred to her. For instance, that love and sex can make human beings do crazy things. As can loneliness. And that beauty is a mineral deposit riddled with deceit, which can give you the world on a silver tray, but sooner or later it's bound to present you with the bill, until you just can't sleep nights. Which is why the real Marilyn died in the poisonous aftermath of an overdose of sleeping pills. But that was never going to happen to her, Milly Gallo, an orphan, alone in the world, but an enemy to all loneliness.

And so when cruel fate took everything away from her for a second time, robbing her of her sweet Filippo, who died in her arms, killed by a neglected case of pneumonia, Milly confirmed to herself that she wouldn't allow herself to be bent low by destiny: she'd do her best to bend destiny to *her* will.

She dried her tears and reined in her grief. She stopped acting on stage and started doing it in life. She used her impatience with shyness to become even more aggressive, more ostentatious, and perhaps even more beautiful. Selling herself on the installment plan would have been easy, too easy, especially now that sex had become of the utmost indifference to her. And men no longer scared her. But she didn't want life's spare change, she wanted to carve out a place for herself in the world that was big enough to hold her new dreams without necessarily having to clear out all her memories.

From a fantastic coworker at the pastry shop—blond, Roman, with stiletto heels and a prodigious laugh—she learned her first rule of life, which ran thus: "Never give blow jobs to men with small dicks if you don't want to get wrinkled lips."

And so it was with judicious care that she selected the lovers she meant to crown. The first one would have to have a fortune. And so she chose Mariano Lupi, building contractor and real estate speculator from the Castelli Romani, nicknamed "Cement" in honor of the much-loved raw material he worked in; she'd landed him during the before-dinner drinks catered by the pastry shop for the inauguration of a major construction project. Mariano was twice her age, so cheerful that he verged on lunacy, and he drank, and cheated, and bribed, and fucked anything that moved within arm's reach, including waitresses. She pretended to yield out of sheer passion, but she had the wit to give in slowly, until he was on tenterhooks, consumed with lust, and finally in love, until he plunged head over heels and she surfaced six years later. At the end of this time, before remarrying the first of his three wives, he was kind enough to put her name on the deeds to six one-bedroom apartments ("an apartment for every year of love, my darling tea sandwich") in a planned satellite community he was building not far from Fiumicino.

Her second sweetheart, three years later, became her first husband: she married José Bautista, who also dreamed of becoming a poet, but unlike the late, lamented Filippo, he lacked the demented patience required to hunt for words. To earn a living, he worked as a screenwriter. He had landed from the Canary Islands in the nocturnal gulfs of Testaccio in search of a little cinema and fortune, and he was handsome with a nice dark smolder, specializing in the two-bit Westerns that lazy Roman producers like Eusebio Reverberi were still underwriting, following in the glittering wake of Sergio Leone, the Maestro. It was during one of those productions in El Desierto de Tabernas, in Almería, that Milly first crossed paths with Oscar Martello, at the time Reverberi's chauffeur, but already giving the impression he knew more than he let on, a specialist in smiles, special favors, and first-rate cocaine at bargain-basement prices. So successful that every night there was a line outside his hotel room, which is where, one night, who knows how, she wound up coming back with him. It was an old Marriott chain hotel, she could still remember every detail of the place, white plaster and red bougainvilleas, with a view of the Alcazaba walls, which she stared at, leaning with both hands braced on the minibar in Oscar's room, while he was screwing her from behind. And she let him do it, entranced by the tinkling of the mignon bottles in the minibar with every thrust of his pelvis, doing nothing more than to play the part of the kitten in heat. But that idle fling did nothing to stand in the way of her engagement with dear old José; in fact, if anything, it hastened the wedding preparations. And with them, the best intentions of living a conventional life, though within the eccentric and melancholy whirl of the Roman movie industry, where Milly came to understand the lash of time as it disintegrates dreams and careers, making high-tone asses sag and shattering already fragile nerves.

That was when she chose which side of the road she would work. Having learned just how to settle the hash of the vast numbers of her penniless tenants, how to fight with the tax authorities, how to grease the palms of the bureaucracy, how to see through the fog of the ordinary world, she realized she was finally ready to run the extraordinary world of cinema, where everyone tries to cheat everyone else, with the excuse that they all consider themselves past masters of make-believe. Including the supreme instance of it: that they're in it for the art, and not for the greed of money and mirrors.

She opened her first office as a movie agent with Diego Locatelli, a Milanese advertising executive, an expert in casting and smuggling cash to numbered Swiss bank accounts, so useful for depositing undeclared income from movie contracts. And then she got pregnant. But the baby girl she had inside of her, whom she planned to call Ophelia, imagining her as lovely as her old rag doll, failed to survive a terrible night of contractions and bleeding at the start of her fourth month, leaving Milly so alone, so empty, that even the mere presence of José Bautista, his body, his stupid screenplays about cowpokes with handguns, became intolerable to her. And so she finally sent him away—even though he loved her and had done nothing wrong—offering as a sole consolation the fact that she kept his wonderful, lovely surname. It was during those months that she started eating sweets, bingeing drunkenly on colorful finger pastries and perfumed custards, just as she had dreamed of doing during the luminous days of the pastry shop, and suffering unexpected bouts of depression. During the longest of those bouts, she decided to give in to the desires of her body and let herself go. She began to put on weight, dye her hair purple, dress up in cyberpunk and grunge style, buying rags for two thousand pounds in London's finest boutiques. Drinking small Camparis during the day. Sampling men and women during the night ("So I'm bisexual, what of it?") and putting them back in the box the next morning. Keeping a couple of grams of coke on hand for emotional emergencies, tucked away in the little amber turtle she wore around her neck. This change of lifestyle worked out well. She became an eccentric personality of the Roman nights, a perennial party guest who had known how to transform her waning beauty into a character, and thus remain magically desirable to men, and even more so to women, especially the younger and more insecure ones.

Over the years, she had saved up enough money to buy the pastry shop on Corso Trieste where she'd once worked. And after that, four more. Changing her mind once and for all about solitude: no longer the source of every ill and ache of the heart, but an unrivaled palliative, an open door to the world, a meadow across which to gallop her daily vendetta, which fed on two sentiments: contempt for the weak and hatred for the strong. And one rock-solid certainty: defense of her territory, which meant her apartments, the pastry shops, and her movie agency. That is why she surrounded herself with lawyers and dogs, both trained to bite. But for certain special matters, she preferred to use her own teeth. And Oscar Martello fell into that category.

⌘

"They say that our movie is half baked," she told him.

"What do you mean ours? It's my movie."

"It may be yours, but they say it's never going to take off."

"Oh, really? And just who says that?"

The music forces them to stand very close, Oscar and Milly, as if they were fond of each other.

"Rumors."

"Pay no attention to rumors, Milly. That movie is sharp as a sword, a surefire hit."

Milly blows out her cheeks and then exhales. "No, please, I'm begging you, don't you go saying 'sharp as a sword' too! I've heard this thing with the sword a million times."

"And where did you hear it, darling, at the orphanage?"

"No, dickhead, I've heard it from con artist producers like you who don't know how to choose a story, pick the wrong directors, and then when the movie goes belly up, put all the blame on my actors."

"Relax. The movie is fine: once it starts, you can't look away. And Jacaranda is great in it."

"I knew that before you told me. You still owe her a final payment, and don't forget it."

"How could I forget it with you there to remind me every twelve hours?"

"Then pay up."

Oscar crosses his forefingers over his lips as if to say, *I promise!*, but his eyes are telling a completely different story. They say, *I'm never in a hurry, to pay or to die.*

For an instant, the DJ halts the electronic tempest of strings and percussion. A gap opens up in which voices, clinking glasses, and laughter emerge, and Andrea jumps in. "Now let's have something to drink, and then maybe we can take a spin around."

"There, that's right, enjoy the party," says Milly.

"What are we celebrating?" asks Andrea.

"The beginning of summer, sweetheart. The full moon. And the fact that we're still alive."

Jacaranda in the Aquarium

Three vodkas later, Andrea is still greeting men and women lounging on the perimeters of the scene. Mirko Pace, the second-ranking muckraker, walks past, with his usual smart-ass demeanor, his sideburns sculpted into arches, and his skin well done from baking in the UV-ray solarium, a habit he's never lost since his days of penniless deprivation, when he read *Novella 2000*, dreamed of becoming a reality TV bachelor, and still lived in the Giambellino neighborhood. Now he gets his tans at the Parioli Sport Village, which is even worse. For this evening he's wearing a silver jacket, an unbuttoned gray shirt, skintight black trousers, a gold Rolex, and an indeterminate number of bracelets and tattoos. As he strolls past Andrea he gives him a wink and a thumbs-up; he looks like a caricature but he's dead serious. Once he's close enough, he imparts his moral support with a knowing smile. "I always said you were a winner."

Andrea eyes him in bafflement. Then it dawns on him: Oscar must have let slip the fact that Andrea's fucking Jacaranda and that before long there'll be something meaty they can sink their teeth into. Andrea stays in character. Aided by the vodka and everything he's had to drink during dinner, he nods his head to show he's caught the reference and underscores it by acting vague. "How's life these days?"

"Never as good as it is for you. Maybe one of these days we can have a little chat with my partner." And since Andrea continues to gaze at him impassively, he adds, "In the strictest privacy."

"With you and your partner, only in the presence of my lawyer."

It's an old line, but Mirko Pace pretends to guffaw heartily. "And just who would your lawyer be? Old man Martello?"

"No, why would you think that? He doesn't defend me. If anything, he's my ball and chain." Again, they laugh heartily together. And for both of them it means that the conversation is over.

Andrea moves on. He's looking for a bathroom. But all the bathrooms are packed with people humping, snorting, snapping selfies, and fixing their makeup. He manages to find a tiny, empty one, though. He makes use of it. Then he stumbles into the main kitchen, the big one, with reggae music at low volume, where everyone's standing up, average age of twenty, swaying and eating all sorts of things, curry meatballs, biscotti, salami, yogurt, pickled onions, chocolate puddings. And they chew, with the assistance of their youthful metabolisms. And they gulp. And they drink.

It's getting late and he still hasn't found her. He glimpses Oscar in an area of sofas surrounded by hands and laughter. He skirts around different densities of crowd. He needs air and silence. He steps out into the garden, amid milky lights and couples concealed in the shrubbery, who snort, whisper, and drug themselves in blessed peace. The full moon riding high in the sky as always

surprises and enchants him, just as it did when he was a little boy
and imagined sailing up there by magic, closing his eyes. He starts
down a path made of sand and stones and lined with palm trees
that runs around the dark side of the villa, where the trees end
and you can hear the backwash of the waves. On that side he finds
a large sliding-glass door that finally offers a patch of silence. He
enters a study shrouded in shadows, decorated with maps on the
walls and shelves filled with books, and in the center of the room,
an immense blue aquarium, illuminated by a shower of white
pearls, bubbles of air rising in single file through the clear water,
past colorful waltzing fish.

Jacaranda appears in that instant. She materializes on the far
side of the aquarium glass, caressed by the shifting shadows of that
sea in a box, making her face undulate. He remembered her with
the long red hair from her last movie. Instead now, it's back to
her real hair: blond, short, brushed back. Her eyes are still honey
colored, the color that the pulps call "Jacaranda gold," and they're
focusing on him from a distance that's not entirely attainable.

"Are you ready to go on set?" he asks her with a smile, doing
his best to close that distance.

She leaps over it. "I don't like this story."

She has a lovely voice, but a nasty tone that suggests alarm,
fragility, hesitation. Andrea has heard it somewhere before, he
can't remember where, but he knows what causes it: psychopharmaceuticals. She looks around. She's beautiful even though she's
not smiling. "I still can't figure out why I accepted. I'd hoped I
was through with Oscar, and instead he always manages to pin my
back to the wall."

He tries to give her a hand, tugging her away from that wall.
"We're just going on a trip, all expenses paid. And when we get

back, everyone is going to want to take your picture, interview you, and offer you stacks of scripts."

"Is that how you see it?"

"I look on the positive side of things."

"The negative side would be that, as usual, that prick Oscar wants to use me to trick everyone."

"Why as usual?"

She hesitates. "That's how he uses people. And then dumps them."

Andrea feels like an idiot, but he goes ahead and says it. "Well, the movies do the same thing."

She contradicts him, but nonchalantly. "The movies are something that resembles a game. Oscar isn't a game. He's a . . . mean person." Once again, that catch in her voice that promises nothing good: neurosis, insecurity, trouble. And, naturally, Xanax in steady doses over time to fill holes of different sizes in the space of the soul. He supposes that perhaps Jacaranda is just a little more fucked up than expected. Or else she's under greater pressure than one might be led to think. Her fragility reinforces him, to an entirely unexpected degree, eliminating all his sense of uncertainty. "How about we do it like this: we're on the set of our movie. Now you and I start acting and we leave. After all, Paris is a better destination than Lamezia Terme, don't you think?"

She ignores the wisecrack. "Is it time already?"

"It's midnight. We've got a thousand miles to cover, heading due north, even if no one's coming after us. We have no baggage, we have no appointments. We've got a nice apartment waiting for us in Paris, and maybe even a ride up to the top of the Eiffel Tower."

She looks at him with a slight intensity of focus, one of those gazes in which you see a person for the first time. "Romantic."

"So it would seem."

"But it's a script. And I've had better."

"Maybe together we can improve it." And he immediately regrets saying it.

She has other things on her mind. "And Milly?"

"What about Milly?"

"Am I supposed to leave without saying anything to her? She's my agent."

"No one can know anything about it. We'll leave and that's that. Unless you came here in your own car."

"I don't own a car. And I don't even have a driver's license." She says it in an irresistibly bitchy tone. Except that an instant later, a goldfish appears in the cobalt aquarium that separates them and spins around, scattering reflections across her face, which, for the first time, seems to open into a smile. She draws closer. Now he can finally see all of her: she's wearing a long silk dress, clinging to her lithe body, with a pattern of pastels, largely pink and white, like Maggie Cheung in the movie *In the Mood for Love*.

She notices his glance. She says, "I know, I can't go to Paris looking like this, people will think I've lost my mind."

"Fuck, you could have thought of that before."

"Well, I didn't."

He ignores her tone. "We'll take care of it. Are you ready?"

To Be on a Trip, To Be in a Film

They've turned off their cell phones. They're walking down the halls of the huge villa toward the music, the pulsing lights, and the living rooms. They angle across them diagonally, ignoring the noise and the crowd that surges and darts, like schools of fish.

Jacaranda has found her handbag, and now she's tailing after Andrea toward the door. He turns to her and says, "Wait for me here."

He goes back into one of the first bedrooms, where the jackets and coats are piled high. He chooses a jacket in amaranthine red leather, evaluates it to guess the size, empties the pockets. He fishes out a black shawl and a small Panama hat, made of pink and white straw. When they leave, he has her try on the hat and jacket, which fit her perfectly. "Where we're going, it's going to be colder." Then he takes her by the hand. They walk quickly past the parked cars. The Jaguar lights up like an ingot out of *Goldfinger*. As the tires slip on the asphalt, they sail past the bodyguard fast asleep on a chair. The gate is wide open, the engine sings, ahead of them nothing but pavement and moonlight.

❧

Four hours later: empty service plaza, except for the two of them sitting at the counter and a sleepy waitress.

Jacaranda has just taken a Xanax. He's had a double espresso. Now she's as dazed and soft as a little girl. "Do you know where we are?"

"I told you: in a movie."

"No, seriously."

"In Versilia. On our left is the sea, on our right the Apuan Alps. Follow your nose and in six hundred miles, Paris."

"And now what's going to happen?"

"The boy and the girl are going to keep on running away."

She thinks it over. "From what?"

"From life."

"Oh, yes, that would be nice."

"I was just kidding."

Her eyes narrow like twin fissures, and she forces a smile. "I wasn't."

"I know practically nothing about your life, except for your work."

She's looking elsewhere and thinking about who knows what. Then she notices him again, and says, "It's better that way."

Andrea goes off to wash his face; she's wearing him out as much as the trip is. When he gets back, Jacaranda is gone.

He waits for her, guessing that she's in the restroom. Then he goes to check: it's empty. He asks the waitress. The waitress awakens from her lethargy. "I've seen your girlfriend before. She's an actress . . . she's a singer, isn't that right?"

Andrea ignores the question. "She's not my girlfriend. Did you see her leave?"

The waitress rings up his bill and ignores what he said. "There's no one else here now."

He sets off down the aisles through shelves of colorful boxes, emerges into the warm air. The emptiness surprises him, as if it were produced by the sudden lack of something.

Cars rush past in the distance, cutting their way through the night with a wedge of light; those too are lives in transit. All of them with an appointment to keep, or else to leave behind. He watches them and considers that he's among those heading no place, even if his place is called Paris, is called Cinema. Paid to act out a strange story without a finale, where no one counts the miles to be deducted or even the emotions, for that matter, but only the deceits to be tacked on. Then he decides that alcohol plays nasty tricks when it fades: it clogs your heart with bad thoughts. And in fact, he'd be happy just to find out where that turd has gone to ground so they can leave and he can stop thinking them.

He finds her stretched out in the back seat, wrapped in the amaranthine red jacket and the black shawl, already fast asleep. She has the face of a little girl, and a look of sweet dreams that he gazes down on for a while until his annoyance subsides.

Part Two

PARIS, OR ANYWHERE

Very Separate Rooms

He was dazed by the fifteen hours of driving, plus three hours of sleep in a Swiss motel with a scalding-hot shower, followed by a gorgeous afternoon driving through the green and blue hills of Chablis. She was worse off than him, caught in a spiral of sleep and wakefulness, freshly squeezed orange juice and vodka, pills for anything you got, an obsession with the complete works of Amy Winehouse, the loveliest and most unsettling and warm voice of the entire European division of addicts and alkies who died of bad living, songs fished out of the Jaguar's audio menu. And she started the playlist over every time it came to an end, without even the slightest courtesy of asking Andrea whether he'd had enough of that languid death on the installment plan.

The GPS took them straight to Oscar's new apartment ("These are the keys and these are the codes. I'm still furnishing the place. No one knows I've bought it; to all intents and purposes you'll be in a clandestine lair: just think how insane that is."). 16 Rue Liancourt, right around the corner from Place

Denfert-Rochereau, fourteenth arrondissement, one code for the gate that leads down to the basement parking garage, another code for the elevator that will take them up from the basement to the eighth floor, and one last code for the alarm, the minute they enter the apartment. All of them pointless precautions, seeing that the apartment contains a luminous, unsettling void; that is to say, highly polished hardwood floors, two windows, a white sofa and a fireplace in every room, but no chairs. Two bedrooms, each with a bath and built-in armoires, never used, that smell of wood. An all–stainless steel kitchen just stripped of its plastic wrap, and an immense refrigerator with one of the two doors stacked full with Perrier bottles.

The minute they got there, Jacaranda shut herself into one of the two bedrooms, the one with a wall-mounted television set that didn't seem to be hooked up yet. He tried to read on the couch, with Paris Jazz in the background, tuned in through a burnished-steel digital radio that was miraculously operative. He fell fast asleep without even realizing it, slipping into dreams of asphalt and flickering grapevines, until the morning after, when he found himself in a room full of sunshine and unmistakably Parisian rooftops.

As soon as he was awake he took a shower, shaved, and went out to get breakfast. When he knocked on her door to wake her up, she grunted at him to leave her alone. In the middle of the morning he went downstairs again to the market stalls on Rue Daguerre and bought warm bread, shrimp, eggs, asparagus, salad, a package of camembert cheese, a bottle of olive oil, a container of vanilla ice cream, two bottles of sauvignon, and a bottle of Talisker single-malt Scotch whisky. He cooked lunch, set the table, and called her. She half opened the door to her dimly lit room, looking

first at him, then at the set table. "I'm not hungry." She was wearing one of the T-shirts she'd bought at an H&M in Auxerre, along
with the sunglasses, the jeans, and all the rest. She was pale, she
was distant. She was out of it. She shut the door again before he
had a chance to reply.

Then Andrea went downstairs again. He called Oscar from a
phone booth and told him, "Your actress is a bitch on wheels. And
she's depressed, too." He told him, "She hates you. She hates me.
She hates the whole world."

Oscar started laughing and caught him off guard: "Do you
want to fuck her?"

"Who? What?"

"You want to fuck her and she isn't even taking you into con-
sideration. Ha ha! Or am I wrong?"

"Stop talking bullshit."

"The great writer! Am I wrong?"

Andrea paused a beat, told him to go fuck himself, and then
asked how the movie was doing.

Oscar was revved up, drunk, or wasted on something. "It's not
doing anything yet. It's too soon, but we'll go down in film history,
my friend, just wait and see."

"Excellent," Andrea said to him, eager to end the conversation.

And Oscar said, "While it seems to me that all you want is to
get between little Jacaranda's legs, I know you." He snickered.
"You want to screw her, all you want is to screw her!" And he just
wouldn't stop.

Andrea hung up. He was so frustrated that he didn't even feel
like going back upstairs. After the sunshine, a brief rain had come,
and now it had moved on. Paris was pure cinema, but with the
perfume of life.

He continued toward the Boulevard du Montparnasse, took a seat at Select, ordered a Ricard, ate eggs and ham with a beer and a coffee. Then he walked over to the Fondation Cartier, where there was a personal show of Jean-Michel Alberola's work. He'd seen an Alberola show at the Galleria La Vetrinà on Via dei Coronari in Rome, and he remembered certain phrases of his painted on the walls in garish colors, the finest of which stated: *La sortie est à l'intérieur*. "The exit's inside." He thinks the same thing.

In midafternoon, after more clouds, the sun came out again. He walked to Raspail, bought a stack of useless but very colorful magazines, went back to Select to read them, drinking a couple of beers. And once he felt better, he went back home.

Jacaranda had slipped on the amaranthine red leather jacket that Andrea had fished out of the pile of coats in Sabaudia and which seemed to have been custom made for her. She sat on the cushions with her legs crossed, in her bare feet. She'd regained color: she'd eaten a little salad and some cheese. She'd downed a bottle of wine and knocked down the level in the whisky bottle by three fingers. On the tray on the floor was a package of Xanax.

"You left me stuck in here without a set of keys," she told him in a drawling, singsong voice, submissive and docile. A voice that immediately got on his nerves.

"Why, did you miss me?"

She looked at him and, looking at him, ignored him.

"Those two things don't go well together," Andrea told her, pointing at the Xanax and the bottle of Talisker.

"No, they go together perfectly, as far as I'm concerned," Jacaranda replied, again with that voice. The voice of a stupid little girl, thirty years old, drunk on whisky, and stunned by an excess of psychoactive meds.

She continued looking at him without seeing him. But he could see her. She must have taken a shower. Her hair was wet, brushed back, her eyes were luminous, as they had been two nights back in Sabaudia. He felt as if he'd been putting up with her for an unnaturally extended time inside this absurd situation of cinematic clandestinity. And at the same time, she always struck him as prettier than the last time he'd seen her. A beauty that was even irritating, given the way it was mistreated. He thought, "You stupid actresses," but instead of thinking it, perhaps because he'd spent the whole day alone, he said it out loud, as if thinking to himself.

She furrowed her brow. "What did you say?"

"Nothing."

"Asshole."

Andrea felt his irritation increasing. "Has anyone ever taught you how to live your life right?"

Her honey-colored eyes filled with loathing. "Why of course, the first one to do it was your friend Oscar Martello." Then she stood up and went back to her bedroom.

In the middle of the night, he heard her sobbing. He got out of bed, knocked on her door, opened it a crack. "Hey, what's going on?"

She told him, "Go away," but softly, without force, without anger, almost supplicating.

He turned on the night-light in the hallway and saw her floating in the darkness, sitting in the middle of the bed, in a black tank top, arms folded across her chest, her face bowed. Her breathing slowly calming. "I had a nightmare."

"You want to tell me about it?"

"No."

"Okay, now it's over."

Andrea boiled some water for her, made a green tea. He went over and sat down beside her, on the bed, and brushed his fingers over her forehead, which was ice cold. "I told you that whisky and tranquilizers don't go together. Now drink this and go back to sleep."

She did as she was told, docile the way that frightened women sometimes are. She drank in small sips, until she'd finished the whole mug. Then she told him, "If I close my eyes now, will you stay here and stand guard?"

An instant later, Jacaranda was already fast asleep, lulled by other worlds that she visited from behind her eyelids, breathing deeper and deeper, as if she were walking through the underbrush of a night that was finally inhabitable and now inoffensive.

Paris Does Miracles

This exhausting, and yet poetic situation, of being stuck, the two of them, on something like an island surrounded by a sea of black roofs and sky, in a half-empty apartment, with their cell phones turned off, could have reined in their bland collisions until they attained a state of perpetual and reciprocal indifference. But instead, the warm sunlight of their third morning there came pouring in through windows thrown open to the city at large and somehow made them both wake up with a new and inexplicable sensation. A state of mind that made everything around them newly lightened, creating a bubble of air, a suspension of time.

Suddenly all that was missing to truly feel like he was free and on vacation were the café umbrellas and the scent of baguette. Jacaranda had suddenly bloomed again. Her nightmares had left no traces on her face, or in her honey-colored eyes. Her skin was luminous and her teeth were white. And as she walked into the kitchen, she said, "I'm hungry."

When they went downstairs, to guard against prying eyes she

wore the panama hat, the sunglasses, and a shawl. They sat down at the Café Noir on Rue Daguerre and ate croissants and omelets. Then they went over to the Bon Marché, where he bought two cotton T-shirts and a pair of jeans. She tried on three dresses, three skirts, three pairs of shoes, and in the end bought a raspberry-red Agnès B. silk blouse that she put on and spun around in twice before the big mirror. She looked at herself and smiled. "I had one just like it when I was a girl."

They walked over to the Cinémathèque Française, where at noon a retrospective of the work of Jean-Marie Straub was playing, but they left after the only scene that could possibly be worth watching, the one where the schoolteacher scolds his pupil in front of the boy's parents for being too impertinent, for never giving the correct answers. In order to prove his point, the teacher points the boy to a framed butterfly under glass and, when he asks him what it is, the boy replies, "A crime."

On their way out, they noticed that scheduled for the next day was a screening of a restored version of Antonioni's *L'Avventura*. She wrinkled her nose. "It's a beautiful film that talks about nothing."

"Are you sure?"

"It always made me feel tremendously sad, it put me into some kind of a bad mood."

"I think that's what Antonioni had in mind when he made it. To put you respectable folk in a bad mood."

For the first time, Jacaranda laughed. "Respectable folk! Nobody says that anymore. It's a word from twenty years ago."

"A lot longer ago than that. It's a word from the sixties. Just like the film."

"There, exactly."

"But as you can see, it still works, it always comes up with the film. Because it continues to put you in a state of alarm."

"Put us? Are you saying that I'm . . ."

"You said it."

"No, I didn't say anything of the sort."

"But you made me think it."

"I don't think of myself as respectable in the slightest. In fact, I often think and do the most disrespectable things."

"That's exactly what being respectable means, completely disrespecting others and completely respecting yourself."

Jacaranda gave him a serious glance. "And in fact, that's the way I am."

"You see?"

They ate lunch at the Café Bonaparte in Saint-Germain. The cinema and the landscape were healing her. She kept looking around as if she were seeing it for the first time. As they were drinking their coffee, she said, "I'd like to do something I've never done before."

"Like what?"

"Something that you promised me."

An hour later, they really were at the top of the Eiffel Tower, surrounded by respectable tourists just like them and Japanese couples on their honeymoons taking pictures of each other. When they got back to earth, a guide offered them a half-price open tour on a double-decker bus leaving for Notre-Dame and the Louvre. Jacaranda started laughing. "That's the last thing we need, standing in line for two hours to see the *Mona Lisa*."

An hour later, they were really were standing in line in the Denon wing, on the second floor, to see the *Mona Lisa*. And as they were waiting to move forward, one step at a time, hemmed in by men in flowered shorts, women in wooden clogs, and fat, annoying children, she said, "I can't take it anymore. When we're done, promise me that we'll go back to behaving like cynical, self-regarding bastards."

He pulled her out of the line. "Let's start over right away. The *Mona Lisa* is overrated."

On their way back home they went into the Montparnasse Cemetery. As they were searching for Guy de Maupassant's grave, they stumbled upon the grave of Alice Prin, better known as Kiki de Montparnasse, an actress, singer, and painter, and Jacaranda stood for a long time in silence, looking down at that grave, and then said, "One time I studied a theatrical script that talked about her life. Her mother abandoned her when she was fourteen, because she was posing nude in the painters' ateliers. Did you know that? She had a purity all her own that no one understood. And everyone punished her for that." She looked at him with a certain intensity, and Andrea had the sensation that she wanted to add something. Instead, though, she said nothing, looked elsewhere, and once again had a change of mood.

Three Knocks and He's There

After another day spent maintaining an intermediate distance, he is drying off after taking a shower. Jacaranda is locked up in her bedroom, and in the living room Paris Jazz is broadcasting Jaco Pastorius recorded live at the Montreux Jazz Festival. Suddenly three knocks threaten to break down the front door. And when Andrea throws it open, in comes Oscar Martello like a gust of wind, with a leather travel bag slung around his neck and a fat pack of newspapers in one hand. "Come on! Get out the glasses and the caviar. The producer has arrived! You don't have any caviar? Of course you don't, you're poor: so I brought it."

He landed just a few hours ago in the airplane of his friend Angelina Casagrande, the Queen of Flowers, who always has new tits. He dumped her on Avenue Matignon, at the Christie's antique jewelry auction, telling her he had to go meet old Gérard Depardieu with his agent at the bar of the Hôtel Lutetia to propose he make at least a cameo appearance in a new European series about a squad of Interpol cops: a Frenchman, an Englishman, an Italian—

"Like in the jokes?" Andrea asks him.

"Exactly! But with a bunch of money from the European Community, just think what a fantastic thing this is, they call it cultural integration or something like that . . . this time I'm in with a one-rock chip, a million euros. But the next series, I'm going to make it all on my own." He went into the kitchen to find the second table in the apartment, one of those small round café tables, dragged it into the living room, unwrapped the two bottles of Cristal, opened a jumbo container of imperial Sterlet caviar, and poured two packets of crackers onto a plate. "When my aging little girl has spent her half million euros for a couple of Victorian-era emeralds and she's finally had multiple orgasms, I'll send her straight back to Rome."

Andrea starts to get alarmed. "Why, are you staying?"

"Would you like that?" Oscar gives him a feverish glance. He must already have stuffed himself full of coke to help him take the stress of the flight and the propositions of his friend. He lowers his voice: "That way I can watch while you guys fuck, and maybe I can lend a hand, I don't know if I make myself clear . . ." Then it occurs to him that there's someone missing at the little party. "Where's Jacaranda?"

She appears at that moment. She put on the raspberry-red blouse that lights up her face. She's beautiful. She's seductive. Oscar takes both her hands and kisses her. "Here's my movie star. Just look!"

He tosses the pack of newspapers onto the sofa. All the dailies have gone for it hook, line, and sinker, and featured it on their news pages, even though we're still not seeing banner headlines. The *Corriere* put it on page 8, below the fold, headline: "The Mystery of Jacaranda Rizzi," subhead: "Lead Actress of Anti-Mafia Film

Vanishes. The Producer: We're Worried, but Not Alarmed." The other newspapers are more direct: "Jacaranda, Where Are You?," "Disappeared!" They all carry photos from her best-known movie, *Dangerous Dance*, in which she's a lap dancer being stalked by a serial killer. Jacaranda's behind, shot at a dramatic angle as she swings from a pole, is beautiful, but it winds up undercutting the alarm. Oscar taps his forefinger on it. "You're making news, my love."

She looks at him, without ever smiling.

But Oscar doesn't give a damn, he's pumping sheer energy. "Do you know how much this publicity is worth? And this is just the first few days. Let's let the baby grow. Then War & Peace will go into action with their sentimental bullshit and we'll be flying high. By the way, how are the two of you doing, are you making war or are you making love? Ha ha!"

Jacaranda gives him a chilly reply: "If you're saving all this money on advertising, maybe we should discuss a serious fee and not this two-bit tip you're paying us."

Oscar shoots back a scorching glare. "Do you know what Brooke Shields once said about Bo Derek? That she was so stupid she flunked her Pap test. There are times when you remind me of Bo Derek."

Jacaranda doesn't even pretend to laugh. "I may be Bo Derek, but you definitely don't rise even to the level of Orson Welles's shoes."

Oscar doesn't take that well. "Hey, I'm paying for you to take a vacation in Paris, I'm putting you up in my own home, I'm giving you headlines in all the papers, and now you're busting my balls?"

Andrea seeks a middle ground. "Let's drink this Cristal and calm down."

Oscar: "I'm perfectly calm. I'm just trying to work for the good of this fucking movie."

Jacaranda: "You always seem to be working for the good."

Oscar: "It's in my nature, sweetheart. What about you?"

Jacaranda: "Well, you ought to know."

Once again, the tension between the two of them flares. Andrea pours himself a drink. Oscar and Jacaranda ignore him. There's some kind of flow of energy between them that emits sparks and fills the air with an uneasy charge.

Andrea: "Let's sit down and you can tell us how things are going in Rome."

Oscar focuses on the situation again. He checks the time on his 170-large Patek Philippe. "In an hour, with your permission, I'll take back my car. So now I have time to tell you a few things that the newspapers aren't saying yet."

"For instance?" asked Andrea.

"That there's a strange cop on your trail. A guy who's going around asking questions."

"And how do you know that?"

"Because yesterday he came over to my house to talk to me."

"Fuck, and when were you planning to tell us?"

"I'm telling you now. Do you want to hear the rest or not?"

"Do you need a written request?" Andrea said.

"No, as long as you pour me a drink and pass me some caviar."

In the meantime, he pulls out a pebble of coke and a credit card. They sit down around the little white hearth, and they take turns serving themselves. And when Oscar tells the story it's already a movie you can watch, even if he doesn't actually illuminate all the details. He leaves things out when he feels like it. He adjusts where it suits him. But in the meantime they eat, drink, and snort. And they fly into the movie.

Enter the Cop

The cop is called Raul Ventura. He comes from the fogs of Milan. He's forty years old or so. His face is haggard and hollow under the cheekbones, his hair is crew cut, his eyes are black velvet, his respiration is calm and slow. He's wearing a hazelnut suit, a light-blue shirt, and a loosened tie. He has shoulders like a refrigerator and the hands of a pianist.

His father was a Communist factory worker for Fiat. His mother stitched hems and skimped even on breathing. They were both depressed and depressing, though with the best of motives. Raul enlisted at age eighteen to get away from home. And at age twenty-three he was already a cop first class in the ranks of the judicial police for the Tribunal of Milan, flushing out wrongdoers for the bloodhounds of the Bribesville investigation. He'd watched the whole world of before come crashing down. Wives wearing leopard-skin stoles bringing a cutlet for dinner to their husbands, former municipal commissioners, who had been stewing for several days already in the Sixth Wing of San Vittore prison. And young whores hightailing it out of the studio apartment with black wall-to-wall carpeting rented for them by their respective lovers on Via Vincenzo Monti or in the Ticinese neighborhood on the Navigli canal, doing their damnedest to swipe for the last time the credit cards issued in the name of the regional government or the municipal government or the party, cards that they'd been using for years to buy *prosciutto crudo* at Peck and silky lingerie on Via Montenapoleone, in the name of the Italian people.

When the corps of Bribesville judges was dismantled by the newly arrived bad guys who had come to take the place of the old bad guys and set up the same political con games in their own names, Ventura dismissed the disenchantment at the injustice of the justice system, which was the kind of thing his father liked to wallow in, and understood in plenty of time that "one season had come to an end, God rest its soul." He managed to get transferred to police headquarters on Via Fatebenefratelli, where he dedicated himself to old-school bandits, thieves, armed robbers, and fences, finding them not entirely despicable, capable at least of distinguishing between good and evil, possessing an ethics of friendship, and a little more respect for the institutions, at least those in uniform, tending to surrender, hands in the air, when confronted by them.

In those years of solitary investigations, Ventura had fallen in love with a Polish girl, Grażyna, who worked at the organic gelato shop across from the San Lorenzo Columns, and who had the melancholy smile, blond hair, and heart of gold of the farm girls of yesteryear. He would go pick her up at closing time and they'd take long nocturnal strolls through the city, in the course of which she'd tell him about the many little things that had happened during the day, and sometimes about her boyfriend in Kraków who stalked her from long distance with his jealousy. And he'd talk, too, as he'd never talked before in his life, though he didn't even know where all those words came from.

Until he discovered that they came straight from his heart. As did the first kiss, when she said *I can't, I have a boyfriend*, but it turned out she very much could, even though she trembled and held him tight, just like on the September night when they made love, in a tent, after climbing a wooded slope in inland Liguria, lighting a fire, eating chestnuts, and looking far out to the distant sea. A night that he remembered as the high point of his happiness, at the culmination of which he asked her to come live with him and she smiled, but said nothing. And she perfected the silence of that night with a subsequent and longer-lasting silence that she vanished into without another word to him, save for three months later, when she sent him a letter to say that she had married her boyfriend, farewell: she hadn't had the courage to tell him in person, and she was telling him now in writing, reminding him to remember her as a friend and adding the loveliest thing, the hardest thing to take, *I loved you that night, you're a wonderful person, Raul, don't try to find me.*

He had slipped into a state of depression, just like his father, but maybe he'd have been able to forget about her if his Grażyna hadn't resurfaced a month and a half later in an Interpol circular, having been beaten to death by her husband, Dobro Tanic, age thirty-three, Serbian by birth, former paratrooper, on the run and reported to have been spotted in Northern Italy, armed and dangerous, "approach with extreme care," possibly heading for the paramilitary camps of Bosnia, or perhaps staying with a cousin in Milan, "urgent assistance" requested. And that urgency became an obsession for him. From Armed Robbery he transferred over to the marshal's service, the Squadra Catturandi, which worked on tiny specks of evidence, vast gaps, and the long term. In front of his desk he pinned up photographs of Grażyna and the swine who had killed her. He learned the relentlessness of waiting and the elasticity of patience. In five years' work, he captured a substantial number of fugitives, a couple of 'Ndrangheta killers, a serial rapist, two former extreme right-wing terrorists, and even a former Chilean officer who had been living for years in a Benedictine monastery.

But no trail for Dobro Tanic had ever lasted more than a few months. Three times the blinking red light of circular reports had flickered on: one in Milan, one in Gorizia, and one in Sarajevo. Then, nothing. Maybe he really had burned to a crisp in the Balkan inferno, as he deserved. But for Raul, the sad bloodhound, as his colleagues called him, the time had finally come to cash in the appointment to commissario, get over the things that can't be gotten over, and take the photo of Grażyna, yellowed now from five years of nicotine, down from the wall. A young actress named Giulia, Roman in both light and personality, had worked the miracle of changing his mood.

∂⁊◌

For that reason, for a couple of years now, Raul Ventura has been shuttling back and forth to Rome. It helps him metabolize the adrenaline of the investigations, and now he knows whom to call when he's fed up with chasing bad guys. In the meantime, he's formed part of an interforce group that specializes in pursuing the glittering tail of the financial system of organized crime. Now he's hunting down not only fugitives on the run, but also the vast patrimonies that sink into the glittering waters of tax havens, thoroughly laundered narcocapital, tax-exempt profiteering and speculation concealed behind aid to the Third World, import-export companies, anonymous financial shell companies, economic cooperation and development institutes, NGOs, art dealers with the traffic in counterfeits and cash, and infrastructure works contracts in developing nations. And of course, international film and television production.

Experience has taught him to let others take him for a fool if it's useful. To seem inoffensive when it's necessary. To pretend to swallow the horseshit that his wealthy marks usually try to palm off on him, thinking they're *sooo* crafty, certainly craftier than the texts of the legal codes, which they just used to make paper airplanes.

When he enters Oscar Martello's ultramansion he looks around carefully, though without allowing himself to be overly impressed by the living rooms the size of polo fields, with Filipino houseboys instead of horses and frescoed ceilings instead of the sky. There was a time when he would have been left with his jaw hanging and his hands in his pockets, afraid of getting something dirty. With experience he's learned that these landscapes of billionaire interiors don't count for anything. He's seen comparable living rooms in the eighteenth-century villas of Venetian bankrupteers, in the palazzi of Lombard industrialists who are equally expert at philanthropy and bribes, and in the sunny country residences of the Sicilian Mafioso nobility, with bleeding crucifixions under their vaulted ceilings, still lifes of the high Flemish school, and quarterings of saints on the walls. Here there's none of that vintage cruelty. Here you find its contemporary opposite, the carefree glee of neon and manga, the latest in million-dollar conceptual art. But the point is the same: a theatrical layout of wealth and power,

designed to intimidate anyone who looks at it—even if occasionally that excessive willingness to show off is a signal of the owner's
insecurity, usually because that money was piled up too recently.

❧

He introduces himself: "Commissario Raul Ventura, thanks for
having agreed to see me in such a hurry." He starts out all bland
and ceremonious, pointing to the newspapers stacked on a glass
table. "Do you have any idea of what's going on?"

Oscar shows him to a seat in front of an immense red-and-bronze
marble fireplace. He looks at him, he evaluates him, imagining
him as a hunter of runaway adolescent daughters, an investigator
of matrimonial problems—in other words, as a complete jackoff.
Even though, as he looks a little closer, something doesn't add up.
And so he decides to wait, and in the meantime he reaches into the
box for a cigar, feels it, slips it between his fingers, but doesn't light
it up.

"Would you care for one?"

"No, thanks."

"Do you mind if I smoke?"

"No."

"Okay. As far as I know, what's happened is that my lead actress has run away with my screenwriter, and they took my car to
do it."

Raul Ventura absorbs that ostentation of triple ownership as a
small sign of insecurity and mentally files it away. Then he carefully chooses a tone of voice that is at once curious and inoffensive:
"And do you think that this is normal or something that doesn't
add up?"

"Love stories usually put me in a good mood."

"Your own, I can imagine. Other people's, too?"

Oscar indulges in a smile. "I don't have any. My wife is very jealous. And I have a simple heart."

Ventura indulges in a smile of his own. "That I don't believe."

"Which of the three things that I told you don't you believe?"

"The first and the last."

Once they're done with the opening skirmishes, Oscar goes and sits down across from him on the big leather sofa, throwing both arms wide on the backrest and enjoying Ventura's immobile face, as if it were a map of something.

Ventura lets him do it. He continues, "And how do you explain the fact that instead of talking about your actress in the entertainment pages, the newspapers are featuring her today in the crime pages? Where does this whole story of Mafia and kidnappings come out of?"

"Ask the newspapers."

"No, I'm asking you, since you spoon-fed them the story."

"According to who?"

Ventura smooths his tie with an instinctive gesture and turns up his tone of voice by a couple of notches. "I'll ask the questions and you'll answer them: that's the way it works. We know things even when we pretend that we don't."

Oscar looks at him and says nothing.

Ventura continues, "Words like 'Mafia' and 'kidnappings,' Signor Martello, have the ability to alarm my bosses very much. They upset them to such a degree that when they go to sleep, they check to make sure I stay up."

"I'm sorry to hear that."

"Really?"

Oscar thinks it over, stands up, snips off the end of the Cohiba, lights it, sits back down, and says, "Okay. What do you want to know?"

"Just what I asked you before: Do you have any idea of what's going on?"

Oscar blows out the smoke. "I think I do."

"Then where does all this talk about the Mafia come from?"

"It's just an idea that is suggested by the plot of the movie."

"Is *that* what's suggesting it, or is *someone* suggesting it?"

"The papers go crazy about stories like this, and we do our best to give them what they want. And by we, I mean the boys at the press agency War & Peace, who are in charge of launching the movie."

"That's better."

"We're trying to pump up the case, do I make myself clear?"

Ventura doesn't change expression. "The fact remains that Signorina Jacaranda Rizzi has had her phones turned off for the past three days, no one knows where she is, and her agent is calling the police—that is, me—six times a day."

"I understand you."

"I doubt you do. So where is she?"

"I imagine happily ensconced with her new boyfriend."

"We're talking about Andrea Serrano, right? His phone's turned off, too. And both of them are driving around somewhere in your car."

"I have three others."

"Lucky you. But why turn off the cell phone?"

"Do you want my opinion? She was having an affair with the director before. Their relationship lasted more or less the duration of shooting and postproduction. Then it ended with a clean cut. Maybe now he's stalking her and she decided to cut him off."

Ventura wants to give him plenty of rope, so he'll talk and give him some impression. "They live pretty fast lives, these actresses, just the way an outsider imagines them."

"Commissario, no disrespect intended, but dogs pee to mark their territory, right? Well, actresses fuck to mark their territory. Is that clear? And not content with that, they marry the men who will issue their future contracts. You may have noticed that at least half of the women who are successful become the wives of directors or producers." He laughs, *ha ha!* "Do you think it's true love or an insurance policy?" He points his finger at him. "I know what you'd like to ask me, Commissario. Well, let me answer before you ask: no, my wife is not an actress."

Now it's Ventura's turn to laugh, and he does it out of courtesy.

In the meantime, Oscar has gotten to his feet. "I want to show you my lily pad tank. It's the place in my home I like best, come along." They reach the other living room, along the short side of which runs a green marble basin about forty feet long and half that width, full of gurgling water, in which LEDs bob along with lily pads that are reflected in the terrace windows from which you can glimpse the rooftops of Rome. All told, a notable display of what it means to live in the Superworld, fill it with water, and savor it. "My friend Hans Op de Beeck designed it for me. Do you like it?" He points to the rest of the living room floor. "I had to have the whole structure reinforced with cement and steel I beams to support the weight of the water. But it was worth it." Not even alluding to the insane cost of the basin, Oscar winds up underlining it as an immense missing detail.

Ventura, just to irritate him, turns around, then goes over and sits in a Ron Arad armchair, the kind made of wrought iron, perfect for backaches, with his back to the basin. "Very cinematic. But you were telling me about actresses in general."

Oscar registers the lack of interest, but pretends to have missed it. "I was talking about the movies. And the fact that people still believe that it is"—with his fingers he sketches out scare quotes in the air—"the 'place of transgression.' Wrong. There's no place more conformist than the movie industry: anyone who can, steals; anyone who manages to pull it off, takes sex when they can get it; those who have political connections climb the career ladder. Everyone else struggles to get by and tries to hang on with the public funds from the ministry. Just like at the post office."

"Did you know about this plan to escape in advance?"

Oscar bursts out laughing. "In your opinion, Commissario, does a producer not know what his characters are going to do?" He actually uses the words "his characters."

"Okay, then tell me about them. Starting with Jacaranda Rizzi."

"What do you want to know about her?"

"What she's like, inside and out."

"She's beautiful. Apparently fragile. In reality, relentless and determined. Meticulous about her work. A first-rate professional."

"Okay. And skipping over all the decorative ornamentation?"

Oscar takes a deep drag, chooses an armchair for himself out of his vast collection, a Gio Ponti Continuum. He sits down. He exhales. "Skipping over the decorative ornamentation? A difficult, unfortunate woman, like all actresses. And I say that fondly, don't get me wrong. A woman capable of being *anyone* on set, but who never knows who she is in real life. And so when the lights go out on set, she deflates and flutters to the ground like a dropped silk scarf. A drug addict, strung out on pills, tranquilizers, and other crap like that."

"A cruel portrait."

"Balanced by the eyes of a doe."

"Could she hurt herself?"

Oscar removes a nonexistent speck of dust from his white shirt. "Commit suicide?" He stops, he savors the pause. Then he bursts out laughing, *ha ha!* "Of course she could. But not with the movie about to premiere, Commissario. No actress, no matter how hysterical, depressed, or whacked out on pills would ever do such a thing."

"Okay. What about the guy she went off with?"

"Andrea Serrano is a good guy."

"A peaceful good guy, or a violent good guy?"

"No, Andrea would never hurt her. Absolutely not."

"Do you know that or are you presuming?"

"I know it, full stop. Andrea is one of the very few genuine friends that I have in this magnificent city of con men and frauds. He has a heart in his chest and a head on his shoulders, if you know what I mean. He loves women. He has only two shortcomings: he doesn't know how to cook anything edible until after midnight, and he has no practical common sense about life. But as far as both those defects are concerned, he has me, and I cook him the best fish soup anybody in Rome knows how to make. And I tidy up his accounts for him. That's why he works for me."

"Are you such good friends that he can take your car without even so much as a phone call to say thanks, much less tell you where he's going?"

"His exit from Milly's party with Jacaranda was impressive, rapid, and surprising. A true coup de théâtre."

"But he left you marooned in Sabaudia, didn't he?"

Oscar lowers his tone of voice and speaks confidentially: "He asked me if he could take the Jaguar in advance, and I told him he could, of course. Except then I told everyone that he just stole it from me, because that made a more entertaining story. And if a story is more entertaining, it travels faster and farther. I needed that story to get to the papers in a hurry."

"For the premiere of the film."

"That's right."

"Now we're talking."

Oscar throws his arms wide. "The two sweethearts are happy. The producer is happy. And tickets are selling like hotcakes."

Ventura forces his neck back hard against the back of the chair. "Now would you also care to tell me where they've gone so we can put an end to all this playacting?"

At That Moment, Helga Shows Up

At that moment, Helga shows up in the living room. Breathtakingly beautiful. Raven haired, dark eyed, dark skinned, red lipped, with a statuesque physique, but light as air on her stiletto heels. She's wearing a black skirt suit, a pink silk blouse, a string of pearls, a diamond ring worth a hundred and fifty monthly paychecks, and the scent of a citrus orchard in full bloom. She looks not Argentine, but Persian. A Persian princess out of the *Thousand and One Nights*, with a voice just a hint rougher than velvet.

"You're a police commissario, aren't you?" she asks him, as if being one must be the nicest and most enviable thing on earth.

Ventura is simultaneously tempted to, first, get to his feet and kiss her hand and, second, just sit there, gazing at her.

She gives him a smile that will warm up the rest of his day. Then she turns to look at Oscar, dropping the temperature of her gaze until his teeth are chattering in the midst of a tiny blizzard. "Oscar, have you offered the commissario anything?" But she doesn't bother to wait for the answer. She calls her personal maid,

141

Miriaaam! She orders mineral water, espresso, and fresh-squeezed orange juice "for the gentleman." She adjusts her pink gold Mont Blanc wristwatch. She takes a few steps, showing off the lithe elasticity of a runway fashion model and the perfidious wiles of a wife in the throes of hatred. "I hope it's nothing serious, Commissario. My husband is always so attentive to everything I do that he often forgets to tell me what he gets up to." Having conveyed the alibi that makes all further questioning entirely unnecessary, she adjusts the bias-cut bangs that dance over her eyes and then issues her irrevocable decision: "I'm going."

This time, Ventura does stand up and brushes her hand, bowing to her loveliness and her bravura performance. "Signora."

"I hope you'll excuse me, Commissario. Such a pleasure to meet you," she tells him, gazing at him as if he were the most warmly anticipated guest of the week. She then disappears in more or less the same way she appeared in the first place, with a trippingly light dance step, merging her soft curves into the shadows of the doorway that leads through the sand-colored wall, between the large flowers by Andy Warhol and a red slash by Fontana.

"Are you interested in art?" Oscar Martello asks him, curiously, when Ventura, in an attempt to cover up his turmoil at the sight of Helga, simulates a corresponding excitement for the two paintings.

"No, I wish I knew more. But those paintings are so famous that even I recognize them."

"You were saying?"

"That I'd certainly like to know where those two characters of yours have gotten to. And why Serrano too has turned his phone off."

Oscar looks at him, calculating the risk of trying to palm off another fairy tale on him, but he doesn't want to say too much to this guy who's sitting in the middle of *his* home and has just screwed *his* wife with his eyes.

"I don't have the slightest idea. Maybe they're on a beach. Or high up in the mountains. Whatever the case, I'm guessing, in bed somewhere, ha ha!"

Ventura doesn't smile.

Ventura plays the tough guy.

And that's when Oscar shifts gears. "As for the Mafia, the Mafiosi, I don't know how they're going to take this film, which is a full-frontal attack, a level denunciation, and allow me to say it: very courageous."

"Really?"

"It's a film in defense of civil society. I'd like to invite you to a screening. Let's say the advance screening for the press, the day after tomorrow, in the evening. And Thursday, fingers crossed, it's opening wide in four hundred theaters. Your boss is coming too."

"My boss?"

"The chief of police. *Alberto* is an old friend. I spoke with him yesterday. And do you know what he told me? That they're keeping their best eyes on the safety of this film."

"Is that what he said?" Ventura wants to see how far he's willing to push it.

"Well, now that I've met you, I can't imagine he was referring to anyone else, what do you say?"

"What *can* I say? I'm flattered."

Oscar gives him a look and a smile, as if he too has found the man irresistible. "Have you ever thought about going into the movies? I mean it: writing stories for film and television. Or even just telling those stories to one of my writers. I imagine you must have seen some incredible things in such a long career. If you ever feel like it, just whistle, we could—"

Ventura starts showing signs of impatience. He's had enough. "Drop it. You were doing better before."

"What do you mean before?"

"Before your wife came in and scolded you for not offering me anything."

Oscar takes the point, stiffens, rolls the cigar around between his teeth, and blows out a plume of smoke.

Miriam, the Somali housemaid, shows up with espresso, croissants, fresh-squeezed orange juice, and mineral water. But neither of them seems to notice. They continue looking at each other, until finally Oscar gives in. "I hope I haven't offended you, I certainly didn't mean to."

Ventura decides that the time has come. "You don't think by any chance that they've gone to Paris to stay in your new apartment?"

Oscar meets and holds his gaze, and then smiles. "You know things even when you pretend you don't know them, don't you? Ha ha! But this time you're wrong. I don't know where you got your information, but if you're referring to a certain apartment in the Montparnasse district, that's the new headquarters of a nonprofit called—"

"Food against the Storm?"

"No, that's the Italian-English nonprofit. The French nonprofit is called Une Baguette pour l'Afrique. A rather picturesque name, don't you think? But who cares about the name if they do their job well. Are we agreed?"

"So the apartment doesn't belong to you."

"I put in a little money, as I presume you know. But the majority ownership belongs to Angelina Casagrande's nonprofit. My part is mere charity."

"Laudable."

"If a person has been given so much by society, then it's only right for him to give back, don't you think? And if that gratitude also happens to be good for a tax deduction, so much the better, ha ha!"

"So they're not there."

"Is it really all that important? I can reach out to Angelina and find out, and I'll get back to you, if you really care so much."

Ventura gestures as if to say, *fine, just skip it*. But he doesn't stand up. "As long as we're at it, let me bend your ear for another couple of minutes: What can you tell me about Attilio Fabris?"

Oscar thinks it over, relaxes. "A visionary director. A first-rate professional. His movie will prove it. Wait and see."

"Would he be capable of hurting another person?"

"Ah, you just won't let it rest. You continue to think that Jacaranda Rizzi is in danger, even though I've told you that there's no problem."

"I like to know how many characters are onstage."

"You're just like me. A perfectionist, congratulations. In any case, no. Fabris wouldn't hurt a fly. And if he were going to hurt anyone at all, he'd probably choose to hurt the producer, ha ha! I know what you're thinking about. That half-baked movie about violence, right?"

"Yes. It was kind of powerful."

"I know. But believe me: directors dream up things, they see worlds with the eyes of their imaginations and try to re-create them. In the old days, with plasterboard, nowadays with CGI. For anything else, they're useless. To make their damned movies they need a hundred people, on my payroll; I don't know if I convey the point. On their own, they wouldn't even know how to plant a tomato plant in a vase. Literally."

"Okay."

"And you're not going to ask me?"

"Ask you what?"

Oscar's eyes light up with delight. "Whether I would be capable of hurting another person."

"No. I don't need to ask you that." He says it with a serious expression. But to Oscar, that answer left intentionally hovering in midair is an irresistible treat, and he bursts out laughing, *ha ha!* Just then, his cell phone rings. He checks the display, and apologizes, "It's my office, just give me a minute, please."

But it's not the office. It's his law firm. They inform him that Attilio Fabris's agent is about to file a lawsuit for threats, battery, and mental cruelty.

From a distance, Oscar looks at the back of Ventura's head and evaluates this strange coincidence. Evidently everyone's looking into that fart in outer space, Fabris. He'll eventually have to deal with him, too, but for now, lowering his voice, he says, "Tell him that if he dares I'll break both his legs, by stomping on them with both feet, and then I'll break the casts when he gets them."

The lawyer on the other end of the line hesitates. "I don't think that's a very good idea."

"No? I find it's phenomenal."

"If I may—"

He interrupts, "I'm afraid you can't. And tell him that I'm his wolf. He'll understand."

Fabris's Wolves

Oscar Martello remembers very clearly the first day he met Attilio Fabris, three years ago, in the offices of Anvil Film: the director had just turned thirty, and he had the face of a rich, spoiled child. A handlebar mustache to give himself a presence, but with a fairly ridiculous overall effect. Dressed in total black. The demeanor of a wily fox who pretends to be introverted so he'll seem more intelligent. He emanated a high-handed arrogance that he clearly struggled to suppress, probably an inheritance from his father, Pierferdinando Fabris, chief physician in the cardiology ward at Varese Hospital, a man in favor of law and order, and in fact, a monarchist, which was a category of assholes that Oscar believed had gone extinct. As for his mother, she was one of those usual noblewomen, thin as a straw, afflicted with nervous disorders, the ones they still cultivate along the dreary lakeshores, like certain competition roses, and who generally wither and decline until they rot away in small vases filled to the brim with martinis.

In the way of loathing his mother and father that Attilio had, without quarter, Oscar recognized his own. And it was the first thing that aroused his curiosity. That was why he had him tell the whole saga of his travels and his turmoils.

Attilio had gotten the hell out of Varese, and wound up in London. And since he didn't know how to do anything, he decided to become an artist and enroll in film school. That was the first sound thing the young man had done—after previously smoking sufficient quantities of Afghan hash oil, he had experienced the infinite expansion of time itself. And that was his second good hunch, the basis for a short film in which he shot the four-second arc of his own ejaculation, and extracted two minutes and forty seconds of slow motion, with a hypnotic soundtrack of electronic music not unlike the old Pink Floyd. The title was practically longer than the film itself—*The Curvature of Space-Time According to Albert Einstein's Theory of Relativity as Applied to the Flight of My Bird*—and opened many doors for him, stimulating the curiosity of the film critics, giving him access to two dozen film festivals around the world, and to a considerable number of young female film enthusiasts who wanted to experience the thrill of getting their faces splashed by the star of Attilio Fabris's new opus.

If anything, his first feature-length movie prompted even more excitement. It was titled *Wolves*. It was the story of three young men with tough-guy expressions on their faces, studded leather jackets, and tattoos, who carry out a home invasion in a super-deluxe villa in the Lombard countryside, the home of a married couple in their fifties, a husband and wife, salt-and-pepper hair, slim, trim, and athletic, who for the first ten minutes of the movie do their best to talk the young thugs into sparing them any violence. But when the intruders snap out their switchblades, instead of dissolving in fear, the older couple whips out two 9 mm Glock pistols, shoots one of their assailants in the head, and then wraps up the other two wiseguys on two chairs, tying them back to back. Then they don leather bondage outfits, bring out whips, pliers, electric wires, and set to work on them, taking their time, forcing them to tell the whole story of their stupid lives, between one scream and the next. Then they make them watch as they engage in spectacularly theatrical sex, and right at the dizzying crescendo, they slash both the home invaders' throats. They cut them up into pieces. They toss them into the walk-in freezer, already stacked high with other human remains. And at last they emerge into the garden, stark naked, smeared with blood, to howl at the moon.

The sheer brutal eccentricity of the story had its filthy effect. A couple of critics wrote that Attilio Fabris, "by turning the old and savory masterpiece *Clockwork Orange* on its head," had illuminated "the unexpected violence that lies in ambush in the kitchen of everyday life, a metaphor for the insecurity of this globalized world that keeps pushing us backward in time, back to primeval tribal violence." Someone mentioned a chilly masterpiece. Someone else spoke of a boiling-hot gothic.

Fabris went to the first TV interview completely whacked out on methamphetamine. And since he wanted to exaggerate in order to astonish the interviewer, a woman who was panting like a Great Dane, he told her that for the two main characters of *Wolves* he'd taken his inspiration in general "from the criminal bourgeoisie of Northern Italy" and, in particular, "from Mama and Papa."

Complete pandemonium ensued. His family and the city of Varese declared him an outcast. His mother wound up in the hospital, under sedation. His father threatened him, waving a scalpel under his nose. He just laughed and egged them on, the way a young, show-offy toreador might do, he was so completely immune to their threats: his grandfather had been good enough to leave him a fortune of 15 million Swiss francs in his will, before putting a bullet through his head in the vault in his villa in Lugano.

At the height of the quarrel, a couple of squad cars pulled up to soothe tensions within the Fabris family. The young man emerged streaming trails of glory. And the next day, at seven in the morning, for the first time in his life, he received a phone call from Oscar Martello, who introduced himself, crying, "I'm your new producer!" And even though it was the break of day, he assailed him, already pumped up with adrenaline: "What are you doing, Attilio, sleeping? Are you goofing off?"

❧

Oscar puts an end to the flashback, and returns to staring at Raul Ventura—who in the meantime has been gazing raptly at the famous Manzoni monochrome, a square of wrinkled white canvas, tending ever so slightly to gray, in turn set in a larger square of wall painted a soft black to make the painting the center of the immense living room.

"Is this it?"

"Excuse me?"

"Is this the Manzoni that you purchased from the Fabris family?"

Before Oscar's face splits into a beaming smile, a shadow passes over it. "Yes, sure it is. And how did you happen to know that?"

"I've heard about it."

Oscar relaxes. "I bet you did. It's a fantastic artwork. And he, too, well, he was a fabulous individual, Piero Manzoni, the artist. They don't make artists like him anymore."

"Really? I read somewhere that he was a miserable alcoholic who died young."

"Poor, but from a wealthy family, a family of counts or something like that. Alcoholic, no question. A solitary revolutionary, the way I like them."

"Solitary revolutionaries usually come to unhappy ends."

"Exactly. Especially if they fail to find themselves an Oscar Martello who recognizes their genius, harnesses it, exploits it, and pays them. I don't know if you take the point."

Ventura takes the point perfectly; it's all right there in the dossier dedicated to Oscar Martello that he studied with painstaking care, including the transaction in undeclared funds that were used for the purchase of the painting, outside Italian national territory, presumably in cash. Cash that reverberates in many of the legends told in the drawing rooms of La Dolce Roma, where it is generally estimated that the much-despised Oscar Martello spent a fabulous sum, roughly €1.5 million, perhaps even €2 million. A juicy detail. But still, nothing compared with the priceless revelation offered up by Massimiliano Urso, the art critic, who diagnosed it to be a counterfeit, transforming that fake treasure into a delectable sting.

"So you find the director. You take him away with you from his home in Varese. And while you're there, you find the painting. Nice."

"The father and the mother, after the scandal unleashed by their son, had decided to drop out of sight. Move to the other side of the lake, in Switzerland. The Manzoni belonged to the mother's family, in Milan, they wanted to cash out in a hurry. I was their golden parachute."

As he tells him the story, Oscar is wondering why the hell they're talking about it. In the end, he asks, "Why are you so interested in it?"

"Mere curiosity."

Oscar looks at his impassive face, his two-bit suit, the shoulders that are too broad for the mind to be sharp. He has nothing to fear. "If there's nothing else. I'm afraid I have to crack the whip over a few screenwriters."

Ventura doesn't move. He's thinking whether he should venture so far as to ask him about the young Fabris's fortune. So sizable that his law enforcement cousins over at the Financial Police sent him an entire dossier, with potential points of contact or banking connections with Martello's assets. But he's already pushed too far. So he sticks his hands in his pockets and decides to skip it. "I need to get going, too. But let's stay in touch."

"Always at your service, commissario," Oscar tells him, by which he means exactly the opposite.

In Scalding Water

I n Paris, Andrea and Jacaranda are in a bathtub full of scalding hot water. They're at the end of their fourth day together and finally at the beginning of something else. Oscar left at eight that evening in his Jaguar C-X17 with its Liquid Gold paint job, without a word as to whether he'd be coming back, or where he was going, or what had become of Angelina Casagrande, her acquisitions, or her airplane. And he'd said nothing about what was to become of them, or how many more days they were going to have to spend in Paris with their cell phones powered down. In other words, what was to become of the three-ring circus that he had set going. As he left, all he said was, "I'll be in touch." And the two of them, relieved at his departure, taking the tension with him as he left, hadn't felt like asking anything else.

This evening they indulged in an aperitif and dinner at Select.

He tried to get a little closer to her, asking her, "Do you mind if I ask what's tormenting you?"

She answered him, with a confidence that almost verged on

distraction, "I'm falling into the void. And there's no one to catch me."

"Is that how you feel?"

"Yes. Surrounded by hostile people."

"Even now?"

"Yes," she told him, but adding a hint of gentleness to the gaze with which she had just caressed him.

Andrea returned the kindness with a smile and, before he had a chance to regret it, blurted out, "According to Sun Tzu—"

"Who?"

"A great Chinese philosopher, an expert on military strategies—"

"And what does he say?"

"That before you can know who your enemies are, you have to know who you are."

"Oh good Lord, I don't know who I am."

Andrea was about to tell her, *Well then, this is your chance to find out*, but he realized that the whole thing sounded like idiotic lines out of a TV movie. And that she would just laugh in his face. Their evening together deserved better: "Shall we head home?"

❧

The quiet after the winds kicked up by Oscar Martello created a perimeter that took them in. And they filled that perimeter with a blast of flame of pure passion, and then with a bathtub full of hot water. But without excitement, without suspense, as if taking a bath together was just one of the possible options for the evening, available in the catalog. For that matter, they'd first met over an aquarium and now more water surrounded them and perhaps even protected them.

"Tell me where you come from. Start from the beginning," Andrea asks her.

"From what beginning?"

"The beginning of it all. Your story."

"It's not that cheerful."

"I don't like cheerful stories."

Not really sure where to begin, Jacaranda looks around at the empty bathroom and says, "My whole story is a story of homes being emptied. A story of moving. Do you feel like hearing it?"

"Certainly I do."

"Then let's start with my great-grandfather."

Andrea's eyes open wide.

Jacaranda *almost* starts laughing. "But I'll keep it short."

Her great-grandfather, back in the twenties, had sold the family's two apartment houses, in Trieste, to buy German government bonds. "He'd done it just before the fall of the Weimar Republic, which turned those bonds into so much worthless paper. Just think, what fantastic timing." Then guess what her grandfather did: "With the last few pennies of the family fortune, he bought a hat factory in Istria and a big house. You know what year? In 1939, just in time for the outbreak of World War Two. And when the war was over, all the borders were redrawn, with the Iron Curtain, and all property that belonged to Italians requisitioned by Yugoslavia under Tito. All lost."

Then it was her father's turn. When she was eight, he vanished from the scene. "He left for Chile, chasing a woman painter, leaving us a note saying he was sorry."

"And you never saw him again?"

"Never. Never saw him, never heard from him. Maybe he's still alive somewhere, rich and happy. Maybe he's dead."

"Aren't you curious to find out?"

"No. All I remember about him were his consequences. My mother crying and the apartment completely empty."

"Why empty?"

"Completely empty like this apartment. Because when my father ran away, he left us penniless, and to survive my mother sold off all our furniture, one room at a time. And then she was so angry that she cut up all the clothing that my father had left in the closets, into strips. In the end, the apartment was empty, and the floors were littered with hundreds of these strips of fabric. I played with them for a whole month. When I ran, there was an echo."

The water in the tub emits flashing reflections. Jacaranda's face is luminous, in spite of the shadow of her stories. Andrea has been yearning to kiss her since a time that now seems lost in the distant past, when what separated them was the blue and gold space of the aquarium at Milly's house, in Sabaudia.

At Select they drank Ricard until late, then his hand brushed hers, just like in an Éric Rohmer film, and she kissed him, and before long they were alone, back in the apartment, in front of the bathroom mirror, making love with their hands. She with her raspberry-red blouse completely unbuttoned, her skirt hiked up, her legs spread, one knee braced against the sink. He behind her. The two bodies clutching each other, reflected in the mirror. Their panting breath. Empty air around them.

Jacaranda's breasts rise half out of the water's surface, as she goes on with her story. "One day we left for Deauville, on the French coast. My mother knew a guy I called Uncle Jean-Luc, the proprietor of a small hotel on the beach, with lots of empty rooms, but never one for me, I had to go off to boarding school, that was the deal they had made."

"Nice of them."

She smiles. "I told you it's not a cheerful story."

"Go on."

"I was in a horrible boarding school in Strasbourg, run by sadistic nuns."

"For how long?"

"Two years. One day my aunt Dora shows up. My salvation. Divorced. Cheerful. After all the men, she was ready and willing to be a mother. She owned a pharmacy that she'd hired someone to manage, so she had enough to live on. Professionally, she was a theatrical impresario. She talked my mother into letting me go back to Italy with her, first to Genoa, and then to Turin, and after that, to Rome."

"More moves."

"I never even managed to learn my way around the neighborhood."

"Poor thing. You were alone, friendless, without a homeland."

She raises her eyebrows. "You can laugh, but that's what it was like. And it still is."

"What are you saying? You're the fabulous star of *No, I Won't Surrender!* All of Italy is worried sick about you. And in the meantime you're having a high old time in a bathtub with your new gentleman friend."

This time she bursts out laughing.

"I finally made you laugh."

"It's just that I usually feel as empty as the houses of my life, as this apartment."

"Emptiness isn't so bad really, if a person knows how to use it."

"Well, I've had enough of it. I wish I had a close female friend. I wish I had a man. I wish I had a child. Not this emptiness."

"You don't have children to fill a void. All you need for that is a PlayStation."

Jacaranda gazes at him for a long while, with the expression of someone discarding one phrase after another. Then she picks the last one. "I don't even know what I'm doing here."

"You're in Paris."

"But I could be anywhere."

"Anywhere wouldn't be the same thing."

"For me it would." Her distance is a rubber band that stretches out and narrows down.

Andrea searches for a handhold to bring her back to where she was. "You're here to complete a movie that keeps going after the final cut. I told you that. And I'm here to help you. We even went up the Eiffel Tower, remember?" He feels pathetic, he can't think of anything better.

She notices, and decides not to pile on. "Right. We're all toy soldiers in the hands of Oscar Martello."

"Why do you hate Oscar? I mean, aside from the fact that he's a bully, a megalomaniac, an ignorant oaf, conceited, and filthy rich, why do you hate him so much?"

She's lost in thought, gazing into the water surrounding them. Then she looks up at him again. "And why on earth are you his friend?"

Yeah, come to think of it, why is he? Out of convenience? Out of self-interest? Because he admires him? Because he'd like to be like him, or for the opposite reason, because he wants to be *completely* unlike him and be as far from him as can be, while still remaining close to him?

Among all the possible answers, he chooses the simplest one: "Because we work well together. He pays regularly. Sometimes, we even have fun. He's one of the very few people who under-stands film and television."

"Television is shit. And film is this stuff here."

"Well, he wallows in it, the others live off it. Including me and you, it seems to me."

"It's one thing to do it to make a living. It's quite another thing to live so you can do it. And anyway, you never answered my question, how can you stand to be such a close friend of his?"

"Well, you didn't answer me either, why do you hate him so much?"

Once again, the lost look, as if the question had caught her off guard. "Because he's a bad man."

"Maybe. But above all, he's a desperate man."

"Is that why you're his friend?"

"That's one reason."

Deep down, it strikes him as an acceptable reply. Surprisingly, she agrees. "Yes, desperate is the right word. But not for the reasons you have in mind."

Oscar, the Top Hat, the Yacht

Oscar Martello is a great deal more than just a magician with a top hat that he knows how to pull rabbits out of. He's all three things at once, including the rabbit. And since it's a routine he's been pulling off for years, he thinks he no longer needs to worry about the audience that's watching him and which, over time, has learned to recognize his tricks.

He left the apartment on Rue Liancourt and picked up his Jaguar from the basement garage. From that moment on, his movements were tracked by a satellite homing device installed in the car by Raul Ventura's men, with a warrant from the district attorney's office in Rome and the approval of the French authorities.

First stop: the parking facilities of the Hotel George V, where Oscar had taken a suite for the night. The next morning, he was tracked through 215 miles of French countryside, until he reached the town of Dudelange, just over the boundary of the Grand Duchy of Luxembourg.

Video cameras monitoring the border zoomed in on the tail of his car as it entered the country. And, four hours later, the front of the Jaguar as it left.

In those four hours, a couple of men from Interpol have photographed him walking into the BNP Paribas branch office at 50 Avenue J.-F. Kennedy with three blue plastic travel bags, which he'd just unloaded from the car trunk. Then they followed him, photographing him all the while, to the tables of the Restaurant Clairefontaine, where he ate lunch with a high functionary of the bank who showed up ten minutes later, white-haired, tall, and thin, wearing an impeccable pin-striped suit. At the exit, the two men went their separate ways. Oscar Martello went into a mansion midway between Grand Rue and the Place d'Armes, a well-known first-class bordello. He emerged an hour and a half later in the company of a blond woman who drove him to the Brussels international airport, where Martello boarded a flight for Rome, just in time to take part in the movie's premiere. The blond and the Jaguar continued toward Paris. The Jaguar went back to the garage it had left that morning, in Denfert-Rochereau. The blond vanished in foot traffic.

⚜

As he was reading the last page of the report, Raul Ventura experienced the usual dizzying vertigo of someone looking down on the men and women scurrying far below, in the anthill of the real world, with their trajectories that seem so random, so messy, but which all have a purpose. His task now was to reconstruct the trajectories of Oscar Martello. Photograph him with his money: one step after another, until he reached the end of the path.

His little stroke of luck—after months of sleuthing in the shadows for tax evasion, clandestine funds, money laundering, and aggravated fraud—is that now he can do it under the simplest of covers, pretending that he's interested in another trajectory, namely the film industry that operates in broad daylight, or rather, in the light of the Internet.

To follow the developments of *No, I Won't Surrender!*, one need only tap on any of the websites that pulsate with news about Jacaranda Rizzi, all of them agog at the coincidence of the movie appearing on screens across the nation and the star disappearing from circulation. The articles yammer on about Mafia, threats, perhaps kidnappings. The uproar even spreads to the print media, which are slower on the uptake, more circumstantial, but also somewhat less naive, never forgetting to point out in their coverage the possibility of a publicity stunt by "that devil Oscar Martello, a producer of many hit movies."

Without this general groundswell of excitement, without this state of fibrillation over the major film premiere, Raul Ventura would never have been able to get close to Oscar Martello without arousing his suspicions and endangering the investigation, and his team. Now he's even set foot in his home, he's met him in person. He saw with his own eyes how far he's come and how he feels: cunning and well protected. But also so high up, on tiptoe atop his narcissism, that just a single false step will send him plunging headfirst to the ground. Or at least so Ventura hopes: that's why he's there.

❧

The preview screening at the Cinema Adriano was an orgy of bare backs, photographers, and crumpled paper sailing across the red carpet on account of the street sweeper strike and the sirocco wind that had sprung up. The general wave of apprehension for the

fate of the leading lady warmed up the embraces and air-kisses of
the entire community, but without ever interrupting the sequence
of selfies. At the end of the projection, applause. With Oscar in a
black suit, walking through the audience to savor his triumph, the
handshakes, the white teeth bared in smiles, and more hugs from
Attilio Fabris, Helga, and Angelina Casagrande, even a hug from
one of the seven kings of Rome, Marietto, hairdresser to the stars,
who told Oscar, "Beautiful! I would have made Jacaranda a little
more sluttish, a bit more of a woman, you get me, a little more of
a hottie, not with the tight curly hair of a schoolgirl, but with the
impressive ringlets of a horny female cabinet minister, even if she
is a Mother Courage type. Bravo, my compliments, fine movie. If
perhaps a tad slow."

Oscar let Marietto walk away, then locked arms with Angelina.
"Since when are fucking hairdressers allowed to be film critics?"

Angelina grabbed his wrist. "Well, they just don't have the
social classes they used to, my dear one. In my day, hairdressers
talked about who was cheating on who and the cooks stayed in
the kitchen."

They laughed. "I adore you, my love, ha ha!"

The next day, Oscar invited ten or so journalists to Fiumicino,
to eat raw tuna aboard his €10 million eighty-foot Magnum Marine, showing them all the plaque on the stern that states: "The
fastest high-performance luxury yacht in its class in the world."
"Fifty-two knots, there's nothing faster! Like its owner, do I make
myself clear?" He greeted them wearing a faded grapefruit-
colored linen suit and a midnight blue T-shirt, with cell phones
chirping, answered promptly by two skinny black-clad assistants
from Anvil Film who lived in the constant terror of being fired,
and the equally constant terror of being rehired the next day.

Once the troupe of journalists had excited itself sufficiently thanks to the chilled white wine, the alcohol-charged mint mojitos, and the pitch and roll of that gleaming white, highly finished floating piece of patrimony, Oscar started reeling off groundless claims about the movie, the plot, its importance as a piece of civil protest, the extraordinary gifts of the director ("the great, great Attilio Fabris, who is unfortunately still at home sick, but you can certainly call him, anytime you like, and in the meantime he sends you all his fondest best wishes"), and naturally the magnificent Jacaranda Rizzi in the role of a woman strong enough to stand up to the Mafia, "a woman that we'd all want as a friend, a sister, a bride, and whom as you well know we're trying to protect from obscure threats."

A shiver runs through all the journalists who are drinking, chewing, and jotting down notes. All of them exchange glances, a little bewildered at the idea that they may have to handle a slightly more serious story than the usual, inoffensive bullshit with which each of them fills their pages and their lives.

They cluster around Oscar the oracle in a semicircle. And, ignoring all the other actors from the cast, hoisted aboard as background scenery, the most zealous reporters venture questions suitable to the occasion: "Can you tell us where Rizzi is?"

"Has she been threatened?"

"Is it true that she's left the country?"

"Are we sure that this isn't a publicity stunt?" ("Ah, no! Now I'm insulted, how dare you think such a thing?")

"Today the War & Peace agency posted that this is a sort of elopement. What's the real story?"

Oscar plays the mystery card and pontificates like a wise old man: "The truth, the truth! The truth is always ambiguous, al-

ways presumed, you all are journalists, you ought to know that."
And as he says it, he pours drinks for them all, doing his best to
get them drunk, to balance on the razor-thin line of uncertainty,
to keep all the fires burning under the fat ass of a movie that, with
all the kerosene he's been dumping on it, sooner or later is going
to have to heat up.

Lea Lori, the film critic whom he keeps on his expense roster
(even though she's "a toilet with pedals," as he told Andrea one
day: "In the old days, I only paid the most fabulous pieces of pussy.
And now look at me. I'm clearly getting old."), did her job on the
blog that she writes every day, in her description of the "power of
this film, based on the rough nature of the story that smacks of the
crime pages. A work of cinema that occupies a worthwhile space
in the realm of what we call democratic filmmaking, but without the tedium of the so-called auteur school." A specific critique
meant for idiots, given the gross defects of the plot, but one that
would exert its influence, shaping the judgment of other anemic
or simply lazy critical minds, which, not knowing what to think
for themselves, would simply think with the well-coiffed little
head of Lea Lori. And Lea Lori thus ensured her daughter's job
security for another six months.

After the umpteenth round of bottles, giggles, lies, and insipid
questions, Oscar declares the boat trip over. "But we never even set
sail!" objects one of the journalists, who had knotted a silk scarf
around his neck for the maritime occasion.

Oscar turns around, trying to imagine what right that complete nothing of an ink-dabbler thinks he has to expect a ride on
his boat. "Friend, I have to work for the Italian cinema. But if you
want to take a ride, stay on board. Go ahead and fill up the tank,
it's only fifteen hundred gallons."

Revelations at Dinner

On their sixth Parisian afternoon, while back in Italy *No, I Won't Surrender!* has opened wide on four hundred screens, Andrea and Jacaranda strolled and chatted. She hasn't taken pills, neither of them has had too much to drink. Night has fallen. Over the darker streets of Saint-Germain all the stars have flickered on. And they have walked in among the mirrors of the Brasserie Lipp to sit at one of the little tables that give you the illusion of having everything within reach, tenderness, food, the city. And sometimes, even the world.

An instant before sitting down, she took off her amaranthine red leather jacket, and the new white T-shirt she was wearing left uncovered her collarbone and her sternum all the way up to the swell of her breasts. The warm light of the dining room highlighted the cornice of her blond hair, the fine, regular features of her face, the gold chain dancing around her neck. As he looked at her, he could make out the pores of her skin, the fine blond fuzz, backlit, and the regular wave of her breathing that seemed to lull her in that instant of unique, never-again perfection.

They ordered steamed fish, julienned vegetables, and a dry white wine. They felt good, they were hungry. They were on the same wavelength.

They told each other about the most beautiful places on earth they'd each seen. For Jacaranda those were the Punta della Dogana in Venice, on a sunny day with a cold northwest wind, and the top of the Empire State Building, at night, in June.

"Why in June?" he asked her.

And she answered, laughing, "Otherwise, you freeze to death."

For Andrea, it's Torres del Paine, in Chilean Patagonia, in the warmest month of the year, January, and without wind. At sunset, when the granite turns red.

"What else? Tell me another," she asked him, like a little girl.

"Any table in any restaurant in Paris, looking into your eyes."

She burst into laughter, threw a crust of bread at him, and asked, "And they pay you to dream up this crap?"

"Not as much as I'd like."

Jacaranda told him that she lived for a whole year in Venice, perhaps the loveliest year of her life, in spite of the fact that she had a boring, jealous boyfriend.

"The architect?"

"Yes. I've always admired architects. Some of them are geniuses."

"And was your architect a genius?"

"I don't know, maybe. But instead of looking at the world, he read too many books and constantly called his mother on the phone."

"Mothers ruin the world."

"Architects are even worse."

"How did you become an actress?"

She had probably answered that question a million times before, but she's thoughtful enough to make it seem like the first time. "Half of the blame goes to my aunt Dora. And half of it was my own choice. By taking me away from that boarding school and saving my life, she introduced me to the theater. In Milan, Strehler was still around, in Rome, Gassman. Lots of things were circulating: ideas, scripts, dinner parties. Those were creative years. In the end, I chose to attend the Rome Film Academy. And that's how the rumba began."

"Don't you like what you are?"

"I like the work. I hate everything that surrounds it."

"Maybe the two things are connected."

"In what sense?"

"At the circus, before going on, and at the end of each performance, you need a lot of sand to clean up."

The waiter brings the fish and the mayonnaise. He fills their glasses and then vanishes.

It's at that moment that their talk heads in the direction they were both expecting. She looks at Andrea meaningfully. "I know where you're trying to steer the conversation."

"Tell me."

"Toward your friend, Oscar Martello, the sand king."

"We also got interrupted before making the deep dive."

"Maybe because I didn't trust you."

"And now you trust me?"

"Maybe the time has come to tell you what I know about him."

If there had been a spotlight in the shadowy dining room of the Brasserie Lipp, this would be the moment to turn it on. Good actress that she is, she senses it. And good screenwriter that he is, he sees it.

"I'm listening. I've heard lots of backbiting about him. Most of it has to do with his manners, his arrogance, and his money."

Jacaranda drinks and thinks it over. "What I have to say about him isn't backbiting, it's his story. You've known him for five years, I've known him for twenty."

"Really? You never told me that before."

She fails to catch the irony; she's too focused on what she's reviewing in her mind's eye and recounting. And the sorrow that she's experiencing. "My aunt was a close friend of Eusebio Reverberi, the producer, maybe she'd even had an affair with him, I never really knew. I remember him from when I was a girl, he'd come over for lunch on Sundays; he'd always bring a box of pastries. And I remember when his henchman first showed up, your friend."

"He was his driver."

"He was his everything, he was always underfoot, at lunch, at dinner, even after dinner."

"That's just his personality."

"No, he was studying him. And you know why? To learn everything he could from him, starting with how you make a movie. So then he could get rid of him and take everything he possessed, ideas, friends, and contacts. Until one day, he actually did."

"What day?"

"The day they arrested Eusebio. Did Oscar never tell you about it?"

"Yes. He told me that the police staged a raid at the crack of dawn. They were looking for accounting documents. Instead they found cocaine, an unregistered pistol, and an underage female."

"Nonsense. The police weren't looking for accounting documents. They were there because an anonymous phone tip had come in to police headquarters. Guess who made the phone call?"

Andrea isn't sure he really wants to know. "Do I have to guess?"

"His lackey and your friend, Oscar Martello."

"How can you say such a thing? You were just a little girl."

"No, I wasn't a little girl, I was sixteen years old, exactly half my age now."

A doubt crosses his mind. "How do you happen to know all these things?"

She turns her gaze away, the way she did in the bathtub. Then she turns back and stares at him. "Because that day at dawn the police weren't looking for Eusebio, much less his invoices or anything of the sort. They were looking for me."

The room spins around once. Jacaranda's face comes out deformed for an instant, before resuming its normal appearance.

"In what sense were they looking for you?"

"I was the underage female."

"Fuck. That was you?"

"Don't start getting ideas. And wipe that look off your face. Eusebio was three times my age; I wasn't fucking him. I wasn't doing anything with him. And I wasn't naked in his bed, the way they said in the papers. I was in the guest room." She looks at her plate, but what she sees is the scene from back then, she hears the sound of excited voices, slamming doors. Then she breathes, "My name was kept out of the news. And in all these years, it's never emerged."

Andrea needs something more to drink. He pours some for her too. "Go on."

"When the police broke in, I was asleep. The shouting woke me up. I came out of my bedroom in sheer terror, wrapped in a sheet. Eusebio was in the hallway, wearing a pair of ridiculous red briefs, bare chested, his face as white as a ghost. But since he wanted to reassure me, he threw his arms around me. Some policewoman started shouting and someone took me into another room and told me not to move. That's where the misunderstanding arose. The newspapers built quite a story out of it."

"And how does Oscar fit in?"

"The cops went straight to the coke, found it with no difficulty at all, it was in a box of salt. And the handgun was in a wooden box, behind some books. Eusebio was positive that it was Oscar who informed them of every detail with that anonymous phone call. I told you: to ruin him and take his place."

Andrea tries to resist this revelation. "The fact that you're convinced something is true doesn't necessarily mean that it's actually true."

"It all fits together. Including the fact that Eusebio was planning to fire him for that very reason, he felt he was being spied upon. He had told my aunt that he wanted to get rid of him once and for all because he'd noticed that the man was devouring his life. Little by little, he was taking over everything."

"When he got out of prison, he really did fire him. But then he died from a heart attack. What did Oscar have to do with that?"

"Everything. The last coke he ever snorted was coke Oscar bought for him. As always. But when they autopsied Eusebio's corpse, it turned out that the coke was insanely pure: a chemical time bomb."

Andrea thinks it over and decides that the plot holds together. So does the motive. "Still, though, fuck: the pistol, the cocaine, the orgies, maybe your friend Reverberi kind of asked for it, don't you think?"

"He was no saint. He was a bandit himself, like almost everyone, but unlike Oscar he wasn't a bad man."

They practically haven't touched their food. On the other hand, they've finished their wine and ordered another bottle. The waiter comes over, looking worried: "Is something wrong?"

Of course not. Everything's fine. I'm on an all-expenses-paid vacation to arrange a piece of cinematic fraud, on the payroll of an unscrupulous producer who used an underage girl and a batch of superpure cocaine to screw a friend, and he did it so ruthlessly that he might have even become his friend's murderer. And that murderer has been my best friend.

"It doesn't add up."

"Oh, yes, it does."

"Then tell me why sixteen years later he decided to cast you in his movie."

Jacaranda shakes her head to underline the simplicity of the answer. "Because he didn't remember me. And because in the meantime, I changed my name."

"I don't believe it."

"But it's true. Nobody knows it, but I'm legally registered as Maria. Maria Rizzi is my legal name. Jacaranda came later."

"Maria is a beautiful name."

"At age twenty I didn't think so, I wanted an artistic name."

"At age twenty people do a lot of stupid things."

"And plus back then my hair was red. I've changed. There's nothing left to link me to that night. Which no longer even exists, no one remembers it now. Except for me and Oscar."

"Then what are you doing in his movie?"

She hesitates, then says, "That story has obsessed me my whole life. I intend to resolve it."

At the table of the Brasserie Lipp, sitting in that tiny portion of the world, Jacaranda is facing her past to try to change her future.

But Andrea is still opposing resistance; he doesn't want to give in to that reconstruction of the facts. "If his plan, Oscar's plan, was to ruin your friend Reverberi and take his place, he'd already done it by sending him to prison. What need was there to kill him?"

"Maybe he didn't mean to kill him, but he arranged for it to happen, with the coke, with the stress, with the scandal. As for his reasons, he had an endless array of them. He wanted to rub out his old life and the smell of sweat that it had cost him. He knew that after he got out of prison, Eusebio would fire him and ruin his reputation. And all his dreams would end before they even began: no films, no money, nothing at all."

No matter which way you turn it in search of a way out or another explanation, Jacaranda's reconstruction is based on pretty solid evidence. And when Andrea tells her, "I have a hard time imagining Oscar as a murderer," the exact opposite idea actually surfaces in his mind. "Does he know about you?"

"Yes."

"Have you talked about it?"

"I did, but only when we were done filming."

"And how did he react?"

"He turned pale, he told me that he didn't remember a thing. He said that he always puts the past in the cellar. But he was acting to conceal his fright. He knows that I know the truth."

"And what do you have in mind?"

"I told you already. I want to get free of this thing. I want to do it for myself, for Eusebio, to tell everyone who thinks they know him who Oscar Martello really is."

"If you're right and things went the way you're telling me, then you have a very dangerous job ahead of you."

"I know that."

Every word in that lengthy revelation has dense emotional implications and carries the jagged weight of consequences. The poison that dried up so many years ago is liquefying right before their eyes. The accumulated rancor is ready to unfurl into vendetta. And the vendetta threatens to turn into an appointment with fire.

Tension floats in the air around them. Because the fire is going to devour everything, from the very first lick of flame. They both know it. But the idea of bracing for the consequences of the imminent roaring blaze isn't sufficiently urgent to dim the light of that instant. Luckily, there's still time, a whole night ahead of them. And there's still wine. Andrea raises his glass. "Well, you're going to need protection when the time comes. So when you're ready, let me know."

She too raises her glass, as well as raising her eyes to look into his. "That's what I'm doing."

No Solution

At home, after dinner, Jacaranda had changed her mood. When he'd asked her if he could call her Maria, she'd told him, "Go ahead, but don't expect me to answer you." She'd turned more off-putting than ever.

"Do you want to be alone?" Andrea had asked her.

And without turning around she had replied, "*I am* alone." She had told him, "I don't like any of what's awaiting me. In fact, it terrifies me."

He was astonished by the rapidity with which her face too had changed, how the sweetness of her gaze had turned to suffering. And Andrea had glimpsed for an instant what that suffering multiplied over time would change in her face, swelling the bags under her eyes, irradiating a web of fine wrinkles around the lips, putting out the lights in her hair, so that the image of her future had finally made her even more desirable to Andrea's eyes in the here and now of the present.

Which was, however, a forbidden present, at least as much as

175

her name from the past. A present that was separating them, at a clip that was visible to the naked eye. Because from that moment of revelation at the table in the Brasserie Lipp, Jacaranda had never let him get near her again, and locked herself up in her room. In the middle of the night he heard her go into the kitchen, probably to take her tranquilizers.

In the darkness, Andrea tried to tune into the wavelength of her eyes, or her last glances. And that wavelength frightened him because it was veering toward the blackness of depression. It was prefiguring no escape routes, it was announcing shortness of breath, it was foretelling panic.

As he heard her move through the apartment, he was tempted to get up, but he didn't do it. Among all the possible options, he chose the Neutral Working Expression: break off communication, close his eyes. Without even imagining how bitterly he'd regret it.

❧

The next morning Jacaranda is gone. On the bathroom mirror she'd written, "Don't try to find me," as if they were two young sweethearts breaking up. But the two of them are nothing. Or almost nothing. They've made love once. And once they gave each other a bath. They shared a strange vacation. Which was actually a well-paid assignment. And during that assignment they exposed themselves more than they thought they would. Especially her. By opening up a part of her world to him. Which has just shut back down.

After all, what does he know about her?

He knows that she lives in Rome over near the Hilton, but he doesn't know where. He knows that she makes her living as an

actress, he knows her filmography. But he knows nothing about
what her life is like: who she has for friends, what numbers are
contained in her cell phone directory. He knows the heft and feel
of her breasts, the scent of her flesh, the shape of her sleep. But he
has no idea whether she's ever been married, or how many people
she's cohabited with. Whether she ever *seriously* considered having children. And if so, how many? Whether she knows how to
drive, swim, or cook. He knows that her anxiety keeps her from
breathing at times. And that ghosts whirl around her. Ghosts that
she tries to capture in packages of Xanax, as if they were chemical
safe-conduct passes capable of staving off that anxiety, until she finally decides to ask the wrong person for help ("If I close my eyes,
will you stay here to stand guard?"), accept the sleep that comes,
sit in her dreams with her ghosts, and then wake up with the light
of a smile and say, "I'm hungry."

He knows that she contains mysteries. Hidden loves, lurking
resentments. And perhaps long series of lies.

He knows her orgasm. Which arrives in gusts and expands,
one contraction after another, the way waves do. But he knows
nothing about the fiber that makes up the slow declension of her
life, the tide that day by day fills the sea bottom with sand, clogs it
with habits, appointments. Or solitude.

He knows that she's thirty-two years old. But he doesn't know
the day of her birthday. The name of her favorite movie. The music
she listens to. What size shoes she wears, a 6 or a 7? What size
jacket does she wear? What's the name of her perfume? Whether
she loves gold best, or coral, or neither of the two. Whether she
loves the black of velvets or the light blue of silk.

Andrea knows that there are unlikely to be any answers to

these questions. The opportunity is gone. The worlds are closed now. In the eyes of Jacaranda, by now far away, this apartment in Paris will just be the thousandth empty home to add to her collection of memories.

Her request is "Don't try to find me." And he complied with it even before deciding to. It's as true for Paris as for anyplace else.

Decompressions

The decompression of Andrea Serrano in Paris lasts two days. What with his endless twirling of the thought of Jacaranda through his fingers, he finally decides that he feels absolutely nothing for her. But that nothing is unexpectedly something. And if he were going to write about it, he'd start with her eyes, with her distance, and with those mysterious electric signals that she emitted from that distance—as if to communicate her position to someone out there listening, as if sending out a call for help. And then deleting every scrap of it just as quickly, passing from the white of a smile to black.

Uncertain whether or not to turn on his cell phone, he went down to the phone booth on Avenue Général Leclerc. He asked his agent for the phone numbers of Jacaranda and Milly. Massimiliano Testa pelted him with two dozen questions. Andrea reassured him with an *I'll tell you all about it later, not now*. Jacaranda and Milly both had their phones turned off. Oscar answered barking and snarling on the twentieth ring, "So it's you! What the fuck are you doing on the phone?"

"Jacaranda left."

"I know, I'm taking care of it."

"How the hell do you already know?"

He hesitated. "You underestimate my muckrakers."

"You're having us watched."

"No, of course not, we're just keeping an eye on the story so we can be ready. Stay put for a couple of days. We'll get hold of the crazy girl and then get organized for our grand return home."

"What am I staying put for?"

"You're on full expenses and greatly appreciated. Enjoy Paris."

❧

The decompression of Oscar Martello—with his film finally out in the movie houses, various fibrillations on the pages of the social networks, cautious, but positive, critical reviews, a sharply rising curve of ticket sales—lasts the entire weekend; the intrusion of that strange investigator, who has penetrated so easily into his sheltered world, has the annoying weight of a mystery and perhaps, also, a danger. That is why this is a more troubling decompression than usual. One that needs a hand, a body, a bit of excitement, to win its way back to the surface, seeing that Helga and the girls have flown off again to Courmayeur, leaving him in the midst of a void. And so he got a girl to fill that void and the girl finally fell asleep on the couch in the study, the glassed-in room high atop the turret, while he slept on the large cushions that slid off onto the floor and now he feels like every one of his bones is broken and his stomach is in flames, burned by his gastric juices and by the bottle of Caol Ila that they drank off, chasing it with rails of cocaine and plenty of hashish, just to keep the thing going. Flames that awaken him with the early sunlight of Sunday morning. With Filipinos gallop-

ing upstairs from the kitchens—in response to a couple of grunts
from him over the intercom—bearing American-style coffee, ice-
cold water, aspirin, and Maalox.

Oscar gets up off the floor, stretches, spits. He looks at the
time, it's six in the morning. He throws open the window onto
the cool air that makes the domes and flowering terraces glitter.
The whole city is still asleep, under the sky that's a special blue
dedicated to men like him, men in penthouse apartments in cobalt dressing gowns that in these moments of secret sincerity and
well-protected solitude ask themselves in their heart of hearts, in
the face of that spectacle of immense beauty and privilege, how
they ever managed to climb all the way up there, what merits,
what alliances, what good luck, what determination, what muscles, what threats, what humiliations, what pills, what lost sleep,
what deceptions, made it all possible. And whether those deceptions have now been adequately concealed.

He knows his own with absolute certainty. They are the faces
of the actors he deceived, the out-of-energy screenwriters he never
paid, the old movie stars he sent shuffling into the slaughterhouse,
the partners he duped.

He remembers the first time he ever saw Eusebio Reverberi
and how much weakness he'd sensed in that man, by now over-
taken by wealth, damaged by cocaine, softened by privilege. And
he remembers when, years later, but at the right moment, he first
saw an adolescent Maria, that is, Jacaranda, and the rapidity with
which he had the illumination: she was lovely, desirable, with her
breasts in flower. She wore a white tank top with a drawing of
a strawberry in the middle, a pink miniskirt, a pair of red ballet
flats. She was a little girl-woman. And there was a light in her
eyes that he recognized because he'd had it too when he was a kid,

when he wanted to escape the gray skies of Serravalle Scrivia. The hard light of those who believe, in solitude, that they've focused clearly on life, that they're clever enough, sharp enough, to snatch it for themselves: now or never.

And he remembers the last time he left Eusebio Reverberi behind him, pumped up with cocaine and fury, barefoot, unshaven, empty gin bottles on the side table, shouting at him that he'd turn him in to the police, he'd ruin him, he'd destroy him once and for all. He buried those images far from his surface life, filed away in the darkness, wrapped in the cellophane of bad memories, and then closed up in a plastic container, stuck in a drawer, inside a cabinet in the deepest cellar of his past, *his special cellar*, where he keeps the worst part of himself.

And if anyone ever managed to track back from one hiding place to another and finally snatched away even that last protection of his first secret, it would still be his word against that of the snoopy intruder, his regret, his gaze of crystalline innocence. And of course, the complete array of his lawyers, with their leather briefcases, the tough tanned hide of their faces, and their dizzying hourly rates. Who can compete with the great producer's team of lawyers? Jacaranda with a couple of tears? Some nosy cop in a hazelnut wool suit?

No, no one, not even the truth in person. *Wait, hold on, are you telling me that there's anyone left alive who's innocent enough to believe that such a thing exists as the truth in person?*

There, it's Oscar Martello asking himself the same question for what must be the millionth time. At dawn. Breathing, all alone, like all the men in all the penthouses. It's the doubt that's been eating away at him for years. That never lets him get enough sleep. The fissure that cracks his well-furnished world, always threatening to shatter it to pieces. That torments him with its tiny and absolute blackness. At least until the phone call at six thirty in the morning comes to save him—the hour when the men in penthouses call each other to talk about everything, everything except the terror that just woke them up—the phone call from the inevitably bored senator who asks for gossip about a new actress, from the bishop's secretary offering him a real estate deal, from the director at BNP Paribas inviting him to come see him, from a certain wealthy swine at the Ministry of Public Works who just saw a little boy in a TV movie and who wants to know how to get in touch with him so they can play doctor.

He listens to them all, one by one. Because they all occupy the steps that will lead to him finally crossing the Threshold in a white convertible. Cinecittà isn't some toy that you can buy with a check or a line of credit. In this country of recommendations and Mafiosi, you need the money, but the money's not enough. You need the go-ahead from everyone who's secured themselves a fucking padlock and a little smidgen of power: the little tycoons of television and the great traffickers of Angelina Casagrande, just for starters. The mayor and the trade unions. The undersecretary and the cabinet minister. The prince of the Freemasons and the cardinal. The English bankers. The American bankers. And in the end, even Three-Fingered Jack, the one who does the Almighty's dirty work.

He heaves a sigh, feels an immense weariness wash over him, and then a jolt of adrenaline—there's someone standing behind him, watching him.

It's a young woman in flesh and blood, who also woke up early and is now looking at him from the threshold of the French door, completely naked, except for the coat she found on the floor and threw over her shoulders, and she says to him, "Are you already at work, kitty cat?"

Oscar, turning around, silently absorbs the question, evaluating the harmony of that body, so young, so smooth, so light, and yet which he has no desire even to touch; she shouldn't be there, not at that moment, not in the middle of that headache. And yet she also stirs a sense of sudden nostalgia deep inside, a heartbreaking nostalgia for the things that are lost once and for all, and a tone of gentle kindness comes into his voice, surprising him: "It's still early, go back to sleep, Domiziana."

The young woman gazes at him, entranced, nods her head yes, like a good little girl, backs away behind the glass door, lets her overcoat slip to the floor, then comes back, reappears in the doorway, and says, "My name is Domitilla."

Offshore Charity

Paul Ventura, stretched out on the Naugahyde sofa in his one-bedroom apartment with a mortgage and faucets that drip time in regular intervals, reads more accounting reports about the superwealth of Oscar Martello. As he does it, he tries not to think about everything that furnishes his life as a public functionary earning €2,200 a month. Giulia, who's set off on tour with her wake of cheerful good humor, has left him with his black thoughts to confront, the first of which is devoted to Dobro Tanic, without even needing to leaf through the dossier that he's memorized by this point. The second thought turns to his father, who flew away a year ago, whereupon he realized that he knew nothing, absolutely nothing about him, and the third black thought is for his mother, who has been taken prisoner by Alzheimer's, and who would be so much better off in heaven, mending clouds, but who instead remains in the hell on earth, nailed in place by certain physicians who torment her with lifesaving pharmaceuticals, even though what she's been living hasn't been a life for years, just a chill she can't get rid of.

He reads that Oscar Martello's palatial Roman mansion is 66 percent owned by an anonymous company domiciled in the Cayman Islands, 9 percent of the ownership is in the name of Helga, and the last 25 percent is assigned to the nonprofit Food against the Storm, where for Italy the administrator is none other than the queen of flowers herself, Donna Angelina Casagrande, who takes in money for an infinite array of charitable pursuits, soup kitchens, and free clinics in Africa, as well as first-welcome centers for immigrants. The same accounting contrivance applies for the ownership of the eighty-foot Marine Magnum tied up at Fiumicino, though it sails under an Irish flag. For the artworks, including the Manzoni Achrome. For the fleet of automobiles, with their respective leasing agreements and insurance coverage. For the houses in Courmayeur, Sperlonga, Milan, Venice, and, *naturally*, Paris. For the twelve apartments collected in Rome, in the quarters of Testaccio, San Lorenzo, and Prati, all of them snapped up at bargain-basement prices in the last years of black economic downturn.

"All apartments," reads the summary of the investigation carried out by his men, "that in the golden years of television drama, were financed and purchased by screenwriters, directors, and actors confident they would be looking at good incomes for years to come. But reckless in their forecasting and unfortunate in their chosen remedies, when the market collapsed and forced them to sell at low prices what they had so lavishly acquired."

That means that they had let their ambitions run away with themselves, some of them to such a degree that they had brought into the world both mortgages and children, both of which grew far faster than they'd expected, especially after the ten sumptuous seasons of *Spells*, *Hospital Ward Hearts*, and *Ibiza* had gone off the air, and the revenues had dwindled as the contracts had failed to renew. Which meant apartments for sale at fire-sale prices. Apartments that Oscar Martello, the producer with a heart of gold of, that's right, *Spells*, *Hospital Ward Hearts*, and *Ibiza*, had been only too willing to pick up, with a little cash up front, an appreciative hug for the discount, a reassurance reported back by "our confidential informant," that said, word for word, "Prices have collapsed, you know it as well as I do, and I'm doing you a favor." Plus, the promise of a first installment of a future contract to write a story about orphans or lusty lifeguards or homosexual couples, a contract that of course they'd never see.

Likewise, the acclaimed Anvil Film, according to parliamentary investigations, has its feet on one side and its head on the other: ownership lies with a Belgian holding company that has its legal headquarters in Ireland, and its tax domicile in London with a tax rate discounted by 20 percent. A modest corporate capital base, less than thirty thousand euros ("thirty large, basically nothing"), total revenue in the last fiscal year of nineteen million euros ("nineteen lovely rocks, do I make myself clear?"), from which to deduct expenses, losses, and prior debts amounting to roughly the same amount. Moral of the story: nothing actually owned by Oscar Martello, except for a small tax liability just to save face and the occasional flash of glory to show he still has the knack and the luck. Or even the other way around.

Ventura starts to wonder whether Andrea Serrano, the man's friend, the least misfit of all the screenwriters, is also implicated in the darker side of Oscar's dealings. And whether he's a knowing accomplice, a member in good standing of Martello's and Casagrande's gang, or just a puppet with an expense account who's looking at jail time with nothing to show for it. To judge by the look of things, though, the man's just a fool.

What's more, dumped unceremoniously at a certain point even by the sad and drug-addled Jacaranda, who had left him to twiddle his thumbs in Paris. Which left him unrequited and restless, wandering from one to another of the art house cinemas that specialize in career overviews of auteur directors, or else out on aimless, aperitif-less strolls, but also reasonably self-sufficient, given the facility with which he was able to strike up acquaintances with young ladies for a morning out in the Luxembourg Gardens, only to give them the slip and tiptoe all alone into the restaurant and hotel Select, whose brown leather armchairs were his favorite place to leaf through magazines. And so it went for two days straight, until he flew back to Rome, where it all began just a week ago, and where it was now bound to come to an end, one way or another.

Part Three

WE'LL SLEEP WHEN WE'RE OLD

Bad News

The flight back from Paris was one long slumber, dreamless, ending in the bright sunlight of broad Roman midday. So warm that the minute he's outside the bounds of the airport, Andrea decides to tell the cabbie to take him not straight to Rome, but instead to the Ristorante Nautilus in Fiumicino, so that he can slowly reacclimate, seeing that it's one of his favorite spots, with boats and fishermen in the background to brighten his mood.

Sitting in the shade, in front of a bottle of white wine and the sea, Andrea finally turned his cell phone back on. And it came back to life with an avalanche of emails, missed phone calls, and text messages. Text messages—all of them super urgent, all of them buried after days and days in mothballs—from newspapers, magazines, journalists, TV shows, web editors. Messages from his agent, Massimiliano Testa, in Milan, from his girlfriend Fernanda, a.k.a. Ninni, and even from Margherita, his elderly next-door neighbor. There was some kind of note from everyone he knew. But nothing from Jacaranda—though hers was the only one he was anticipating. And he realized, as he hunted for it, that Jacaranda had taken a little piece of his heart. In just a few days. In an hour. In a minute. Perhaps because she had showed him just how unattainable, how off-putting, she could be. Distant even when she seemed close, in those few minutes of intimacy spent in front of the mirror, in the bathroom, seeking each other with desperate hands, practically without undressing, and looking at their reflections, she with an intensity bordering on pleasure, but also on yearning nostalgia.

Or else it was the loneliness of those last days in Paris that pushed him over the threshold of a strange emotion, that of thinking of Jacaranda in a past that he'd like to relive in the future.

The telephone immediately started ringing, all the calls from unknown numbers, probably journalists hunting for news. But just as he's about to turn it back off, he sees the number of Massimiliano Testa, his agent, again, and when he answers, the man doesn't even give him a chance to speak, but tells him, "Fuck, Andrea, I've been calling you for hours, for days, and you never answer. Do you mind if I ask what the hell kind of mess you've gotten yourself into? Okay, don't say anything on the phone. I've found you a lawyer, his name is Giovanni Soffici, he's wide awake, good at his job, with plenty of connections in the district attorney's office. I'll send you his phone number, call him immediately. Do you need money? I don't like anything about this story."

"What the fuck are you talking about?" he finally manages to get out after drinking in those sentences that struck him as so meaningless.

"Have you just landed from the moon?"

"No, from Paris, I just deplaned."

"Then you don't know anything."

"About what?"

"About Rizzi."

"About who?"

"Jacaranda Rizzi. Are you drunk?"

An airplane soars past and into the sky, its shadow slipping over the sun. "Jacaranda what?"

"They say she's killed herself."

The sea off Fiumicino turns black twice. And Andrea has to breathe deeply twice. "I don't believe it, that's impossible. She was with me until the day before yesterday."

"I know that. But this is something that's been circulating since last night. I've been trying to reach you for hours."

"Who says so? When did it happen?"

"I don't know. They're saying it on the Internet. Facebook says so. I'm getting one phone call after another. Everyone is looking for you."

"That's complete crap. What does the Internet say? And why would she have killed herself? And where?"

"In Amsterdam. They found her body in a canal. That is, they say it could be her."

He shuts his eyes. He can feel his heart pounding. He needs a drink, he needs to think. "Bullshit. I'll call you back."

He rejects two incoming phone calls. First he calls Jacaranda. The phone's turned off. He calls Oscar Martello. The phone's busy. He calls Anvil Film. The phone's busy. He calls the landline at Martello's house. The phone's busy. He calls Milly Gallo Bautista. The phone's turned off.

He's just stood up from his table when he sees him screeching to a halt aboard a dark blue Yamaha R6 motorbike. He's wearing a black leather jumpsuit with yellow trim. When he takes off the full-face helmet and the pirate bandanna, Andrea recognizes the expression of a bird of prey that has just spotted the prey in question: it's Mirko Pace, the muckraker. He gets off, lights a cigarette, and waits.

Andrea doesn't have to be asked twice. He goes over to him. He's terse and unceremonious: "What's all this about Amsterdam, another one of your fucked-up inventions?"

His phone has started ringing again. He rejects the call.

"No. It's a rumor that's running from one venue to another."

"And what does this rumor say?"

"That a woman has been found floating in a canal. Blond, with short hair. No ID. If you like, the description could match."

The phone goes on ringing, with calls from unknown numbers. He rejects them.

"But why should it be Jacaranda, of all people?"

"Because someone saw her picture, she's an actress, isn't she? And when she left you in Paris, she showed up in Amsterdam, didn't you know that?"

He starts to lose his patience. "No, I didn't know that. What was she doing in Amsterdam?"

The muckraker answers a call: "I've found him, it's all good. I'll call you back." He turns and looks at him. "But it's still just a rumor, without any solid confirming evidence."

"And why have you been repeating it?"

"That's obvious. We're still under contract for the movie, right? We're just trying to keep up."

The phone rings.

"Turn it off, trust me."

Before turning it off, Andrea tries another round of phone calls, Jacaranda, Oscar, Milly. All without results. So he powers down. Then he looks Mirko in the face and it's as if he'd just noticed his existence in that instant: "What are you doing here? Who told you where I was?"

Mirko hands him his second helmet. "We didn't know how to get hold of you. Starting yesterday I sent one of my guys to check all the flights arriving from Paris. He saw you half an hour ago. He took a file photograph and then called me. Shall we go?"

"He took a file photograph of me, for Christ's sake . . . No. I'm going back to the airport and finding a flight to Amsterdam."

"Don't talk bullshit. My partner has sent one of our boys to talk to the ambassador's underling. We'll be the first to hear about any news. Oscar is all wound up. He wants to hold a press conference."

"When?"

"Right away."

"And are you supposed to take me to this press conference?"

"No. He sent me to keep you from attending. He wants you to remain missing, that way we can stoke the mystery."

"Fuck. But if Jacaranda—"

"Hey, my friend, he doesn't give a shit about Jacaranda, do you get it or don't you? He cares about the movie: the more people talk about it, the more money it brings in."

He's tempted to lunge at him and punch him in the mouth. Instead he just stands there. "What the fuck was Jacaranda doing in Amsterdam?"

Mirko Pace looks at his watch, lights a cigarette, and hands it to him. Andrea refuses the offer.

"Okay, I'll update you." He tells him the bare necessities. He tells him that two days ago at dawn Jacaranda was picked up by Milly Gallo Bautista, her agent, who appeared and was photographed on the Parisian scene covered with plumes and shawls as if she'd just stepped out of a cedar chest from the 1930s, and that she'd taken custody of her client protégée. She pushed her into a taxi and then together they boarded a high-speed train for Amsterdam, setting up housekeeping in a neutral zone, the apartment of a girlfriend, more or less midway between Dam and the Sofitel. "Don't ask me what they planned to do, I have no idea."

Connections

Twenty minutes later, Andrea is traveling at top speed along the beltway, heading into Rome, glued to the oblique back of Mirko Pace, with gusting wind exploding on either side. As he holds tight, he's telling himself that he absolutely has to meet with Oscar, look him in the face, figure out how the fuck he ever reached that point, and then maybe throw him down the stairs. Because with the proliferation of mirrors onstage, Oscar is stripping him of his sense of orientation. The initial contrivance, at least somewhat amusing, of the escape to Paris and the love nest there, hatched within the harmless fairy tales that La Dolce Roma feeds off of, now strikes him as lit by an increasingly grim glow, one that Jacaranda actually did plunge into. Swallowed up, devoured as if in the blink of an eye. She, who was not only the woman he suddenly realized he'd fallen in love with—or something like that— but also the sole witness to Oscar's past, as well as a formidable resource for the accounting of his own immediate future.

They roar through roundabouts and down straightaways, they zip past the aqueduct, they turn onto the Via dei Fori Imperiali: Andrea tries to free his mind of the image of Jacaranda's honey-colored eyes and of the void that now scares him. He wants to stay cold. But his head is spinning. They sail at full speed into the siege of traffic emerging onto Via del Circo Massimo running along the Circus Maximus, and then onto the riverfront embarcadero along the Tiber.

He wants to think. With Jacaranda's death, the box office will explode tenfold, and then a hundredfold, burning through all records in terms of ticket sales. By now, all the online venues will be feverishly lunging at the last photographs of her taken by the henchmen of War & Peace. Photos of the party at Sabaudia at Milly Gallo Bautista's house. Photos of a dinner party at Oscar Martello's. Photos of the wrap party for *No, I Won't Surrender!* And maybe even the "file" photo of her last boyfriend, who'd just landed at Fiumicino.

Along the banks of the Tiber, processions of dark-blue government cars, sirens blaring. They veer over onto the sidewalks, whip around buses stopped in intersections and tourists plunging into traffic.

Starting tomorrow, the print editions of the newspapers, the afternoon newscasts, the breaking newscrawls all over the channels, will take care of the rest. Revealing details, plot twists, mysteries about "this sad tale of loneliness." Everyone will rush out to their local movie theater to see it. And then they'll set off on the manhunt for the villain. All the journalists, the sorrowful female anchors, the tear hunters—they'll each dig their own little section of the collective grave.

The stench of diesel exhaust and the smell of burned gasoline fills the air. Every jerk of acceleration from a stoplight cramps his stomach and his neurons.

Perhaps someone will trot out the Mafia at some point, with the supposition that it was a hit made to look like a suicide. The others will choose to illuminate the paths that lead to Jacaranda's heart, the real or imagined love affairs, the depressions, the psychopharmaceuticals. Every trail has its own script already written, like automatic fairy tales with high levels of hypnotic intensity.

And he, Andrea Serrano, "mediocre writer of screenplays and TV series, an artist living a messy life, currently under the investigator's examination," will land in the middle of it. After all, he was her last, ill-conceived love story, with a midnight drive to Paris and other associated mysteries. They'll put him in the spotlight and roast him over a slow flame: *Hey, everyone, do you think Jacaranda killed herself over this nutjob?*

They'll rifle through all the file cabinets in search of his past as an unstable traveler, crime reporter, and not entirely reassuring writer. They'll examine all the various strata of life experience, scrutinizing spots on his personal history, analyzing alibis, grilling family members, friends, enemies, ex-girlfriends, and they'll pore over his relationship with Oscar as a friend, employee, and accomplice.

Mirko drops him off at his apartment building. He takes back the helmet, he tells him, "Don't show your face for a while. You'll be all right." It's an order, not a suggestion. And since he doesn't expect an answer, he squeals out, engine roaring.

Stunned as he is, Andrea simply obeys.

When he walks into his apartment, the place he finds is silent and tidy, nothing's happened, the roofs of Rome and the refrigerator in the kitchen are still in their places. The thought of Jacaranda comes in waves. What always happens to him happens: he has the sensation of having just come back from a very long trip. He tries sitting down while his thoughts gallop along. Is this another one of Oscar's tricks, fine-tuned by his muckrakers? For a second, he hopes it's true, but that would be too much, even for him. And yet Jacaranda meant to avenge herself, not kill herself. Right? He circles the thought. He searches for a motive that he finds convincing. He finds none. In fact, actually, he does find one as big as a house, but it's Oscar's motive. More or less the same motive that pushed him to get rid of Eusebio Reverberi: to delete his past, free up the future, and up his earnings a hundredfold. But then Andrea's stomach cramps when he remembers the note that she left him on the mirror. "Don't try to find me": as simple and straightforward as a farewell.

✑〇

The piping-hot shower relaxes him. After drying off, he opens his laptop and surfs the various news sites. Jacaranda looks out at him from every photo. In one she's walking the red carpet of the Venice Film Festival, in a light-blue dress and the same gold chain around her neck that she wore in their days together in Paris. In another one, she's about to dive off a motorboat, it's a scene from a movie, and she's so young and alive she could drive you crazy. For half an hour he reads the same news about the suicide over and over, not that it's really news, it's just a theory that is gathering around this anonymous body found around the same time as the new mystery of Jacaranda, reported in Amsterdam by the henchmen of War & Peace and then vanished from their radar. He tries to make the same round of phone calls again, but all he finds is the same cell phones, turned off. The whole world of instantaneous interconnections has coalesced against him, isolating him and holding him prisoner in a neutral but highly anxiety-inducing space.

There's no cannabis in the apartment. With twenty drops of Valium, he tries to break the sense of isolation. He adds some vodka. The effect is an enchantment of sleep and wakefulness. Suspended between one and the other, he tries to call Jacaranda until his cell phone dies. When he wakes up he doesn't know if he really called or if it was a dream. On the other hand, day has dawned. He makes an instant coffee, shaves, and then stands, dreamily, looking out over the Tiber that puffs mist into the air where the seagulls play. He needs air, he needs to walk. He buys newspapers that are already a day old and tell the same stories as last night, before the Valium and after the vodka.

An hour later, after passing Via Barberini, he stops on Piazza della Repubblica, where the city buses swing around the large roundabout. He goes over to sit on the steps of the portico to make a phone call he's been holding off making for two years now.

This time the phone rings free. She answers on the third ring with a harsh voice. "What do you want?"

"I need to talk to you."

"Well, I don't."

"You're always so courteous, Helga."

Helga in a Bubble

It happened only the one time. They'd never spoken about it, but that thing still floated between them. It was a bubble inside which, on one special occasion, the two of them might have found or smashed into each other.

It happened late one morning in June, two years ago. They'd chanced to run into each other—if there is such a thing as chance—outside his apartment building, on Piazza di San Lorenzo in Lucina. She was just leaving the Louis Vuitton store and he was about to enter the Bar Ciampini. He'd just bought a paper from the newsstand, and when he turned around, he saw her. She was alone, without Oscar, without her two little girls, without her chauffeur. He'd called her name. She'd smiled in his direction. Which was a new development from what he was used to.

She was wearing a silk dress with a fine pattern of little flowers, a beige jacket and beige scarf, light suede boots, sunglasses. And a vermilion lip gloss that highlighted all her loveliness. She kissed him on the cheek, then she said, "I've had it up to here with your friend, he's driving me crazy."

"That's the effect he has on everyone."

"But the rest of you don't have to sleep with him at night. We've been fighting for three days."

"Where is he now?"

"He's in Milan. He's coming back tomorrow. I hope that at least he's fucked one of his television starlets, maybe it'll improve his mood."

"And what are you doing?"

"I'm finally breathing."

The conversation flowed intimately, without obstacles. There was sunshine, there were children and nannies, there were people riding past on bicycles. It was an ordinary day, but it seemed like the Sunday of the world.

They exchanged smiles. And a little burst of euphoria had locked arms with them both. "Turn off your cell phone and take the rest of the day off."

Helga had lifted her sunglasses and looked him right in the eyes: "*Roman Holiday*, why not. Maybe you even have a Vespa?"

"No. No Vespa."

"Well, I have the rest of the day off. Are you heading home? Why don't you offer me something to drink?"

Helga is one of those women who are always seductive, a natural gift, a reflex, even when they've just woken up and are brushing their teeth, looking at themselves straight on and in profile in the mirror, or at a restaurant, when they're ordering a mineral water and they amuse themselves by knocking the waiter to the floor with a sidelong glance, or in a Roman piazza, with their husband's best friend. And do it without ever expecting the slightest interference with their will, so unsettling as to stun any attempt at self-defense, so sure of themselves that obeying their slightest whim, even the most dangerous, comes naturally, never seeming as if it's the result of some request of theirs, but quite the contrary, a kind concession on their part, accompanied by a little flutter of the eyelashes.

When she and Andrea go upstairs together to his apartment, they drink an espresso, then a vodka, then another. They turn on the music. They smoke some grass. They get comfortable. The grass makes them laugh. The grass burns away all senses of guilt. The grass makes them fly through the air. And when they land, what they want are all manner of sweet things, honey, dried fruit, and more vodka. And what with all the drinking, they both understand what they're doing there, without any need to speak of it.

At a certain point she stands at the center of the big window, the one that overlooks the Tiber and Rome. She reaches her arms straight up, pressing her hands and her forehead against the glass, and then just turning her head ever so slightly, she says with a sweet smile, "Come here. It's so pretty you could lose your mind."

Andrea is next to her. He smells her perfume. He's thinking of stepping away and instead he stays right there. He's thinking about Oscar's account of the savage blow jobs that Helga would give him, squatting down on the floor in front of him. And without even realizing he's doing it, he brushes the back of her head with his fingers, feeling the shiver of a wave that dissolves all the tensions, warming his fingers and respiration. She flexes, as if struck by that current, lowers her head, and starts telling him in a low voice, "My first man was a bodyguard. He liked having his flesh burned while he was fucking me. He liked having his neck throttled with a belt until he almost suffocated. He liked taking me brutally, from behind."

"And did he hurt you?"

"Yes, a lot."

He presses his fingers a little harder and slides them down from the back of her head to her neck. He tells her, "Don't move." And then he continues descending, fingers running down the central line of her back, making her shiver in a way that arches her body like a rubber band being stretched, pushing out her hips, sheathed in the softest silk of her dress, which yields to the pressure of his fingers, revealing the point at which the thong begins and where it ends, where Andrea presses harder as she emits a little moan and spreads her legs to better accept that pressure, let it slip in deeper. She gets wet. She touches him. She sighs, exhales, murmurs, "Lift my skirt and fuck me."

"What do you want?" she asks him over the phone now, and her voice is very different from what it was then.

A police car goes screaming past at top speed, heading across the piazza toward the Termini station. He has neither the time nor the inclination to take on Helga's bad moods.

"I want to talk to Oscar. I want to know what happened to Jacaranda. She disappeared, he disappeared, I have newspapers calling me continuously, can someone tell me what the fuck is happening? Oscar can't just disappear like this."

"Sure he can. He's always done it."

"Is he there?"

"No."

"Well, this time a woman is missing, for fuck's sake. And she might be dead."

"The police have already come to the house twice. Oscar screwed you, what did you expect? He told them everything."

"Everything what?"

"The truth. That Jacaranda was in Paris with you. That the last person who saw her was you. That he has no idea of what happened between the two of you."

Andrea feels the rage build up inside him in surging waves. "But I have a pretty good idea of what happened between Jacaranda and Oscar many years ago, tell him that."

"And what should I tell him that he doesn't already know?"

"That that's a motive the size of a house."

"A motive for what?"

"For hurting Jacaranda."

"More than what your stupid Jacaranda already did to herself? And anyway you're talking as if I give a damn about Oscar."

"Don't you?"

Helga answers him, icy and off-putting, "Get your friend to update you, when you see him. I've left him."

His anger turns into frustration. "Why would you do that? Are you already done chewing the flesh off him?"

Helga absorbs Andrea's venom in silence. Then she calmly says, "Fuck yourself. As for you and your friend, I don't know what you did to that girl. But I hope they come and haul you both off by the balls."

Andrea knows the calm that makes her imperturbable. "But do you seriously think that you're out of this mess? If this thing goes sideways, it'll run you over the same way it does all the rest of us. Do you understand that?"

Silence. He hears Helga breathing. He imagines her furious face, creased with tension, electric. Then he hears her issue her verdict: "If you want to screw Oscar over, go right ahead, I couldn't give a fuck. But if you come after me and my girls, I'll kill you. Don't you ever call me again."

The Quarrel, the Blood

When he's in a bad mood, Oscar Martello detests all living beings of the vast Western world. He is willing to grudgingly concede the occasional exception to, say, those who do backbreaking menial labor, farmhands in large landholdings, steelworkers who man blast furnaces, orange harvesters in Rosarno who earn five euros a day, prostitutes working the beltway emergency lanes who get their asses slammed for ten euros, nurses assigned to wards full of the terminally ill, caregivers for senile old Alzheimer's patients.

Towering high above the other 90 percent, ranking even a little higher than film critics, is Helga, when they fight. The other night she found him drunk and flying high on coke, when they were supposed to be getting ready to leave for a gala banquet held by the Friends of the Museum, €10,000 a table. She'd paid for a table that seated eight, and among their guests would be the Argentine ambassador with his wife and teenage son, a personal apotheosis for Helga, who'd come up from the dust of the Buenos Aires barrio.

Oscar screamed at her, "I have other things on my mind, you bitch. There's an actress who hates me and has gone missing, and I have no idea what the fuck she's up to. There's a piece-of-shit movie that I'm trying to save. There's a goddamned cop who's buzzing around me, I don't know if you've noticed? He dropped by to get a whiff of the prey. And the prey would be me."

Helga raised both hands to stop him. "I don't want to know anything about your dealings."

Oscar was sweating. The cocaine was accelerating his gestures, the alcohol was slowing them down, and the contrast between the two left him swaying. He had to brace himself against whatever sofa came to hand because his head was spinning at warp speed. "Ah, you don't want to know anything about them? Too bad that you live off my dealings, you good-for-nothing hobo cocksucker."

She too was swerving. But she did it by standing perfectly still, trying to choke back the waves of hatred she was feeling for Oscar, for his wrecked face, his bullying, the smell of him. "You're nothing but a pathetic fucking drug addict and drunk, a miserable, hopeless son of a bitch."

"Look who's talking. The crazy woman is talking!"

"I was certainly crazy to get hooked up with someone like you."

"Then go see a psychiatrist, but pay him by turning tricks. You want to donate to the museum? Pay for it with blow jobs. Sooner than go there with you, I'd cut my dick off."

She remained impassive. "For all the good it does you, *cojón*."

He smacked her with the back of his hand, but with the hand armed with a ring, the old twenty-buck skull on his pinky, and it opened a slashing cut across her cheekbone. Three large drops of blood spattered her white linen blouse. She screamed, staggered backward. And as she staggered backward, she hurled at him his precious humidor of Cuban cigars, and the box glanced off his shoulder and then smashed against the Plexiglas front of the Manzoni. The Manzoni shook but remained in place. Oscar started shouting. Two of the three Filipino houseboys appeared in the living room doorway, then softly vanished, leaving the masters to settle their own disagreements.

Oscar was ranting. Helga was bleeding. And in the meantime she was threatening him with the metal poker that she'd found next to the red marble fireplace, holding him at bay: "You bastard. You swine. If you touch me again, I'll run you through the heart with this."

He stood there, nonplussed. She left the living room and went to take shelter in the most sacred precinct of the house, the room where the little girls slept, a place he'd never violate.

She locked herself in.

This morning she was ready to leave him, "but once and for all, you filthy *hijo de puta*." She succeeded around eight o'clock, holding Oscar at bay—in underwear and bathrobe, still stunned by his sleepless night and drunken binge—and holding the two little girls by their hands, the two little angels Cleo and Zoe, who, as she glared daggers at him were dutifully waving *ciao ciao papi*, their faces lit up with their smiles so gleeful, so utterly defiant, that they forced him in place, forbidding him to seize their mother by the throat and kick her savagely in the gut.

"Don't use the girls as a shield, you damned Argentine slut," he snarled at her, while two giant pistons hammered away at his temples.

Helga burst out laughing right in his face. "I'm taking the girls to the amusement park, isn't that right, girls?"

"Ye-e-esss!" Cleo and Zoe replied in chorus, following their mother out the door and into the metallic-finish Porsche Cayenne parked in the courtyard, which then screeched out in an expensive cloud of rubber smoke.

Andrea's phone call arrives in those very same minutes, catching her already stuck in traffic around the Pyramid of Cestius, still seething with adrenaline. She doesn't give a flying fuck about him; he doesn't have the guts, or the money, to afford a woman like her.

But Andrea's right about one thing: she hasn't yet finished chewing the flesh off Oscar. In fact, she hasn't even gotten started. And so, while the little girls were singing in their car seats, she called the most respected and notoriously vicious divorce lawyer on the market, a woman who was callously abandoned by her own husband years and years ago, and who has only women on her unrivaled staff, all of them armed with legal codes and vaginas dentata. Helga arranged her first appointment, the one where they would lay out the topographic maps and charts to lay siege to the vast possessions of her soon-to-be ex-husband, Oscar Martello, the great juggler capable of making houses, apartments, land, companies, cash, even actresses, vanish into thin air, but not the traces of the young sluts that he still brings home and screws under the shelter of the conjugal roof. The divorce lawyer welcomed her phone call like that of an old long-lost friend, and in seven minutes of conversation, she comes straight to the point: "As far as your husband's assets, we need only wait. Much publicity and great envy tend to awaken the curious. And awakening the curious is never a good thing, especially when the curious tend to have handcuffs well within reach."

Helga focuses as the light turns green and the whole line of cars starts honking its horns: "In fact, some guy did come to interview Oscar. But he was looking into the case of that missing actress."

"I doubt that very much. That was probably just his cover story."

"What do you mean?"

"As far as I know, Commissario Ventura investigates money, not actresses."

She smiles. "You don't say."

Having tucked that information away, Helga manages to get the phone number of that same Raul Ventura who just the other morning was eyeing her with trousers full of appreciative zeal. She gives her name to a well-mannered police headquarters staffer. Three minutes later, her call is returned: "Please hold, ma'am." When she's put through, she doesn't even give him a chance to speak: "Commissario, maybe you and I can help each other out, what do you say?"

The News Comes In,
Late in the Morning

The body found floating in the canal in Amsterdam is that of Jacaranda Rizzi, actress, star of the movie *No, I Won't Surrender!* The autopsy report says that her death was due to an overdose of barbiturates and drowning.

Oscar Martello has just stepped out of the sauna in his personal bathroom when all his cell phones and landlines simultaneously begin to ring. One by one, he takes delivery of the details. He lays them out in a row, he memorizes them. Aside from a slight sense of tension, he feels nothing in particular. His only care is to steer the consequences, ensuring that they are favorable. He agrees to a couple of interviews then and there: "I cared for her dearly. She was one of my finest discoveries." "Yes, of course, she was a fragile woman. And the world out there is mighty damned hard-edged, have you noticed?"

He issues instructions to War & Peace: "Kick up all the dust

and tears that you can. I want the details of the whole story."
They've already got some juicy tidbits: Jacaranda was in Amsterdam with her agent, moving in a circle of vegan lesbians. They were doing meditation and bullshit like that. There was generalized muff-diving. Milly was trying to get her committed to rehab. They fought. Milly took a flight home while Jacaranda was left behind. *Jacaranda was left behind* is practically a piece of gallows humor. "Good work, you even write your own jokes. Anything else?"

"Nothing else for now," Mirko Pace tells him over speakerphone. He asks, "And what about poor old brokenhearted Serrano, what do we do with him?"

"What do you mean?"

"Should we keep him out of it?"

Oscar thinks it over. Maybe bringing him into the case as the triggering cause of the suicide could turn into a good story, a new script, a new film. Technically speaking: a spin-off. Or not, too sad, too *boooring*.

"Let's leave him out of it for the moment."

"That's fine with us."

Oscar is mapping out the scene. "Suicide note?"

"The drowned woman? No, no suicide note."

"Too bad." He knows that people usually prefer suicides with an explanation, because at least then they know what to think.

Mirko is telling him, "Maybe we can post one to the web."

"Like what?"

"I don't know. There's a guy with an archive of two thousand of them, and he's put them all online."

"What guy? Huh?" Oscar doesn't understand what the fuck he's talking about.

"A Dutch doctor who's been studying suicide notes for the past twenty years, I'm not kidding."

"Christ on a crutch, a Dutch doctor. How do you know that?"

"We've already used his archive once before."

Oscar laughs. "Fuck, are you saying you need an archive to write a suicide note . . . Just take a look in the mirror: You must have some good reason to kill yourself, don't you? Just use that."

Mirko Pace laughs, even though he's not sure he's understood.

Oscar ends the phone call. The large eye painted by Cristiano Pintaldi, which is of course Naomi Campbell's left eye, stares at him from the middle of the wall running along next to his bed, on Helga's side. But now there's no more "Helga's side of the bed." That's a revelation that catches him off guard, freezes him in place for one long instant, and finally stirs him back into action. He picks up the phone, and after a blackout lasting many days, he calls Andrea Serrano.

Who answers by barking into the phone, "It's about time, you son of a bitch. It's about time!"

But he is Oscar Martello, and he knows when to turn more tractable than a babysitter: "You can't begin to imagine how sorry I am, Andrea, this is just a terrible thing. Until this morning, I didn't want to believe it, I swear to you. But weren't you two doing well together? When I was there you looked even—dare I say it?—happy. I didn't understand why she dumped you either." The silence that follows means that he hasn't gone too far, and that Andrea's sharp edges have vanished in a puff of mist.

Even still, Andrea tries to insist on his point: "You and I need to talk."

"Sure, why not. We'll talk. But in the meantime, let's think about Jacaranda, let's not just file her away as if we never cared about her. After all, the two of you were together for the last few days of her life, weren't you?"

Oscar doesn't even really have to try. Reshuffling the cards on the table is a specialty of his. While Andrea, who's still navigating through the fog, can't even formulate a reply: "All I want is to—"

"I know what you want, Andrea. We all want the same thing: to honor Jacaranda's memory the way she deserves. And I'll see to it."

"I want to know what happened."

"We'll reconstruct events. Everything, trust me. The only reason I didn't call you is that bitch Helga left me. They all leave me eventually, damn it. She left because she claims I beat her, but it isn't true, I swear to you, I spoke brusquely, I was under pressure, everyone's piling on, and when she's not the center of attention, she makes up stories, she invents sheer bullshit so that she can be in the spotlight, she and she alone, she drives me crazy, you know what she's like, don't you?" As he rattles on, he senses that talking about it is doing him good, it's reducing the pressure oppressing his heart, his respiration. "She left and took the little girls with her, my two tiny angels," he's saying, and as he says it, he can also sense that between his heart and his respiration, between his respiration and his two tiny angels, between his two tiny angels and that tremendous slut Helga, suddenly as if generated automatically by his anxiety, Angelina Casagrande has poked her head up, along with their accounting of travel and good deeds, their far-distant banks, their secrets, too close. He needs to hang up on Andrea, whom he's just quieted down, and take care of her. "Hey, maybe I'll swing by and see you soon. We can take all the time we need to talk. But do me a favor and stay holed up at home until you and I get a chance to talk. And steer clear of journalists, understood?"

And then he called Angelina. He heard her steaming, and already steaming on the phone, with all the eavesdroppers listening in, isn't a good idea, so he told her, "I'm taking care of everything."

"What do you mean, everything?" the stupid woman asked him, but in the tone of a hyena.

"We need to talk about it face to face."

"Is that your work, the actress who killed herself?"

"Hey, I said we need to talk about it face to face."

"Too bad she didn't do it in Paris. The French police are relentless."

He heard her breathe. "Take it easy," he told her.

Then she said, "I'm going to see my masseuse at De Russie. I need to relax for an hour."

"Good for you."

"Then you call me. Call me and we'll get together."

"All right. Now get going."

As always, someone else's weakness strengthens him, feeds his resources until at last Angelina's anxiety has swept away his own.

Oscar is pumped up again; he calls Giovanni Cotta—known as "Rat Face" because of his pointy little nose and mouth—the most important Italian film distributor. "Starting tonight and until this weekend you have to find me seven hundred movie houses to run the film. And I don't want to hear excuses, or reasons why, do I make myself clear? Seven hundred. Evict whatever you want. Toss some of that American crap in the toilet. And thanks for the condolences."

This is how he plans to honor the sad loss of Jacaranda Rizzi: by multiplying the movie's box office, first tenfold, and eventually a hundredfold. This is the big chance he's been waiting for. The stratospheric earnings that are going to allow him to make the great leap forward. He can already envision the first ten films that he's going to produce on his own—no, make that with the Americans: *Bye-Bye, La Dolce Roma*, Anvil Film is setting sail into the great open waters. He can feel the bow wave, he can glimpse the ass of the *Rex* under full steam: that's part of what he's going to buy.

As for the missing suicide note, well, he'll write it in Jacaranda's name. A note without a lot of frills, without any fancy phrases, like this: "I just don't feel like it anymore. Have fun without me. And try not to gossip too much about me." It's terse, detached, and sad. *Try not to gossip too much about me* resembles something he's heard somewhere before, but where?

Andrea wanders aimlessly around the apartment. It's been such a long time since death passed so close to him. He remembers his father's dead body lying facedown on the floor of their home, even though all these years later he couldn't say if he really saw it or just imagined it. And then his mother's face, white as a sheet, the last night in the hospital, encapsulated in her oxygen mask, already so far away from him, though he sat next to her, holding her cold hands in his, no longer even recognizing the feel of them, but unwilling to let them go, convinced that in that grip of skin and fragile bones and infinite memories and endless fear lay the last thread still linking him to his mother. And linking his mother to life.

Those two deaths were part of his story, and now so was Jacaranda's. The others that he had seen on the asphalt of crime reporting, or the horrible deaths in the rubble of Chechnya, were fragments, flashes in black and white, vignettes that had passed before his eyes, only to be sterilized in the ink of a narrative that made sense of everything that completely lacked it.

But there's no way to distance ourselves from the deaths that concern us. Andrea knows that, because he felt them enter into him, become part of the time he breathes, marking a before and an after. And now Jacaranda's peach-colored skin, which he'd seen from up close while they were eating at the Brasserie Lipp, the gold chain around her throat, the fine blond hair on the back of her neck, backlit, her morose smile, will forever be a part of him.

⁂

The radio stations broadcast the news, the online editions of the newspapers publish the biography "of our dear Jacaranda Rizzi," lists of her movies, interviews from the archives, television footage of "her beautiful, flourishing career," the story of her loves and losses, the testimonials of friends, male and female, colleagues in tears, inconsolable directors. And then the chagrin of the film critics: "She was so young," "She was so pretty," "She was such a good actress," all of them predictable and foreseen. So zealous in serving the lives of others that they feel a sort of authentic regret when those lives shuffle off this coil.

One critic notes "the macabre coincidence" of the film's premiere, and another writes about how "treacherous fate will have its way." And what if it had been a murder disguised as a suicide? What if this was a Mafia vendetta?

Andrea knows that this isn't going to stop until the day of the funeral, the supreme obscenity of the applause that he can already picture to himself, in the nave of Santa Maria in Montesanto, the church of the artists in Piazza del Popolo. A serial apotheosis that is renewed from one corpse to the next. The last time he went there was with Oscar for Mariangela Melato, and he hadn't even wanted to go in; all he'd needed was a single glance at the crowd thronged out front. The universal exposition of sunglasses and Prada overcoats. The pack of photographers. The high theatrical performance of collective grief. Which is, after all, a way of celebrating with tears the circumstance of all of us still being alive, and savoring in blessed peace the remorse for someone else's death.

Funeral Rites with Pastries

Dinner is the most enduring ritual of this permanent cinematic newsreel that is La Dolce Roma. It comes from the hunger of the postwar years, when even the picnic baskets of Cinecittà were precious troves, when actors had the calloused hands of the former bricklayers so many of them were, actresses mended their worn nylon stockings, and roast chicken was a rare Sunday treat. In the years of political opulence, the ritual bulked up, enriching itself by a thousand other proteins, contented to stuff its maw not only with cinema, but also television, photographers with flash guns, clientelism, familism, factionalism, but never losing its initial and primary vital function, the pleasure and delight of nourishment. That is why—in contrast with the constipated meals of Milan, where advertising executives and fashion models snort more cocaine than roast pork—Roman dinners call for lengthy mastication of *pastasciutta*, long and short, with meat sauces, ground meats, and roast meats, occasionally large fishes served on platters with sauces, fine-grained fries of anchovies with lemon or freshly shelled shrimp called *crudità di gamberi*, vegetables raw and cooked, boiled and sprinkled with lemon or boiled and then sautéed with garlic and chili peppers, great fat round mozzarellas like the August moon riding over the Colosseum, Roman pizzas, Neapolitan pizzettas, Genoan focaccias, Turinese breadsticks, sweet buns, wood-fired baguettes, multigrain biscotti. And then there are the sweets. The sweets!

"Hooray, here come the sweets, come on!" The glorious finale of any self-respecting dinner, with a brightly colored array of fruit mini pastries, cream mini pastries, Neapolitan pastiera tarts, gelato, semifreddo mousses; and then there are the chocolates, hot and cold, in wafer or in chips, with or without whipped cream, the puddings, the crème brûlées, the spumonis, the marmalades, the little dry puff pastry confections, the moist ricottas topped with candied orange peels, sweet raisins, dried fruit with honey, vanilla beans, and powdered cinnamon, Sicilian cassata, Tunisian sesame treats, resulting in a manifold display of delicacies from every latitude, as a compendium of all the various weaknesses of the character, of the soul, and of the palate, but without the tedium of guilt or restraint, which is, after all, the holy vocation of La Dolce Roma. Those thousand faces rendered immortal by the portrait photographers of Dagospia's *Cafonal*—the bible—the photographers who narrate the festive Roman ruckus, who celebrate in every shot the luxuriant scandal of those groaning banquet tables and exhibitions of foods and gaping mawfuls of teeth ingesting every mouthful, dripping sauce and *sugo*, revealing every detail, including the cavity-ridden molar of the divine diva and the sweaty politician, the senile old contessa, the formerly starving poet who chews all alone, in the corner, the only one to give truth its due, capable of whispering into his own ear, "We're all just horrendous, haven't you noticed?"

But a dinner complete with funeral rites like the one conceived by Oscar Martello in his palatial mansion was something that hadn't been seen before, if not in the occasional Caribbean embassy, perhaps in Haiti, obscured by the shadows of extraterritoriality and the mysteries of voodoo rituals. Especially not at a dinner honoring and commemorating an actress whose body covered with violet skin still lies in a fluorescent-lit room in the Amsterdam morgue, and who in the meantime has become the top box office draw of the entire movie season, just to point out how death can come as a surprise for the living. Especially in this unfortunate case of youth scattered to the winds—or rather, dumped into the black waters of a Dutch canal—with all the evidence still pinwheeling through the air in relation to the reasons for her suicide; that is, if suicides really ever have reasons, explanations, rather than being a predisposition that finally comes to pass, a vice that perfects itself, leaving aside the suspects, the men in her past and her present, numbering among them none other than the man holding the dinner, the immensely wealthy and arrogant Oscar Martello, who is proud and pleased to summon the entirety of La Dolce Roma with a single line of ink: "Nine P.M.—I await you in my home—Aventino—Rome, RSVP," *répondez, s'il vous plaît.* With this overblown conceit of not even bothering to put the entire address. But to do justice to the truth, who, among the inhabitants of La Dolce Roma, doesn't know where "that tremendous son of a bitch Oscar Martello" lives?

✐

This is what an overwrought and torrential Milly Gallo Bautista has just finished spouting out to Commissario Raul Ventura, both of them sitting among the red furnishings of the Caffè Doney, the down-at-the-heels heart of the Via Veneto, swamped with Russian tourists, Romanian hookers, and Calabrian wiseguys: anyone and everyone from the vast world, except for real Romans.

She, as always eccentric and very much up to the strength of her fame, decked out in an absurd pair of black palazzo pajamas with purple velvet hems, in perfect broken-grief style, with sunglasses to cover her puffy eyes and highlight the cascade of gold around her neck.

He, on tenterhooks for the flashy duds Milly's wearing and the glances that she's drawing, endangering what he had hoped would be a private meeting, but which now looks from one moment to the next as if it's going to be immortalized by some passing camera flash.

She, already on her second healthy rum and Coke, with the addition of a nice wet rum baba and plenty of tissues, applied judiciously with her pudgy beringed fingers, to dry off, when and as needed, the tears and the snot.

He, still on his first sip of a sambuca with ice water on the side.

She, overexcited by her suffering and the impending dinner.

He, awaiting revelations.

She, well aware of the fact that she was the very last person to see Jacaranda alive in that lair of lesbians from which she had promptly fled, leaving her friend alone in Amsterdam: "I'll never be able to forgive myself."

He, consoling her by reminding her of the unpredictability, but also the inevitability of suicides.

She asks him, point-blank, "You want to see her?"

"Who?"

"Jacaranda." Milly pulls out her iPhone. "Fifty seconds of video recorded in Amsterdam, the last seconds filmed of Jacaranda." She taps, clicks, and says, "We were talking about ourselves. Without telling me, she turned on her cell phone and set it on a pillow between us and recorded. It pissed me off. But now it's of no importance."

The video starts up. Jacaranda appears at the edge of the frame, sitting in a red armchair with her legs crossed, cut tattered jeans, her voice slurred. She's saying, "The truth is that I've never fallen in love with a man. Never, not even once."

Offscreen, Milly's voice: "And when you're with one, what do you think about?"

"Nothing."

"What do you feel?"

"Nothing."

"And the sex?"

"And the sex is nothing, too. But I'm good at pretending. At least when it comes to that, I'm a great actress."

"Then why do you go to bed with them?"

"With men? Because they expect you to."

"That's it?"

"I'm trying it out with women, but it works better when I do it by myself. What about you?"

"Well, I've ridden plenty of those horses, sweetheart. In lots of different ways, when I was young I . . . Hey, what the fuck! Are you recording me? Give me that . . . Turn it off. What the hell got into you, hey!"

The video sizzles and fades to black.

Jacaranda goes back to the afterlife.

A big tear wells up in Milly's eye.

Ventura takes a drink.

Milly rattles on about the ultimate meaning of life.

Who can say why, but Ventura thinks about his Grażyna, whose life was taken from her so cruelly, and the time that the two of them awakened at dawn on the high-elevation mountain meadows of the Valle Argentina, above Bussana Vecchia, and they'd made coffee that was so bad they'd had to laugh, and then they'd drunk cold water from the stream, as if they'd turned into children in a bygone century.

He tries to sound out the how and the wherefore of the thing that chiefly interests him, to hell with unstable actresses: "If it turns out that Martello pays your clients in cash without declaring it to the tax authorities, and you help us prove it, we'll take that into account."

She says, "Of course I'll help you. I knew him like I know the back of my hand, the inside of my pockets. Or make that, the inside of *his* pockets. From the days when he sent plenty of skilled workmen, actors, and agents to pick up their salaries in cash in London in certain cubbyhole offices of shell companies, without receipts, without documentation of any kind. These days, the whole shadow economy is moving to Luxembourg."

Ventura focuses and pushes a little: "And maybe you'd also know how he does it?"

"I imagine with the air taxi service of Angelina Casagrande, his partner. Or else old school, via mules, transiting through Switzerland."

"What do you know about Angelina Casagrande?"

"That her money is dirty, that first she obtained it from criminal husbands, and then in the field of international aid. For every euro she lets drop down a well in Africa, she keeps a hundred for herself. Oscar has his own dealings, using her foreign connections."

"What do you know about her business dealings?"

Milly widens her eyes. "Except for you, the same things that everyone in Rome knows: cash, cocaine, artworks."

"Do you know for certain, or are you just guessing?"

She heaves a sigh of irritation. "I'm not an investigator, you know." She thinks about it, bursts out laughing, and points a finger at him. "But I can help you to find some good leads. Tomorrow come to the dinner; if you need, I can help you get in—you can definitely have some fun there."

He tries to remain impassive. "You have a strange way of saying things without saying them, Signora."

Milly is flattered. Milly is drunk. Milly is reciting, or actually, singing, "To say, not to say, perchance to dream . . ."

Milly is out of her mind, and Ventura puts up with her. "Go on."

"I can only tell you that there's going to be a big surprise."

"At the dinner?"

"Exactly."

Ventura is starting to get irritated. "Signora, this isn't a game, this isn't a movie, there's an investigation under way concerning money that appears and disappears, illegal patrimonies, and—incidentally—a woman who has died in circumstances that remain quite unclear, many miles away, while you were with her."

Milly blows her nose. And she takes her time before clarifying: "Don't be unjust with me, Commissario. I took her to Amsterdam to protect her. Then I made a mistake and left her alone. I haven't slept in two days and two nights. I loved Jacaranda like my own daughter."

"Then let's try to respect her memory with the truth." He can't believe his own ears, as he listens to himself.

Ma Milly drinks it down to the last drop: "You can be sure of that. I think that there's going to be a reckoning at the famous dinner."

"What is that supposed to mean?"

"That at a certain point the comb hits the knots, Commissario. It happens in everyone's life, even Oscar Martello's. Andrea isn't going to keep his mouth shut."

"Andrea Serrano?"

"I think that this time he's going to grab him by the neck."

"Does he or doesn't he have anything to do with his business dealings?"

"No. But you have to look at the whole picture. Andrea has something to do with Jacaranda. I think he was in love with her."

"And so?"

"So now he's furious at Oscar for how he treated her."

"Get to the point."

"And now maybe he'll pull out some old story of Oscar and Jacaranda that is really less than edifying for Oscar."

Milly winds up by taking a sip of her rum and Coke.

Milly needs to smoke.

Milly wants to leave, but she still isn't done. Now she can talk about what she cares most about, but without entirely exposing herself, as if she were doing it in Andrea's name, not her own: "It's an old story, but it's worth the time. Have you ever heard of Eusebio Reverberi?"

Oscar's Homily

At the far end of a terrace covered with flowers and flickering candles, under a heart-shaped wreath composed of ten dozen red roses, a luminous phrase enjoys pride of place: "We miss you, Jacaranda." Before an audience of sixty or so people already pumped full of alcohol, pills, and emotions, Oscar Martello is declaiming his homily, in a sand-colored suit with a light-blue silk dress shirt and white French-style calfskin shoes: "The cinema," he is saying, "has many arms, many heads, but just one heart." The wind buffets his bandit face and then continues along, caressing the shoulders of the women in plunging necklines, for the most part actresses, who gaze upon him, enchanted by his impressive market value, especially now that Helga, the Argentine slut, has left the field wide open. Slender women, still ready for the race, many of them with small tattoos on their ankles but great plans for the future in their heads, sprinkled throughout the ranks of manly jaws that chew, arms crossed, all of these manly men broadcasting a not particularly reassuring demeanor, their stomachs trained to digest the rocks of power, and when necessary also ready and willing to hurl them at their fellow men, whether those are the first or the second stones to be cast.

There are directors and actors, all of them poised to express exquisite emotions before the camcorder wielded by Attilio Fabris, readmitted especially for the occasion; Fabris is working the crowd in search of tears to pack into his video condolences for Jacaranda, to be titled *Letter with No Return Address to a Friend*. Less prominently situated are the producers and the lawyers who are evaluating the movie's box office—record ticket sales of another €6 million on the second weekend, with average box office of more than €4,000 a screen, almost freakish in these times of grim downturn—but they only whisper about it among themselves, as if they were talking about hookers in church.

In the front row, in a prime spot, the undersecretary for entertainment, Roberto Neri, tanned and fit, has taken pride of place, with a sweet-smelling entourage of blond assistants and the keys to the gates of Cinecittà in his pocket. Next to him sit another half-dozen Roman bankers and CPAs with whom Martello has dealings, and among them are the men who financed the film, the happiest few there that evening, even though they can't let it show for fear of committing a gaffe and stirring envy.

There's Angelina Casagrande, who in the afternoon calmed herself down and is now dressed to the nines in a black Von Dutch dress and silver René Caovilla shoes decorated with mink pompoms and river stones. After her massage at De Russie, she met with the lawyers, who for the past two days and nights have been war-gaming Helga's imminent assault on Oscar's personal fortune, which, after all, is also hers, and just how much damage she can really do ("the slut") by unleashing who can even guess how many private investigators in search of their treasure. All the more so now that a certain Commissario Raul Ventura has caught a whiff of something and is circling the money trail, too.

There's the entire cast of *No, I Won't Surrender!*, with the lower-ranking members clearly intimidated by this overarching display of wealth. Accompanied by their whores, two Russian investors, who are openly courting Oscar to become involved in their plan to build a cinema multiplex with twenty-four screens between Rome and Ostia. A former rock star who's since become, simultaneously, a Buddhist and a methamphetamine dealer. A Roman Catholic monsignor with reddened skin, the result of psychosomatic eczema. A homosexual fashion designer skinny as an anchovy, his face camouflaged by the jungle of cosmetic incisions, his body now displaying all the elasticity of a wind turbine that, when it turns, it all turns. A bald, black-clad, megalomaniac architect, accompanied by his wife, who's gone completely hysterical from the doses of amphetamines that she takes to lose weight, even though she's just downed a double shot of Campari and gin, doing her best to see if she can drown in it.

Oscar is saying, "This isn't a party and it isn't a funeral. It's an opportunity to gather, all together, in the presence of the great mystery that can only ever make us feel alone. The mystery of our sell-by date, of the sand that continues to drizzle downward—" A buzz of superstitious disapproval among the guests. "I know, I understand you, it's always hard to hear that what awaits us all is that great leap into darkness. The mystery from which no one ever returns. But we are movie people! We make movies! We manufacture a way out, ladies and gentlemen, friends all. And that way out will still be there even when we, knock on wood, are no longer around, if not actually dust in a few years, or relegated to someone's memories, or even an unpaid debt, ha ha! And every film we make will be just one more lasting sign that we haven't passed through this world entirely in vain. This evening we're paying homage to a great actress who is no longer here among us, among her fellow actresses and friends, among her working companions, even if she really no longer is here." A pause to gaze out at the faces looking up at him. "But instead, my friends: she is here!" He says it in something approaching a shout, beckoning for the applause that is beginning to spread somewhat hesitantly, only to grow as Oscar greets it with a smile of gratitude. He continues: "I sense that she is here with us, and you sense it too, I feel certain. Just as I'm certain that Jacaranda hasn't left us, that she's just shooting a movie far, far away from here, maybe a love story, and before long she'll be back among us, isn't that right friends?"

"Yessss!" they all reply in chorus.

"And we'll all be here to wait for her. Won't we?"

"Yeeeees!" The applause surges again, and a few tears even roll down the cheeks of the more fragile attendees, among the drunkest and highest of the guests.

Oscar savors the reaction, and when he's had enough, he throws his arms wide. "All right, all right," he says, "now, drink, eat, and enjoy yourselves. Jacaranda is looking down on us from on high, I feel sure of it . . . It would be so nice if anyone who has something to say about Jacaranda would now come forward with a memory to share." A great many hands shoot up, so many that Oscar immediately changes tack. "Ah, there, you see? There are too many of you. Let's just tell each other our memories and entrust them to just one person . . . Where is the director? Fabris, where are you? Here you are, my good friend." He sees him, he harpoons him by the shoulder, and he gazes at him with an imperturbable smile, while he struggles to resist the impulse to squeeze him until he crushes the bones. Fabris hesitates, returning the hatred, but in the meantime smiles back. "Would you like to add something in conclusion, I imagine?" But Oscar's question is really an order. "Here you are, ladies and gentlemen, the great director Attilio Fabris! Our box office champion!"

Once the master of the house has left the spotlight, half the audience turns its back on this Fabris ("Who the hell is he, anyway?"), scattering into smaller groups in search of waiters, alcohol, finger food, and conversation, each individual battling only for his or her own survival. Oscar enjoys the scene, and to whoever asks him he replies, yes, all things considered, this Fabris is a great big nobody.

Jacaranda Hadn't Told
the Whole Story

Andrea Serrano is there. And he looks down on the funeral party from on high. He recognizes the hairdos of the special occasions, the buzz and hum of the Filipino waiters in red jackets tonight, flitting from flower to flower with their trays; he catches a whiff of the blend of perfumes that the small crowd emanates as an olfactory signal of their own exquisite existence to the rest of the world.

He's entered the villa with Milly Gallo Bautista, and to keep from meeting anyone else before it's the right time, he has immediately moved off down the side hallways, to the stairs that lead up to the highest floor in the turret, Oscar's Castle.

The study is furnished in wood and sage-green velvet. There are four windows, which look out over the world at large. There is a messy desk, a green leather sofa, two chairs, two armchairs, bookshelves crowded with DVDs and those absurd little statuettes they give for awards in excellence in television (cats, sea horses, honeybees, dolphins: the "teledickheads," Oscar calls them), which, along with the fireplace tools standing by the now-cold hearth, are all weapons lying ready for their impending clearing of the air.

❧

When he called Milly to ask for a ride, the fat woman finally answered. She told him no problem—"Where do you want me to pick you up?"

An hour later, she showed up at the Janiculum Hill, where the usual thousand or so tourists were milling around in the throes of photographic fervor, admiring the specialty of the house: the sunset. She was riding in a metallic silver Audi A8, with a tattooed skinhead chauffeur, tinted side windows, and leather seats the color of crème caramel so cozy and comfy that Andrea sank into the upholstery, after hours of walking around Rome.

She had him sit next to her, in the back seat.

He told her, "I'm happy to see you," but he was lying.

Milly hugged him and looked him right in the eyes. "She loved you. She told me," and she was lying, too.

They got comfortable in their respective places. Milly was emanating a mixture of Chamade perfume and sweat. She was holding both his ears between her soft, fat fingers, as if she were about to shake him, or bite him, or kiss him.

"You were in Amsterdam with her. Do you know why she did it?"

Milly gets emotional. "Maybe because she was too frightened of what was awaiting her."

"She told me that she couldn't wait to get that burden off her chest."

She sniffs. "I know. But then she imagined the consequences.

The press would treat her like some insane liar. They'd dig into every chapter of her life. And Oscar would destroy her with waves of lawyers and lawsuits. She was tired, she was fragile. And I didn't understand that."

"You shouldn't have left her alone."

"I know that."

"You should have protected her."

"I was stupid, I was impulsive. It's just that she had exhausted me with her doubts, her pills, her weakness. I can't stand weakness. So I reacted. We fought. She turned and left and told me she never wanted to see me again, so I went back to Rome. I was a bitch." This version—right down to the heartfelt overtones—was brand new for her. She'd just made it up, and she liked the sound of it.

Andrea sat motionless, listening to her. It struck him as an acceptable truth. He knew from experience that all relationships in La Dolce Roma emit sparks when they cross the boundary of the other person's sphere of privacy. And they usually stop outright when they start looking too much like a plea for help. Because, if you answer that plea, you'll have a momentary friend and an enemy forever: gratitude feeds feelings of guilt, and feelings of guilt, over the long run, feed hatred.

Could it be that Milly, in the face of that declaration of weakness by Jacaranda and in view of her hysterical intemperance, should simply have decided to take off, leaving her to her fate, and then issue statements of regret for what she'd done, in her silver Audi A8?

Milly blew her nose and fixed her makeup. From the minibar she extracted two small bottles of ice-cold vodka and glasses, and poured for two as the car slid into traffic. Looking at herself in the mirror—and throwing back the first gulp—restored her full self-awareness. She's had it with playing the penitent: "Why is it that all of a sudden you need my help to get into the home of your friend Oscar the Giant Pig?"

"Because I don't know if I still want him to be my friend."

"You've been hanging out with him for what, six years, five? And you still hadn't noticed what he was like? Or else as long as he was ripping off others, but not you, you were fine with it?"

"There were a lot of things I didn't know."

"Maybe because you didn't want to know them, but they were circulating, and how."

"A lot of lies and exaggerations were circulating, too."

"Not really. Truth be told, your ex-friend never wanted for a thing, and he made damned sure of it. Think about it. He stole ideas and scripts, threatened directors, and blackmailed actresses. He purloined apartments in collusion with priests, pilfered construction permits with all the mayors of Rome and even with the camorristi of Sperlonga. He bought other apartments from people gasping under the burden of debt and never bothered to finish paying for them. He sued plenty of people even though he knew he was in the wrong, and he won those lawsuits by hiring lawyers who bribe judges. Is that enough, or do you want me to tell you about when he earned his first money by dealing cocaine at parties?"

Milly had poured out more drinks; she was feeling fine even if she felt unsteady on the curves. "And did you understand the story of Jacaranda, or does that seem made up to you too?"

Andrea feels like an idiot. He says, "She told it to me that last night in Paris. No, I didn't know anything about it."

"Well, that fucking story marked her life. And I'm betting that Jacaranda only told you half the story."

"What do you mean, 'half the story'?"

"Think about it. You're a big boy."

They were traveling at walking speed along the Tiber toward the synagogue. Before long they'd turn up the Viale Aventino and then continue uphill through the succession of curves. "Half the story" could mean only one thing: that the truly odious part had been left out. And the truly odious part was also the most obvious part: sex between a sixteen-year-old girl and a producer in heat, maybe two horny producers. Rubbed down and polished by both of them, "like a waxed floor," as they say in Hollywood. Which was, after all, the oldest story in the books: sex in exchange for the mirage of a career.

"Jacaranda told me that it was the newspapers that whipped up the scandal and that she hadn't . . ."

Milly looked at him, almost enchanted at the sight of such naïveté. "Fuck, it's a good thing you covered the crime beat for ten years, isn't it? And that you write detective shows for TV. So you're saying you've never heard of young girls raped by their fathers, uncles, or even *film producers*, at age sixteen, or fifteen, or fourteen?"

Andrea had felt a stabbing surge of grief and rage. "Well, she could have told me about it and I wouldn't have—"

"You wouldn't have what? You wouldn't have judged her?"

"No, I certainly wouldn't have judged her. I'm only sorry that she didn't trust me."

"Jacaranda never trusted anyone. Over the years, she grew more and more closed. She was terrified at the idea of losing other people's respect."

Andrea was stunned. "Then why are you telling me about it? Just to make me feel like an idiot?"

"I'm telling you because deep down you seem like a decent man.

Because I want you to know just how fragile Jacaranda was. And so that you can help me make that swine pay for what he did."

This new fragment of the truth, which he was now turning over in his mind, actually didn't strike him all that hard: it was the logical conclusion to the never-ending story of access to fresh flesh in the meat lockers of La Dolce Roma. That constant flow of work for the youngest women stepping into the spotlights for the first time—with the perfection of their bodies and their gazes already well trained, ready for anything, armed with desperate determination, plus stiletto heels, smiles, plunging necklines, all of them believing themselves to be stronger than the sense of weariness that will follow—to take the seats already warmed up by the older women, the used-up ones. Who in the meantime have toughened up, like the skin on your feet, calloused from the hard work of supporting the body's weight. And now they need ointments, treatments, cosmetic surgeons, alcohol, tranquilizers, psychoanalysts, and even gurus from some sect, to ward off depression and win themselves a favorable position in the archives, perhaps with a second or third marriage, the last one on the shelf.

Sixteen years ago, Jacaranda too had set sail for the usual island of dreams. And it had taken her as many years, from one success to the next, before going down in a shipwreck. She had built herself a career as a professional actress, she'd smiled on a hundred or so magazine covers, told practically nothing but lies, supposing them to be harmless. Instead, the dirt from their tiny wounds had infected her a little at a time.

❧

Now Andrea is looking out the window of Oscar's study, and he has a complete vision of the ritual that is being staged out on the terrace. He would have liked to have made his presence known at the very instant that Oscar had thrown wide his arms and asked if anyone had a memory to share. He has plenty of memories to talk about concerning Jacaranda's honey-colored eyes, about Oscar's latest con jobs, and, for that matter, his earliest. But he doesn't want to confront all those faces down there, which would turn in his direction. He wants to confront only one face.

A Two-Bit Romantic Story

Clinking glasses and a buzz of conversation has scattered the crowd after Oscar's homily, and the people are sorting themselves out among the blooming lantana plants. The waiters are opening the dining rooms with trays full of raw fish and salads already laid out on tables, with wines, hard liquor, ice buckets, savory pies, risottos, mozzarellas.

At the window, Andrea has lost sight of Oscar's light-colored jacket.

Milly has found a box of chocolates and bottle of whisky. She's opened them both. She serves herself. She gets wound up: "I'm going downstairs now, and I'm going to find him for you."

"Tell him that I'm here waiting for him."

Milly takes a drink, clenches her jaw, gets to her feet. "With pleasure."

❧

When they find themselves face to face, high up in the tower, the clash is rapid and harsh. With half a bottle of vodka in his body and the coke pumping in his brain, Oscar is the first to attack: "I don't recall inviting you here. In fact I told you to stay locked up at home. I would have come to see you. We needed to agree on a few things first, if I make myself clear. Hey! Do you mind telling me what the fuck you're looking at?"

Andrea is in front of him and doesn't move. "Agree on what? She's dead, asshole."

"You came all the way here to give me the news? Well, talk to her psychiatrist about it," he says, pointing to Milly, who has once again redone her makeup and is now darting flames from her mascaraed eyes. "Or else ask yourself whether what happened isn't your fault."

"My fault?"

"What the fuck! I'd asked you to help me launch the movie, not to screw the star and shatter her brain into pieces."

As always, Oscar so overstates things that he leaves Andrea frozen in astonishment. Then he retorts, "You're a son of a bitch! I don't even know why I'm listening to you. You know perfectly well that—"

Oscar greets his outrage with open arms, the way priests do when they're pretending to be goodhearted. "I don't know a damned thing. Except for what you can see with the naked eye: that you, Andrea Serrano, spent a whole week with her, that you certainly plied her silly with questions; that you certainly commiserated with her for her damned awful youth instead of telling her, look to the future, sweetheart, the world's moving along, so hop aboard. And that in the end, when all is said and done, you made a mess of everything, the way you do with the screenplays that I have to toss in the trash."

He looks him right in the eye, turns the half Cohiba, now dead, in his fingers. "Yours is a two-bit romantic story, but at the end the suicide heats it all up. Maybe I'll use this story to make a movie."

Andrea remains standing, facing him. "Well, I have an even better one."

Oscar tilts his head in understanding. "Ah, yes, tell me the story, I might even like it, and if so I'll buy it. Remember that I've already given you an advance of five large, though."

Andrea ignores him and goes on. "It's the story of a guy who comes up from the street. He becomes the gofer of a producer. Once he feels he's ready he gets him into trouble with an underage female that he's already screwed, has him arrested, pushes him into the abyss to steal his soul, his profession, and his Jaguar."

Oscar's face remains impassive. "That's exactly how your Jacaranda told it to you, and now you come and repeat like a good parrot. No, I'm not buying it. I don't like it."

From the other end of the room, Milly makes an exasperated noise. "Now cut that out!"

Oscar pours himself a drink, clucks his tongue, and says, "Quit busting my balls, fatso."

She gives him a hard glare. "One of these days I'm going to stick it up your ass, trust me."

Oscar bursts out laughing in her face. "But I already did that to you, or don't you remember?"

She gives him the finger.

He swings around now and focuses on Andrea. "So let me tell you the other parts that you evidently haven't heard yet. Eusebio Reverberi had squeezed himself dry, down to the last drop. He was done for. He was a dead man. He'd run well past the closing credits, I don't know if I make myself clear. His movies weren't making a penny of box office anymore. He was just stealing money from his financiers and ideas from me. The coke had burned through his hard palate and his brain. And the whores were eating his heart. All I did was I cleaned up after him."

"Of course. Custodian of the year."

"Fuck yourself. As for your girlfriend Jacaranda, she was looking for a quick way to climb. I taught her the fastest way of all: descend."

"Fuck, she was just sixteen!"

"So what? I didn't ask her to spread her legs. There was a line waiting outside. They were selling tickets outside. That was her shortcut to heaven."

"Did you take her there?"

"What?"

Andrea raises his voice and asks again, "Answer me, did you take her there?"

"Why should I even remember? There were dozens just like her. All of them looking for candy. All of them with braids, white panties, and condoms in their teddy bears."

Andrea tries to grab him by the shirt, Oscar steps aside, Milly screams, the shirt tears: "Did you take her there to Reverberi's house, yes or no?"

"Fuck, my shirt!"

"Yes or no?"

Oscar is beet red. "I don't know. Yes, maybe yes! Are you happy now? What the fuck does it change? If it's a crime, well, by now the statue of limitations has run out."

Waves of fury make Andrea clench his jaw. Then the adrenaline subsides, replaced by weariness for this filthy world. He goes over and sits down in one of the armchairs. "You threw open the door for her. You shut her in. Then you screwed your friend Reverberi by making that anonymous phone call."

Oscar is sweating, he takes a deep breath and considers whether to grab him by the neck and keep him from unearthing those long-buried years. But he's afraid that the damage has been done, that the phantoms have been raised, and that Jacaranda's death is only the first of many consequences. He looks at his torn shirt, he starts unbuttoning it. "You don't know shit. I didn't make that phone call. Eusebio had plenty of enemies, but I wasn't one of them. Now do me a favor and go fuck yourself."

Andrea turns around and heads downstairs; he's had enough of that party. When he's halfway down the hallway, heading for the secondary exit, his cell phone rings. "Is this Andrea Serrano? Would you have ten minutes you can spare me?"

The Farewell in a Digital Story

Half an hour later they're both leaning against Ventura's car two intersections away. The street running past Martello's house is barricaded, as it is at every party, by the city police, with signs reading FILM SET, which seems more like a caption than the privilege that it is. Those signs are there to keep the parking places clear for the guests, a thoughtful gesture from the municipal traffic commissioner, a former Fascist enforcer, to his longtime friend Oscar, who on summer weekends takes him and his little wifey, both of them with the eyes of wolves, out for rides at forty knots aboard the Magnum Marine all the way to the island of Ponza, and after a nice swim stuffs them full of amberjack at a reserved table at Acqua Pazza.

Far from the lights of the mansion, the sky is still full of stars, and the other villas on the Aventine seem to be dreaming untroubled dreams.

Ventura has watched Andrea stroll down that brightly lit sidewalk and has evaluated that studied elegance—a plum-colored corduroy suit, English shoes, a soft orange vest, and a vanilla-white shirt—as a token of membership, a sign that he too can claim a spot in the Superworld.

He lets him come even with him and then gets straight to the point: "Will you tell me why you went all the way to Paris?"

Andrea identified him at first glance as someone who always carries that police headquarters light on him, in the cut of his clothes and in his gaze. And so he tries to slow down. "It's a long story."

"Tell it to me anyway. I have plenty of time."

"We were supposed to save a movie. We had invented a sort of game."

"And that's it?"

"And then things got out of hand and what we thought was a game turned into a tragedy. But I couldn't tell you why."

"Do you think smuggling cash out of Italy is a game?"

The question disorients him entirely. "What cash?"

"You tell me."

Andrea looks at him in surprise. "I don't know what you're talking about, seriously. I thought you wanted to ask me about Jacaranda."

"I'm not interested in Jacaranda Rizzi right now. I'm working on Oscar Martello and the money that the two of you illegally smuggled out of Italy."

Ventura's words once again change the whole picture for him. "Who did?"

"You two did. On that trip to Paris."

"I don't know anything about any cash."

"It was in the three blue plastic travel bags in the trunk of your automobile."

"Jacaranda and I didn't have any—" but as he's saying it, Andrea stops and his expression changes.

Ventura takes a deep breath. "So you see that now you remember?"

At that exact moment, Jacaranda's farewell comes over the Internet. Both their cell phones ping out simultaneously, notifying them that a text has come in. Milly has just forwarded it to Andrea. Police headquarters has forwarded it to Ventura. The sender's name has made them both jerk in surprise. They try to open the message, but the web is so bottlenecked that nothing is downloading.

Andrea breathes in, tries to slow his heartbeat, and calls Milly. "What is it?"

"Take a look at it. It's more discombobulated than the other one. But still, it says things."

It takes them several long minutes to download. It's a selfie video a hundred seconds long, shot by Jacaranda in Amsterdam, scheduled to post and parked somewhere on her digital cloud or on some server two or three days ago, presumably shortly before killing herself. Given the content—an actress and superstar, giant box office draw, announcing her own suicide—it's literally breaking the Internet.

Jacaranda appears sitting barefoot on the edge of a bed, wearing her usual torn denim jeans, her face white with tension, her eyes the color of honey, her blond hair swept back. Reciting her farewell message, she gets the tone and the pauses wrong, everything turns out to be dramatically slurred and, at the same time, utterly clear.

This is what she says:

*I've decided to go away and leave it all behind me even life
itself which has been nothing but covering myself with thorn*

branches which wound up suffocating me if I want to free myself from them I have to cut them off at the root and I'll go away with the roots.

Many years ago they took my body I was sixteen years old and I won't say I didn't consent I was an accomplice I believed that the money and the success were worth it but if you're seeing me now girls, please, please don't do it.

In these matters there's always a guy who casts a spell with his stories, in my case the guy was called Oscar Martello, and by using me he ruined a person I cared about and I let him do it.

Sincerely, I don't know if I understood at the time how much harm I was doing I was stupid but it happened, that person, in part because of me, is dead now, his name was Eusebio Reverberi and maybe he too cared about me.

That betrayal was something I thought I could forget as I went my way but instead that betrayal no longer forgot about me, and year after year it became my great remorse until remorse became my sickness.

Today my sickness is ending and with it I too am ending my name is Jacaranda Rizzi get someone to tell you my story my misbegotten love affairs I'm an actress and because of that some of you may think you know me but it's not true I don't even know myself.

The audio ends. The frame veers for a moment into the vague whiteness of a light that might perhaps be that on the ceiling in the room, and then darkness.

Andrea is done watching and he's on the verge of tears. Ventura puts away the iPhone, sticks his hands in his pockets, and says, "Maybe we ought to take a look-see at what's going on in there."

Andrea stops him. "Does Oscar know about your investigation into the money?"

"Maybe he does, maybe he doesn't. But seeing that I've just told you about it, I'll be talking about it with him too."

"I don't give a damn about the money."

"Really?"

"I loved Jacaranda."

"You've told me that already."

Andrea is thinking about how quickly Jacaranda's world closed down, and how little her face, as recorded in that video, matches the face he remembered. Aged by years in just a hundred seconds.

He sees her again at the Brasserie Lipp, sitting across from him at that tiny table, closer than if there had been no table. The waiter had cleared away everything and brought them the hard liquor. Her fingers were knit, her face was luminous, her voice was tired. She was saying, "I've been bought and sold a bunch of times. And you want to know the funny thing? I was always the one who set the price."

The image vanishes.

"I shouldn't have let her go. I should have gone to look for her, gone to Amsterdam to get her."

"So why didn't you?"

"For the stupidest reason, you want to hear? Because she had written on the mirror in the bathroom, 'Don't try to find me.'"

Ventura feels a yank at his heart. Grażyna had used the same words. He knows exactly what Andrea Serrano is feeling. And he knows that he's not lying.

"It's time to go back to your producer."

"He's not my producer anymore."

"Since when?"

"Since tonight."

"That's a good decision. Shall we get going?"

"Actually, I was planning to go home."

"No. I really don't think so."

⚜

In the villa, lots of other people are simultaneously receiving on their smartphones the same video, chain-posted and propagating horizontally as the juiciest novelty of the evening, an unprecedented development taking place before the eyes of one and all: the dead woman, just commemorated, who takes the lectern at her own funeral to mock and ridicule the officiant.

Beyond belief—if it wasn't La Dolce Roma.

The guests emit a buzz of noisy chatter.

The guests have a good laugh.

The guests text and post and text and post, all of them bowed over their smartphones, without even touching each other, as if it were some sort of game. But it *is* a game.

Unleashed by this unforeseen plot twist, all their resentments against Oscar the bandit bob to the surface. They believed—the guests had—that they were being invited to take part in an innocuous but advantageous ritual, to sit without obligation at the steam table of righteous sentiment. And instead the small-time celebrities of Roman nightlife, dressed to the nines, suddenly find themselves chewing over the remains of a suicide at the home of her persecutor. And this is not strictly speaking a good thing, but it is certainly a juicy piece of gossip, and starting tomorrow it's worth putting on your CV.

War & Peace, trained as they are to catch the slightest whiff of blood in the air, immediately start taking pictures of the most prominent guests and archiving the pictures in the new file—"Here's Who Was There That Night," bound to sell at decent prices.

Undersecretary Neri is the quickest to react: "Remaining in the home of Signor Martello can mean only one thing: complicity." And he orders the withdrawal of his retinue of blond assistants, with handbags and overcoats all grabbed on the run, everyone out the door without so much as goodbye to anyone. A couple of lawyers trail after them. The skinny fashion designer flounces out too. Other guests scatter out onto the terraces, while the more curious take their places in the living rooms, clustering around to savor the scene.

Oscar appears, drunk and furious.

Oscar walks long distances between sofas filled only with people who are looking at him.

Oscar wishes he could just kick them all out. He's lost Helga, he's lost his little girls, and now he's getting ready to lose all the rest.

Donna Angelina Casagrande tracks him with a long gaze until she feels her eyelids tug, then she speaks resentfully to the banker breathing beside her: "Too much rancor and too much noise is bad for business."

Attilio Fabris wanders through the crowd filming everything with great brio; it's all first-rate stuff for his vendetta and for his next film, once all his bruises have healed and he can finally get a new producer.

Milly Gallo Bautista is sitting in an armchair and, full of rum, she's finally crying over the milk spilled. After all, it was she who took Jacaranda to Amsterdam, believing she was saving her from that swine Oscar, never imagining that the gray skies of Holland would be the last straw, shattering that frightened little heart and making the irreparable well and truly irreparable.

Andrea has come back and now he's sitting next to her.

Many of the main lights in the other living rooms have been turned off, replaced by needlelike LEDs—from painting to painting, from sculpture to sculpture—to offer greater intimacy in the dim light to the guests gathering in small knots to converse.

Commissario Ventura roams freely like an explorer among the exotic parrots and the oversize ferns on the terrace, worried that his netting might be swept away by this new groundswell of clamor, along with his prey. Now that Oscar has publicly besmirched himself with the crime of having shut Jacaranda's eyes forever, accusing him of tax evasion and illegal exportation of capital funds outside the country strikes him as being in poor taste. Even though these are the only crimes, since the days of Al Capone, that can at least ensure a stay in the national prison system and a bit of social censure; not so much for the commission of the crime as for the weakness of having allowed oneself to be caught.

Now behold the great Oscar Martello, who, in spite of his rage, never forgets his golden rules of screenwriting, and so in the moment of darkest affliction of this entire evening's entertainment complete with funeral, he therefore organizes the turning point, the hero's redemption, or at least the redemption of his party. He orders his housemaids and waiters to turn back on the main lights in the living rooms, one by one. To turn up the music. To throw open the doors. To move in single file from the kitchens toward the sofas with an orgy of trays stacked high with gelato, cassatas with candied fruit, and mini pastries.

The sugary distractions work perfectly. The depression passes: Here come the sweets!

A Film with Three Blue Plastic
Travel Bags

Sweets are forgetfulness. They are the enchantment that dissolves bad thoughts. That makes everyone regress to the carefree innocence of childhood, makes them cluster around groaning tables, even outside, on the terraces. It attracts them around an edible form of happiness that also makes their hearts race, the way flags do when they flutter in the wind, the way national anthems do when they blare out over the crowd: the sweets of La Dolce Roma. In that festive interlude—while Oscar Martello, having successfully pulled off the plot twist, has gone back to his tower study, and Andrea with Milly is following him, and Ventura has left behind him the crowded terraces to make sure he doesn't lose them—no one notices the way the sky is changing color. That the sky is now a contagious black.

❧

Andrea is the first to speak: "Fuck, I'd love to know if you feel even the slightest sense of guilt."

Oscar looks at him, his unbuttoned shirt hanging out of his trousers, his face a wreck. "I don't know what you're talking about."

Ventura intervenes, fed up: "If you like, I'll be glad to explain, but not here."

Oscar struggles even to focus on him, or at least so it seems. "What do you mean by that?"

"That maybe it's time for all of us to go have a nice long chat, but at my place, police headquarters."

"I'm not going anywhere with anyone, half the world of Roman cinema is here in my home, I don't know if you missed that fact. And you're not even on the guest list."

"Would you like me to call a couple of squad cars?"

"Would you like me to call the chief of police?"

"Go right ahead. Maybe you could explain to him the reasons for that trip to Paris."

"What on earth are you talking about?"

Andrea breaks in: "Cut it out, Oscar. After sixteen years, you've pulled the same trick with me and Jacaranda!"

"I've pulled what same trick?"

"Betrayal. The same betrayal! You brought us onstage and then you locked the door behind us."

"If I were you, I wouldn't talk about betrayals."

Andrea ignores him, turns toward Ventura. "Go ahead and tell him, Commissario. He still doesn't know anything about your surprise."

Oscar also turns to look at Ventura. "What surprise?"

Ventura wants to enjoy the sight of Oscar's face, now that he has his full attention. "We at the police department make films of our own, sometimes. Little films. Maybe not as lovely as yours, but I assure you: gripping."

Oscar pours himself a drink and waits. He feels his heart empty out and fill back up.

Ventura has breathed for a full pause. "I'm talking about a film with three blue plastic travel bags that travel to Paris and then on to Luxembourg."

Oscar Martello allows the revelation to settle into the silence, amid the sage-green furnishings of his study. Then he throws both hands in the air and bursts out in a boisterous laugh, *ha ha!* "And that's your plot twist? Not bad. Nice work, Commissario. I like it, I told you that you had talent." He looks at Andrea, sizes up Milly, defies Ventura. "My fucking no-talent screenwriters always go the long way round. Or they take the most expensive route. I'm always telling them: You don't have to knock down the Twin Towers to make your audience jump in its seats. It's enough to just lift a stone and find a scorpion. Do I make myself clear?"

Ventura plays along: "So did I find one?"

"Sure you found one, Commissario. I put the scorpion there. I'm the producer, aren't I?"

Andrea recognizes Oscar's style when he slips into the role of the oracle. He tells him, "Give it a rest."

But Oscar pays him no mind, he walks up and down, driven by his enormous self-regard and also by the alcohol, by the coke that has renewed its chemical cycle in his bloodstream and respiration. Up, up, all the way up to the brain.

"Okay, then, the producer sends his two characters to Paris. Each of them has a motive for going, the producer actually has two: launching a piece-of-shit movie and taking some cash out of this fucked-up country, hard-earned cash that the state wants to take away from him, not to build roads or hospitals, but to pay for hookers. Okay. The writer's motive is the most banal: he wants to take a little trip, all expenses paid, and fuck the actress. The actress's motive is the most complicated one. She wants to use the movie's success and the clamor stirred by her disappearance to tell the world about her sad and stirring story. She wants to cleanse the shame of the abused minor. Unleash a full-blown scandal. Wipe away her remorse and perhaps even her shame. Punish the wicked producer. And, naturally, increase her fee for her next movie. The three stories would have all worked with a bang. No, what am I saying: a nuclear explosion!" He turns around, finds the vodka, hunts around for his glass, fills it up, takes a drink. "But that's when things start to go horribly wrong. Instead of taking the stage, the actress goes into a tailspin because, like all losers, she's terrified by the responsibilities that await her. And so, instead, she makes up her mind to take off with her fat friend. But you know how it works, right? Even if you run away, life chases you and nails you down. And so she winds up the way we know, bobbing in a canal full of lurid water. The writer had his adventure, he may even have fallen in love, he believes that he deserves a third act of a romantic comedy, with plenty of kisses and yummy snacks, but instead he finds himself in the crushingly tedious black and white of a film by Lars von Trier.

"While the producer, on the other hand, wins on all fronts: he's launched his movie, he's gotten rid of the actress, he's safeguarded his money. And if there are any cops who might think of subpoenaing him, well, keep cool and keep your powder dry, guys, because the producer is rich and powerful, there's no flagrante delicto, and the cop is going to have to climb over a wall of lawyers."

Andrea watches him stroll back and forth—*He's dictating a screenplay*. "Christ, your head's coming unscrewed."

Oscar ignores him. He raises his glass as if he were toasting his own birthday. "Am I right, Commissario?"

In the silence that ensues, the first thunderclap explodes in fury. And in a split second, the whole scene changes.

After the Thunder, the Rain

Out of the vast Roman sky the wind springs up. Black clouds descend from the north, swollen with water and muscles. Gusts of wind shake the tops of the maritime pines that rise high above the villas, shiver the streetlights. The temperature plummets. Women in plunging necklines and stiletto heels are the first on the terrace to take fright. The jasmine flowers fly off. So do the mini pastries, blown off their trays. Then the trays themselves.

The first fat drops begin to fall. What follows is a sudden, massive microburst that floods the already overloaded tables and washes over the gelato. In an instant all the candles are blown out. Now the guests rush inside, screaming and shouting, knocking over waiters who are trying to save vases, bottles, and glasses that fly away into the night. A woman has just slipped and fallen, cutting her hands on the glass. No one stops to help her. She struggles to get to her feet. She's drenched, bleeding, and sobbing.

The cypresses and the olive trees in the garden below wave and toss furiously, pushed by the wind that's shaking them with grim and forceful rage. More thunderclaps explode. The iron fretwork lamps fly away, along with the cushions, the canvas hangings of the gazebos. The water pours down, forming streams, and then a river in spate rushes across the terrace, overrunning everything, even the French doors leading into the living rooms. One of the doors slams and shatters into shards.

The hurricane thrashes down, lashing the streets, ripping branches off the trees, causing manholes and storm drains to overflow, overturning automobiles. The traffic lights stop working. Sirens wail, and so do burglar alarms. Via Marmorata becomes a river. Piazza Sant'Anselmo, an overbrimming lake. The wind whips and pursues everything. Sheet metal, terra-cotta tiles, and antennae fly off the roofs. Cornices tumble into the streets below. The underpasses fill up like tin basins under some giant spigot, traffic on the overpasses grinds to a halt due to multivehicle, chain-reaction pileups. Garbage bobs everywhere, choking the outskirts of town, from Torrevecchia to Cinecittà. Cascades of water gush down from the roofs, from the walls, from the bridges, but this is no cleansing water; if anything, it tears and rends, it devastates.

Seen from above—from the four windows of the tower study where Oscar Martello still reigns on high—Rome is an expanse of gleaming scales pelted with rain, besieged by rumbling thunder and windspouts. The blue lights of the ambulances, the fire trucks, the police squad cars, flash here and there and don't seem like announcements of impending rescue so much as warnings of shipwreck.

Oscar Martello follows and memorizes his party with an unperturbed expression, as it collapses into catastrophe—and along with his party, perhaps, his life—in this apocalyptic sequence of torn flowers, bent shrubs, overturned chairs, guests and napkins flying away.

At his side, Andrea Serrano experiences a growing sense of anxiety in the face of that burst of meteorological fury, as he thinks that perhaps it is Jacaranda shaking off this ridiculous party. She who, from the world of death, flips over the real world after doing nothing but take it all while she was still alive.

Then it ends.

Just as quick as it came, the cloudburst moves on and peace returns. In a few minutes the dark sky shreds the clouds into fragments, the rain ceases, and the wind becomes a gentler, softer swell, and glowing stars once again shine overhead.

Now, in the new silence that spreads, it is easy to make out all the noises arriving from different distances: the car horns, the blaring alarms. And over them all, the sound of water that continues restlessly, flowing, dripping.

From the living rooms, human voices can now be heard, many of them complaining, some even calling piteously for help. Life recovers from the shock that has just blasted it.

Andrea goes back and sits down in an armchair. Milly hasn't moved. With every flash of lightning she shut her eyes, immobilized by the thunderstorm; they have terrified her ever since her years in the orphanage. Now she has started drinking everything she can find again and chomping on chocolates to slake her nerves.

Raul Ventura's cell phone rings: because of the natural catastrophe, there's an all-hands emergency meeting at police headquarters. There is a vague interlude. Then the final reckoning will come.

The Scandal Comes Flying

t comes into the nation's homes with the morning news reports. It brings with it, as its dowry, the corpse of Jacaranda, accelerating the stratospheric success of her movie *No, I Won't Surrender!*, already leading the rankings with its €9 million of ticket sales. For good measure, it also brings revelations concerning the tax evasions of the great producer Oscar Martello, with his undeclared funds hidden in cash in Paris, London, and Luxembourg, along with the money of Donna Angelina Casagrande and her various nonprofits.

Banner headlines scream "Money Without Shame." "Filthy Rich Scoundrels!" blares the TV news. Money that instead of flowing to the needy in Africa, circles the globe to wind up in certain horrible tenements in Pomezia, Torvaianica, Marina di Ardea, and from there to Palma de Mallorca, Formentera, and points north, coming to rest in the now-sanitized safes of Swiss and Luxembourgian banks.

Angelina Casagrande clings firmly to her pedestal. She weeps through lawyers and says she knew nothing, couldn't have imagined. And in the first few hours of the scandal she is protected in the soft, yielding arms of the Vatican, in a secret house on Via della Conciliazione, no media pillory for her.

With Oscar, it's quite another tune. Paparazzi with video cameras lay siege to his villa. The TV news reports carry in heavy rotation the sequences of his black Jaguar emerging from the villa, escorted by squad cars, and traveling toward the depositions with the magistrates, the aforementioned Martello, Oscar, present here today, born in Serravalle Scrivia, producer by profession, who when questioned responds, et cetera. There is talk of tax evasion, fraud, export of capital funds, swindling, trafficking in artworks. There is talk of thirty million euros. Then fifty. Then a hundred. There is talk of the fact that Oscar denies all charges, heaves deep sighs, spits, loses his temper, because he is responsible for so much money invested and pays so much in taxes that they ought to thank him instead of tormenting him like that. Why don't they give a thought to all the jobs he creates and what would become of all the actors and actresses and directors and screenwriters that he tucks in every night, slipping under their sweaty pillows a ration of large and a smattering of human dignity? "The dignity that comes with a job and a salary, do I make myself clear?"

But the magistrates scoff cynically at that banal rhetoric of the good-hearted millionaire; they want other explanations; for example, what was the nature of his relations with the poor, deceased Jacaranda Rizzi, "named Maria by her parents," whether he too had abused her when she was still a minor, whether he'd sold her, whether he'd blackmailed her, and with what psychological violence, and for how many years. Because it is from that first act that all the other acts descended, her complete anomie; that is, if

Oscar Martello even knew the meaning of the word "anomie."
And subordinate to those questions, they'd like to know the source
of the money found in the three blue plastic travel bags, and for
that matter of a fiberglass Bonalumi worth £380,000, a Castellani
worth £500,000, and a tree by Penone worth £265,000, all purchased last year at the London Italian Sale, and documented in
photographs taken by Commissario Ventura. Paid for with what
money, earned when and how? From some offshore source? Or
a numbered bank account? Or some other piece of clandestine
banking?

He looks at them, smiles, and says, "I don't remember."

"Really?"

"Really. I buy so damned much stuff. Can I smoke?" Deep
down, he still assumes his back is covered by the incredible success of *No, I Won't Surrender!*, which is now teetering vertiginously
close to the all-time box office record, €21 million last week and
then almost €30 million the week after that, everyone rushing to
see Jacaranda's gold. And adding the price of the ticket to Oscar
Martello's swag, though of course it no longer belongs to Oscar
Martello, since all of it is under seal of confiscation by the investigators of the Italian tax office, damn them, who nailed down the
perimeter all around Anvil Film, driving one stake in at a time,
and now they're erecting one bar at a time to cage it all in, gnaw
every last scrap of the booty, and hand over whatever crumbs remain to Helga's gleaming white teeth.

Donna Angelina Casagrande, the queen of flowers and of ne-
groes in Central Africa, of Roman nights and of little orphans
suffering from malaria, reappears, heartbroken and already *quite
distant* from the abominations of Oscar and his filthy mud. When
she sits down to talk with the investigators—lips and tits sagging,

no high heels, a cunning little Hermès in virginal white—she already sings like a bird at the first interview. And she blames everything on her unfaithful functionaries and, of course, on Oscar; he's the demon in this story, who, by promising that he'd double her revenue for laudable charities, subjugated her for deplorably evil purposes with his black soul and his *morbid* sex appeal, even going so far as to undermine her virtue, elderly and now defenseless woman though she is: "As God is my witness." And along with God, a great many others are her witnesses, witnesses to her guiltlessness and, more important, to her pure, good heart, among them the usual bankers, lobster eaters all, plus a couple of ambassadors with noble blood and rotten hearts, as well as Undersecretary Neri and certain old matrons of the Roman aristocracy, they too willing and ready to vouch for her virtues of blameless altruism, exercised in more than a half century of honored service on Roman terraces, sofas and couches of social occasions, and sacristies of the highest Vatican hierarchies. And "Vatican" is the extra whisper of penicillin that already sterilizes the entire deposition room at the first breath, transforming a sordid confession into an immaculate repentance, "that is, if I have anything to repent, save perhaps for my excessively trusting heart."

In response to a question, Andrea Serrano replies that he knows nothing about Oscar's money or about any blue plastic travel bags, or any of the other illicit traffics he's accused of. He really did think he was saving a film out of friendship and undertaking that trip because, quite simply, he didn't have much else to do and Paris was more amusing than the boredom of Rome. Is that it?

"That's it." And that it's the truth that Jacaranda Rizzi touched his heart in a way not even he expected, even though as far as the magistrate who watches him from behind a pair of tinted eyeglasses, sucking on a menthol cough drop, is concerned, Andrea's heart is of absolutely no interest; what he wants to know is how Oscar paid him and his other employees. "But I'm not Oscar Martello's accountant, I'm not a money smuggler, I'm not a financial professional of any kind!" Andrea states brusquely. "I write screenplays for television," he adds, as if that circumstance added some significant weight to his claims of innocence.

"Ah, that claptrap!" was the brief reply of the magistrate who ultimately decided to find him believable and inoffensive, in part thanks to that detail, and therefore no longer subject to incarceration. "Just make sure we can get in touch with you. Get hold of the invoices. And don't even think of trying to travel."

No sarcasm for Oscar Martello, but instead a substantial list of articles and clauses from the penal code, seeing that the evidence against him included photographs and stakeouts by officers of the law, wiretaps, accounting gaps, eyewitness testimony, as well as a shameless flaunting of wealth and success as vast as the envy aroused. All were matters that conspired to throw open for him the gates of Regina Coeli prison, and a cell at the far end of the second wing, white walls to suffocate him, to make him spit due to rattled nerves and general disgust, as in the bad old days of Serravalle Scrivia, given that by now he's accustomed only to raw fish, warm bread, and gleaming white linen napkins. And instead here he is, imprisoned behind filthy walls, walls that are indifferent to his ravings, walls that are accustomed to drinking in time in silence and spewing it back out as an exceedingly slow, fine gearing that wrings the convict's neck, depriving him of oxygen a millimeter at a time.

A detention that was clamorous in many ways, considering the legal talent deployed, and the barefaced resistance of the prisoner, who continued to send out messages of indignant innocence to the free world, arousing in the rest of La Dolce Roma the sneer of an obscene curiosity that galloped from mouth to mouth, from one conjecture to the next: "What does that old pig eat behind bars, lobster linguine?" "Does he do his hour out in the prison yard?" "Do you think he bought a high-impact asshole protector?" All of them calculating how soon and how brutally Anvil Film would collapse into a thousand pieces, and how much energy that would free in the airless atmosphere of Italian cinema, and whether that energy would take the form of life-giving oxygen or poisonous radiation, and how many producers would battle for the spoils, lumbering off to digest them in blessed peace.

Milly Gallo Bautista organized in that same period receptions at her villa in Sabaudia to celebrate the awesome event of his detention, and wept by night in memory of her grief and mourning, while the two gravediggers War & Peace had promptly collected the second installment of their contract in record time, before scampering over to the other side of the barricades. And on the other side of the barricades, they found none other than Attilio Fabris, who had just taken his seat, finally cured of his bruises, but not of the bruised feelings over the humiliations undergone. And in fact he had hired them to write something injurious against Martello—a shameless, sarcastic version of Jacaranda's farewell note, clicked on 11.5 million times, and transcribed and published by all the papers—and what with great brainstorming and much erasure and rewriting, what finally emerged was a long rambling rant in the first-person singular, delivered by an actor who, from the shadows, fondling a blow-up doll, might perfectly well have been the despised producer himself, the same bandit face, cut by the line between blackness and light, chewing on the stub of a smoking Cohiba, spitting and hacking and, meanwhile, reciting his own eulogy, it too a hundred seconds long, entitled "An Oscar-Worthy Monologue." It began, amid much coughing, with these words: "I steal and I make films. I sideline half of the production budget, I invoice in London, I conceal in Luxembourg, I spend in Rome. I stir the pond muck of life and I stir the economy, I don't know if I make myself clear."

And it went on:

My finest film is the one that nobody can see. It exists in the scenes that I cut from the scripts. In the actors I don't hire, in the benefits I don't pay my film crews, in the money I skimp and save.

I steal and I don't understand all this scandal. A clockwork scandal, if you ask me. The political use of scandal. The media pillory. And if we wanted to be true guarantors of civil rights, every scandal would be considered innocent until proven otherwise, through appeal up to the supreme court, through due process and taking into account all extenuating circumstances.

Because after all, we ought to have a little more patriotic pride, you nasty sons of bitches, seeing that now we export scandals around the world, like olive oil, pasta, and tomato paste. We lead Europe with sixty billion euros, half of all the corruption on the continent—I don't know if I make myself clear.

I steal and I call it the real economy. I call it adrenaline, a lust for life. Look at the dreary face of a Finnish producer, without bribes, and look at the cheerful face of one of ours who makes films full of belches, farts, and cheating wives: this is life! And look at the bellies and jaws of our politicians, of our businessmen, of our bankers, of our Mafiosi—yes, their jaws and bellies too—as they marry off daughters, celebrate lavish public contracts, visit Padre Pio and the Maldives. Once again: this is life! Listen to the laughter. Admire the digestion.

Pay no attention to those who say: There's plenty for everyone. It isn't true. I steal a hundred lives in order to live my own. And believe me, I don't give a flying fuck about the other ninety-nine lives. You should do the same, if you can.

The monologue continues at rap velocity, with syncopated percussion backfiring and spare change falling into the cash register, and it was feverishly popular online. Diffused by dozens of social networks and darkened by thousands of comments that demanded strict penalties and harsh suffering for this filthy rich son of a bitch, this bastard, this piece of shit thief, rapist, pimp, former king of producers now spinning into a ruinous taildive, serves you right, you son of a bitch, fuck you, you deserve to die.

The downward trajectory suddenly comes to a halt when Oscar, quietly, but with four lawyers at his service, is released from confinement at sunset, "because he no longer represents a threat of contamination of evidence," and is loaded into a police car to evade the attention of lurking TV cameras, and is taken into house arrest at his palatial mansion on the Aventine. A development that then and there fills him with a blend of euphoria and a looming sense of foreboding. And the foreboding bears itself out the minute he sets foot in the villa, when he senses the void.

Not some existential void, but a physical void, because of how Helga managed to spirit away the finest paintings and the costliest artworks, the slash by Fontana, the flowers by Warhol, the butterflies and the shark by Hirst, Burri's combustion, and even the tree by Penone and the Bonalumi, all under judicial seal, but not the almost entirely white Manzoni, which hangs there on its vertical stage, a reminder of that long-ago humiliation, his own personal fatal flaw, and in short, the hero's wound inflicted with that throwaway line ("When you find another fool, sell it to him"), which once again burns him, since Helga clearly left it there as her own personal contribution to the ulcer that has just begun to flower in his stomach. And then his collection of watches, all vanished, including his very first pink gold Vacheron Constantin and his last Patek Philippe. All gone, along with the three Filipino houseboys, the housekeeper, Miriam, the entire array of silverware, the damned bulldog, Napoleon, the cat without a name, and another one of his beloved Jaguars.

In the black thoughts summoned by the void, suddenly there also yawns before him the revelation of the grimmest of all possible coincidences. In prison, he counted his detention one day at a time, but only now does it dawn on him that his grimy time behind bars lasted nineteen days. The same number of days as Eusebio Reverberi, sixteen years ago, as if it were a plan, or even worse, a destiny, that in order to culminate was required to respect that exact span of time, whereupon it could proceed to lay out a suitable aftermath. Like, for instance, summon three Brazilian hookers, and have them stuff three grams of coke up his ass, and then take off toward some hyperuranion, leaving his heart behind him, along with all his dreams of glory, Cinecittà included.

Imprisoned by evil thoughts as well as by house arrest, Oscar Martello is not allowed to do anything more than to wander aimlessly through those silences. Forbidden to make phone calls. Forbidden to go out. Forbidden to meet with strangers, save for his crashingly boring lawyers, who scurry back and forth, along with the lawyers of Angelina Casagrande and her highly placed protectors, urging on him the greatest possible caution, take our advice, sooner or later it will all be taken care of, we need only wait for that zealot of a hardliner to take his eye off the ball or find some other bone to chew on.

But Oscar Martello is no bone. And he wouldn't be living on top of the Superworld if it wasn't intrinsic to his nature to do whatever the fuck he pleases. And so on his second night of house arrest, he calls Andrea on one of Helga's old cell phones, a phone he uses when he doesn't want to be recorded, waits for Andrea to answer ("Hello? Who is this?") just to make sure he's home, and then shows up directly on the landing outside his door, at two in the morning, to bark at him, "You left me all alone, you filthy sons of bitches," but with his hands in his pockets, his legs slightly splayed, in a foul temper though inoffensive, or at least seemingly so, and dressed with great elegance, a midnight blue suit, white dress shirt, black leather overcoat slung over his shoulder, a gray silk scarf.

Andrea gazes out at him, entranced, from the doorway. He'd throw him down the stairs if he could. He'd like to erase him from the frame. Instead, who knows why, he steps aside and invites him in. "You've got a lot of nerve to show up like this."

Andrea's Dream

During the days when Oscar was behind bars, the rain had continued to flood Rome. This piece of early summer was over. The Tiber rose twenty feet, flooding its broad banks.

Andrea Serrano had returned permanently to his home, and from there he could look down and watch the river waters flow past, carrying trees and mud. Signora Margherita, his next-door neighbor, had kissed him on both cheeks, as if he were a grandson back from a long trip. She'd told him, "I'm so sorry about that poor girl. Whatever can have happened to her? And you, are you all right?" It was so surprising to hear those words of ordinary everyday kindness that Andrea was on the verge of tears. In his microworld, people used words as sharpened stones to be wedged inside the lives of other people, as weapons to feed cruel emotions, cultivate envies, unveil secrets, insinuate, defame, mock, humiliate. And almost never to ask, understand, and console. Only old Signora Margherita, there on the landing, was still capable of handling with the proper care that example of age-old kindness, which had so surprised him. And which had also, to a small extent, consoled him.

Massimiliano Testa found him a gig to write a TV movie, quick and dirty. "To help you make ends meet, what do you say? Are you still interested in making ends meet?"

"How much?"

"Thirty-five thousand, but you have to split it with Ivano Dotti."

"Oh, no!"

"I know."

Ivano Dotti, a.k.a. Invain-o, a former denizen of Oscar Martello's stable of talent, is a screenwriter who might even be good at his work, but he's touchy, pompous, whiny, and when he's off track, he's capable of writing idiotic things like, "Alessandra was traveling with just one piece of hand luggage: her heart," or else, "The lights of Los Angeles were the new guardians of his loneliness." And he'd defend those lines to the bitter end. You needed a hammer and chisel to get those things out of the scripts and psychiatrist to console him for the loss.

"What kind of story is it supposed to be?"

"A romantic comedy involving a sex therapist and an impotent painter."

"Are you kidding?"

"No. The producer is Tripla Film, ten thousand euros on signature."

"Delivery?"

"The script in sixty days."

Seeing that he was climbing back up out of the very abyss, everything seemed acceptable, the gray sky, the rain, even working with Invain-o. And even the idea of an affair between a nymphomaniac sex therapist and a guy with a limp dick.

"I'll think it over."

"Good boy. And don't be a stranger," he said.

♫

After the wake—grim and fake, at the Casa del Cinema in Villa Borghese, with the film critics playing their usual role as the bereaved, the fellow film professionals all happy not to be dead, and Milly Gallo Bautista in tears—Andrea dreamed of her. He remembered nothing about the dream except for the instant when, on the banks of the Seine, Jacaranda lit a cigarette, shielding the flame with one hand. The glow had illuminated her face like in an old black-and-white movie. She had looked at him as lovingly as any diva, and then she had exhaled the plume of smoke and had said to him, "Shall we go, my love?"

When he woke, he thought for a second that she was beside him. Instead he finds himself in his bedroom in Rome, in the only available real world, where she is gone forever and never uttered a phrase of the sort, certainly not with that unsettling grace. And instead of her face, there is a void. He'll have to learn to treasure that void. To keep it for himself. To gaze at it slowly certain evenings the way you do with old photographs when you're in the mood for nostalgia. And to put it away during the day, to keep it from spoiling, to keep from wearing it out. And then, without haste, he'll have to forget about it little by little, until he can remove it from his thoughts entirely.

That's what he promises himself, while deep down he is amazed at the depth of his grieving over a love story that lasted no more than a day, a dinner date, a one-way trip.

Since when has he become so fragile, so romantic? If, that is, we're actually talking about romanticism, and not some banal nar-

cissistic wound at the thought that he'd been unable to keep Jacaranda by his side, to give her the feelings of trust that might have
helped her cling to life. Or perhaps it's just the fault of the synapses
that tend to break down with age, leaving him here so weak and
bewildered.

The voids left by abandonment, his friend Ginevra, an expert at
living life on the surface, used to say are the most persistent and painful ordeals. They can drag you down with no chance of recovery. Or
push you toward the bridge that can get you back on the road.

He wants to get back on the road. And the bridge that he needs
to find is an agenda, obligations to meet. He'll agree to write that
idiotic movie. He'll make a call to good old Fernanda, a.k.a. Ninni,
who loves him, before she comes back from London, and maybe
he'll even fly to join her and inhale a lungful of new life in the
latest art galleries in East London, going to drink beer after six in
the evening, while the traffic flows past the wrong way under the
light, steady drizzle.

He'll throw dinner parties. Maybe he'll invite the underworld
of the Superworld, a world where he feels more comfortable,
bands of misfit screenwriters, all of them vodka drinkers, accompanied by their lovers and squads of black-clad cinephiles clogged
up with darkness, full of stories that they've never actually lived.
And he'll invite new faces, new people, owners of other lives who
will finally make his own life light up in their embrace.

Because deep down, this is what he's looking for now, an embrace and a little light. And he thinks it without knowing that
at that exact moment, Oscar Martello himself, abandoned by all
good fortune, oppressed by the same void, is looking for the same
thing. Even though on a much grander scale. And in the least ordinary way imaginable. That is, his way.

The Rumba Has Just Begun

"Maybe what I've got isn't nerve. It's desperation, ha ha!" says Oscar, stepping past Andrea and walking into his apartment. He's completely wrecked and he staggers and weaves, he stretches out on an armchair, he closes his eyes.

"If they find you here they'll arrest you and this time you won't get out," Andrea tells him.

"And your heart couldn't take the pain of it, right?" he asks, veering from laughter to a snarl. He feels like a fight, but he's too full of drugs to have the strength for it. "I'm just looking for a little coke, do you have any?"

"No."

He looks at him. "If you had some, you'd give it to me, wouldn't you? I'll pay you."

"Stop talking bullshit."

"Why, I've always done it. I've always paid you."

"Oh, go fuck yourself, Oscar."

Instead of reacting, Oscar limits himself to opening his eyes

276

wide. "Bravo. But this time you're the last one to say it to me. After Helga. After that homely slut Angelina. After the television networks that have torn up all my contracts, inasmuch as I am now persona non grata, and those worms of lawyers of mine, who weren't capable of keeping it from happening."

The newspapers and the Internet took care of the rest. They fished out of the news files an old Carabinieri report concerning a certain Oscar Martello, "driver and all-purpose assistant in the film industry," suspected of being a small-time coke dealer. They dragged up the old story of Eusebio Reverberi. And of course the matter of the "mysterious underage female," who, after all these years, finally has her proper identity, the unfortunate Maria Rizzi, known to the moviegoing public as Jacaranda, may she rest in peace. They reexhumed the suspicions of illegal smuggling of funds out of Italy that were prompted by one of his first trips to London, suspicions that were ultimately laid to rest. The first investigations of his business relations with Angelina Casagrande, who is now collaborating with great alacrity in the hunt for Oscar's money. They dusted off the first dossiers assembled by the Financial Police concerning the acquisition of artworks paid from one foreign account to another. The first banking investigations, with black holes the size of metastasizing cancer cells. And so on and so forth.

Oscar knows that the rumba has just begun. Soon everyone he's kicked in the ass over the years will start piping up. The newspapers will broaden the scope of the story. His wiretapped conversations will come out, his unconfessable business deals, his lovers. Including the especially dangerous ones, who'll put their ass out in the open air just to drum up a little free publicity. Then the politicians will pile on, insulting him, especially the ones whom he fed carelessly, tossing them a chunk of filet mignon at a time. The great vomitorium of the Internet will open wide, and hundreds of anonymous posters will spit out their slanders and libels, the weapons of the small and frustrated and the greatly depressed.

Then it will be up to Helga to haul the nets full of fish back to shore. And all she'll have to do to crown the entire take is ask one small question: "And would you, Judge Your Honor, be willing to entrust my little girls to the paternal authority of such an appalling monster?"

Strip the flesh off his bones and forget about him, that's what she's going to ask them. There will be no way out for him. Or for his creation.

It's just a matter of time.

And with those thoughts, Oscar sits down in one of the pink armchairs and watches the Tiber flowing past, intuiting at that moment that every river, but especially this one, which runs with its mud between the banks of History, is the caption of any and every life. "Do you think I don't know how it's going to end? We make films, we make children, we buy houses, we pay debts, we fall in love, we pull down our pants for a colonoscopy. And then, one night, all alone, we'll end our lives like dead dogs, every last one of us."

Andrea looks at him. "I don't feel sorry for you. I don't feel even a little sorry for you."

"I don't give a damn whether you feel sorry for me or not. All I wanted from life was a hot bath now and then."

"You're a pathetic liar."

He rubs the back of his neck and ponders. "No, you're right, I wanted everything from life. And you're a complete dickhead."

"And you thought you could get it by betraying everyone, me, Jacaranda, and even Helga?"

"Don't you dare talk to me about betrayal and Helga. I've told you once before."

Andrea says nothing and waits.

Oscar levels his forefinger at him. "Did you think that she wouldn't tell me, you damned piece of shit? Oh, she told me. The very same night she left me. And to think that between you and me, you were the one who was all clean and respectable. The one who knows how to read, knows how to write, brushes his teeth and washes his cock every morning. But instead you had the sheer nerve, the cowardice, and also the questionable taste to fuck your best friend's wife. Your benefactor's wife. The man who made sure you had enough to eat, with his own hands."

Andrea doesn't feel like talking about it, much less trying to justify himself: it happened by accident, it happened because he wasn't thinking. And most important of all, it happened in another life, the life from before, the life that no longer means anything, not after Jacaranda and all the revelations that followed. And while Oscar is still trying to cling to it, Andrea knows that in this new life the things from before are no longer of any importance, including their friendship. And there's nothing more to add. Quite the contrary. There's only one thing to add, and if he were to utter it, this is how it would sound: "Go on, get out of here! Just go home!"

But that too would be superfluous.

Oscar's Nightmare

But Oscar really has gone home. And now he's walking through the dim light of the deserted living rooms. How long has it been since he noticed the iridescence of the great basin with the lily pads reflecting the light from the windows, projecting the moving shadows of the city onto the cream-colored ceiling? Now they enchant him like an image lost and finally rediscovered. He searches for alcohol. He calls for houseboys who are no longer there. He finds three fingers of gin, half a bottle of cognac, and half a bottle of Cointreau. He sits down.

He drains all three bottles.

When he falls asleep, he too dreams a dream. In the dream he's walking at night on the median of a broad avenue that seems to have no end. He recognizes the location at the blink of an eye, he recognizes the buildings and the straightaway of *his* Cinecittà. Out of nowhere a car comes racing, veers, almost hits the curb along the sidewalk, flips over onto its side as the windows explode into shards of broken glass. The metal body slides along the asphalt, emitting sparks of blowtorch flame, while the scent of gasoline spreads in all directions. The sparks set off the *whoomp* of fire that goes rushing out. Oscar waits frozen in terror for the sliding car to hit him at any instant, crushing him and sweeping him aside. His heart explodes in his head and his lungs suffocate him. Instead, however, the impact never arrives. The car sails past him with its tail of fireworks, sliding along the perimeter wall of Cinecittà. Fire that becomes roaring flames illuminates the interior of the car, where Oscar sees himself rolling and burning, covered with blood.

Just then, he opens his eyes.

Just then, he shakes off all fear.

Just then, he knows what to do.

_&_

Before dawn, he emptied the large pond full of water lilies. He gathered all the flammable liquids he managed to lay his hands on, from all the cubbies of the house: alcohol, kerosene, gasoline, varnishes, paints, solvents. Now he pours them onto the curtains in the living rooms, onto the carpets woven with Sufi techniques in Kāshān and Tabrīz, over the Flemish tapestries and the Shirvan hall runners, down the hardwood parquet corridors; onto the beds in the guest rooms, onto the towels in the bathrooms, onto the plastic and wooden toys left behind by his little daughters, Cleo and Zoe, whom right now he only wishes he could have within reach, so that he could hug them close, remembering one of the last times he saw them, at this point a good thirty days ago, at night, stretched out asleep in their little beds, arms spread, small faces serious, lulled by a slumber so profound that he went over to first one, then the other, to make sure they were still breathing.

Now he knows it too: that was another world, the world of before. It was a vast, wealthy, well-furnished world, where he had carved out for himself a dizzying place at the very heights, among the winners of the competition.

Now that they've uncovered him—tracking back from one hiding place to another, until they reached his special cellar, the one where he had buried the worst part of himself, or perhaps the best, certainly the most useful—all the consequences of those secrets that in the time before redounded to his advantage are now only accelerating his fall. The formidable energy that everyone acknowledges in him from now on will be interpreted, looking backward, as the intolerable arrogance of a cokehound. His courage, a reckless assault on the world. His creativity, shameless luck. His determination, an ambition that wound up devouring him.

The truth is that, after Jacaranda's corpse, his path turned around on itself, like in a freeway cloverleaf, and from now on he and his destiny might do nothing other than to slide down down into the world of losers: the world he escaped so long ago. He can't allow it, he can't accept it. He is Oscar Martello, he still has a stiff, hard cock, and he can use it to screw that herd of hypocrites and gutless whiners who, in the world of before, came running to his dinner parties and marched in procession to admire his god-damned Achrome by Piero Manzoni, which now, at last, he'll take down off the wall and set atop the pyre. If they think they can take it all away from him, they're missing their bet. He'll beat them to it. And he'll do it all on his own.

If It Weren't for the Wind

I f it weren't for the wind, the Chinese say, the sky would be full of cobwebs. And there would certainly be no roaring house fires, only slow, moribund flames that simply peter out before achieving their destiny.

But the north wind that's blowing over La Dolce Roma tonight has lit up Oscar Martello's villa like a gigantic torch on the Aventine Hill.

Oscar runs into the smoke. And the denser the smoke becomes, the clearer he can see. Suddenly he's back on the stage of the Living Theatre, with all the force and the rage of his early twenties. He's driving his very first Jaguar, the Executive XJ6, with the windows rolled down, in the passing lane, sailing toward Sabaudia. He's at his first party on a Roman terrace, surrounded by scents he's never smelled before and flowers he's never seen. For the first time in his life, he's reflected in Helga's eyes, having run into her at the stables of the Quirinal Palace, at the inauguration of the Antonello da Messina exhibition, and she is the loveliest and certainly

283

the most expensive of all the costly artworks on display. He says to her: *May I know your name?* And laughing, she replies: *No, but you can help me find out yours.*

The flames gallop forward in bursts of heat. And the black smoke whirls and climbs toward the ceilings, in hot blasts that fill the hallways with clouds as big as ghosts. The hardwood floors burn and the stairs up to the turret study burn. The study, the sage-green couches, the interior decorator–chosen books, and every last one of the teledickheads burn to so many crisps.

Everything burns that his enemies would have liked to take from him. It all burns the way the papier-mâché burned in that unforgettable masterpiece *Quo Vadis?*, before the laughter of Peter Ustinov in the guise of Nero, he too the emperor of a Rome that had turned its back on him.

He has no recriminations to make. He's had his run. He's fucked the most beautiful women. He's discovered that people at the top of the world are every bit as rotten as those at the bottom, but at least they're richer. He started from the street and now he's back in the street, all alone. But in the meantime, he had himself a lot of fun.

The fire deletes everything, the reasons, the wrongs, the vendettas. Even the prison. Devouring everything right down to the bone, and then also the bone.

Right down to the ash that flies away, whitened first by the heat and then by the flame-retardant foam sprayed by the firemen who are arriving in force to surround the blazing dragon that fights its last war against the dark-blue night sky only to dissolve, bit by bit, until the dawn of the next day, followed by the closing credits.

And the closing credits really do seem to trend toward the

black with which these stories all end, sooner or later. Except that in La Dolce Roma the house lights only come up to announce the beginning of the next show.

❦

And so, on a certain day many months later, Andrea Serrano's phone rings. It's dawn. He opens his eyes in the dim light and on the display appears an unknown number that, instead of stopping ringing, just goes on. And when Andrea answers, "Hello!" he hears a voice from far, far away.

"Are you going to answer or not?"

The distance of a call from across the ocean, an unmistakable voice.

"Oscar!"

"Good job, it's me."

"I can't believe it."

Instead he believes it, and how: the corpse of Oscar Martello was never found among the ashes of the Aventine. Ventura and Interpol have searched half of Europe for him. For some time now, they've come to the conclusion that he's fled to Argentina, or Chile, or else New Zealand, but in order to continue the search, they'd need personnel and resources they don't have. Moreover, bankers and churchmen got involved, men specialized in carding that airy wool used to blunt corners, lull all imprudence to sleep, and suffocate all curiosity in the name of live and let live.

Not even Helga and her hyena of a divorce lawyer are interested in pursuing the manhunt any longer. Helga has paid off her law team, inaugurated new alliances, and has gone back to living in high style, after auctioning off the paintings that she'd carted away and then taking possession of the bank accounts and apartments that were also in her name as well as Oscar's. She sold her version of the story, entitled *The Martello Scandal: The True Story*, to a weekly TV news show, but more for revenge than for the money, which was small change anyway. She now has two lovers, a young builder for the present and an elderly Supreme Court judge for the future. Two incomes, two sources of protection, both useful in different ways and inverse proportions.

The actors and actresses of Anvil Film's stables have been absorbed into other scripts. The lawyers have started the routine processes of clawing back debts, but without kicking up too much dust, to keep their fingerprints from being noticed.

Aside from Ventura and Andrea, no one else really cared what had become of Oscar and his story arc.

"What are you doing, sleeping?"

"At five thirty in the morning? Why would I be?"

"Ha ha! It's nice to hear your voice."

"Here people might not say the same thing to you. You didn't leave a very good memory when you got out of here."

"It's just because they're fucking jealous."

Oscar feels no shame whatsoever at showing up again. And Andrea feels no resentment about sitting there listening to him. The way it is throughout La Dolce Roma, where everyone is so damned guilty that no one ever really is. And at the end of the day—betrayed and betrayers, robbers and robbed, priests and pimps, wives, lovers, hookers—all go out together to Il Bolognese for dinner.

"How are you?"

"I can't sleep, I can't shit, I can't fuck, I have an ulcer, and I drink too much. Otherwise, just fine."

"I'm not going to ask you where you are, I don't want to know. But how you're getting by, yes, tell me."

"I had some money set aside. And some people who owed me."

"Do you plan to come back?"

"There's plenty of time for that. Right now I have a better idea."

"Which is?"

"Do you remember that time I took you right up to the gates of Cinecittà? We stopped right out front. I told you my plan, my secret plan. I told you that I already had decided what the first movie I would make would be. It was nighttime."

"Yes, I remember, it happened in the other life."

"Fuck that. This is still my life. And it ain't over yet."

"So then, what do you want to do with your memories, make your next film?"

"No, not a film, a book."

"Jesus Christ, Oscar, do you want to write your memoir?"

"No, I want you to write it for me, you adorable little dickhead."

"Are you joking?"

"I'm not joking in the slightest. A book about my rise and then my persecution."

"Persecution? The victims of persecution are generally innocent."

"As usual, you get tangled up in details: guilty, innocent, nobody gives a damn. The book will be a tremendous success, and success, as Liz Taylor used to say, is an excellent deodorant."

"Why me?"

"Oh fuck, you asked me the same thing that other time. In all these years, you haven't changed a bit."

Andrea reviews the scene in his mind, and tells him, "I know what you told me, too: 'Because we're fast friends.' But we're not anymore."

"*I* still am, you asshole. And anyway, you know the characters. And the characters are what make stories."

"If I wrote it, I'd be on Jacaranda's side, not yours." He really thinks it. After all, he doesn't give a damn about Africa, about the undrilled wells, the fake hospitals, and the money that Oscar embezzled from the community, it's all just one more drop in the bottomless sea of cruelty.

In the pause that follows, Andrea can hear that Oscar is smoking, and he imagines him surrounded by his cloud of Cuban smoke, as he hacks and spits.

"Not once I've told you the part you still don't know."

"What's that supposed to mean?"

"That Jacaranda wasn't what she seemed. She was a junkie. She was a nutjob. She was in love with me. That's what it's supposed to mean."

Andrea doesn't feel like listening to him. He doesn't feel like befouling himself with more venom. Instead he just sits there. "It's a little late now for this sort of bullshit. Maybe it would be better if I just hang up and we decide to be done with this."

"But think it over: If she hated me so much, why did she make the movie with me? Why did she come to Paris? She knew all about the money in the car."

Now he's awake. "What?"

"Half that money was for her."

"What the fuck are you saying?"

"The truth. She was blackmailing me. She wanted me to leave Helga and marry her."

"Fuck, we're in a soap opera. Before long, you'll be telling me that Jacaranda was your niece and that you're the Count of Monte Cristo."

"If you want to know the truth, in those bygone days I even screwed her aunt. She was the one who introduced me to Jacaranda. Otherwise how the fuck was I supposed to have met her? Are you listening to me?"

He's listening.

"And it was Jacaranda who couldn't wait to suck old Eusebio's dick. People do things that they later regret or are ashamed of. But they still do them, am I making myself clear? You just need to have the guts to leave them behind you. Instead all she ever did was obsess over them. And I became the worst part of her obsession."

Andrea hunts for a gap in the logic of Oscar's words: "Did you think up this escape hatch all by yourself? Or is this your new script?"

"You don't believe me? Well, she was calling me three times a day from Paris, did you know that? No, of course you didn't know that. You didn't know anything about anything. While I knew everything about the two of you. The strolls, the dinners. That you went up the Eiffel Tower to take pictures of the Japanese tourists. That you had dinner at the Brasserie Lipp. And also that you fucked in front of the bathroom mirror."

Andrea takes in the full weight, word by word, wound by wound. And as he does, he sees the images of those days in Paris pass before his eyes, days that he thought he'd spirited to safety, in a dry spot at the center of his heart. And just to do himself more harm, he thinks back to the last words recorded by Jacaranda, which have never stopped echoing in his mind: "Today my sickness is ending and with it I too am ending my name is Jacaranda Rizzi get someone to tell you my story *my misbegotten love affairs* I'm an actress and because of that some of you may think you know me but it's not true I don't even know myself."

Not even in that last message to the world did she have the courage to tell the truth. Or else that was all the truth that she had the stomach to take.

Oscar is talking to him from far away: "Are you there?"

Andrea takes a deep breath. "Yes. Everything you're saying is bullshit."

"You know for yourself that it's all true."

No, he doesn't know it, he doesn't want to know it. "Jacaranda detested you."

"Maybe she did. But that doesn't mean anything. She detested me and she loved me. Don't ask me why, but she loved me. And she enjoyed hurting herself. Are you listening to me?"

Yes. Instead of hanging up, he listens.

"There are people whose wounds never heal, and in the end they just die. They're called hemophiliacs or something like that, did you know? She was like that, the wounds never healed. Forget about her. Together we'll write a great book. And we'll make the book into a great movie. I already have a title in mind, but I'm not going to tell you. Hey, Andrea, are you listening to me?"

He hears him. He says, "I don't have the time."

"Of course you do. And if you don't, you can find it."

"I'm sleepy."

"You're sleepy? Life is galloping over the hills like wild horses and you're sleepy? There's no such thing as being sleepy, Christ on a crutch: we'll sleep when we're old."

Andrea thinks that this would be a good title, but he doesn't say so.

He wants to hang up, but he doesn't.

Oscar keeps talking, but he's not listening to him.

He's looking at the leaves illuminated by the first rays of sunlight on the terrace. And he's thinking that if it weren't for the wind, the leaves would hang motionless. Instead they move so much that eventually they fall. And the same thing is true for men and women.

About the Author

PINO CORRIAS lives and works in Rome. He was a special correspondent for *La Stampa*, one of the most prestigious newspapers in Italy. He has produced several successful investigative reports and dramas for Italian television. He also collaborates with various important newspapers and weekly publications, including *Il Fatto Quotidiano*, *Il Venerdì di Repubblica*, and *Vanity Fair*.